PUFFIN BOOKS

YOUNG SAMURAI

THE RING OF FIRE

'A fantastic adventure that floors the reader on page one and keeps them there until the end. The pace is furious and the martial arts detail authentic' – Eoin Colfer, author of the bestselling Artemis Fowl series

'Fierce fiction . . . captivating for young readers' – *Daily Telegraph*

'Addictive' – *Evening Standard*

'More and more absorbing . . . vivid and enjoyable' – *The Times*

'Bradford comes out swinging in this fast-paced adventure . . . and produces an adventure novel to rank among the genre's best. This book earns the literary equivalent of a black belt' – *Publishers Weekly*

'The most exciting fight sequences imaginable on paper!' – *Booklist*

Winner of Northern Ireland Book Award 2011
School Library Association's Riveting Read 2009
Shortlisted for Red House Children's Book Award 2009

Chris Bradford likes to fly through the air. He has thrown himself over Victoria Falls on a bungee cord, out of an aeroplane in New Zealand and off a French mountain on a paraglider, but he has always managed to land safely – something he learnt from his martial arts . . .

Chris joined a judo club aged seven where his love of throwing people over his shoulder, punching the air and bowing lots started. Since those early years, he has trained in karate, kickboxing, samurai swordsmanship and has earned his black belt in *taijutsu*, the secret fighting art of the ninja.

Before writing the Young Samurai series, Chris was a professional musician and songwriter. He's even performed to HRH Queen Elizabeth II (but he suspects she found his band a bit noisy).

Chris lives in a village on the South Downs with his wife, Sarah, his son, Zach, and two cats called Tigger and Rhubarb.

To discover more about Chris go to *www.youngsamurai.com*

Books by Chris Bradford:

The Young Samurai series (in reading order)
THE WAY OF THE WARRIOR
THE WAY OF THE SWORD
THE WAY OF THE DRAGON
THE RING OF EARTH
THE RING OF WATER
THE RING OF FIRE

For the Pocket Money Puffin series
VIRTUAL KOMBAT

YOUNG SAMURAI

THE RING of FIRE

CHRIS BRADFORD

PUFFIN

PUFFIN BOOKS

Published by the Penguin Group
Penguin Books Ltd, 80 Strand, London WC2R 0RL, England
Penguin Group (USA) Inc., 375 Hudson Street, New York, New York 10014, USA
Penguin Group (Canada), 90 Eglinton Avenue East, Suite 700, Toronto, Ontario, Canada M4P 2Y3
(a division of Pearson Penguin Canada Inc.)
Penguin Ireland, 25 St Stephen's Green, Dublin 2, Ireland (a division of Penguin Books Ltd)
Penguin Group (Australia), 250 Camberwell Road, Camberwell, Victoria 3124, Australia
(a division of Pearson Australia Group Pty Ltd)
Penguin Books India Pvt Ltd, 11 Community Centre, Panchsheel Park, New Delhi – 110 017, India
Penguin Group (NZ), 67 Apollo Drive, Rosedale, Auckland 0632, New Zealand
(a division of Pearson New Zealand Ltd)
Penguin Books (South Africa) (Pty) Ltd, 24 Sturdee Avenue, Rosebank, Johannesburg 2196, South Africa

Penguin Books Ltd, Registered Offices: 80 Strand, London WC2R 0RL, England

puffinbooks.com

First published 2011
003

Text copyright © Chris Bradford, 2011
Cover illustration copyright © Paul Young, 2011
Map copyright © Robert Nelmes, 2008
All rights reserved

The moral right of the author and illustrators has been asserted

Set in Bembo by Palimpsest Book Production Limited, Falkirk, Stirlingshire
Made and printed in England by Clays Ltd, St Ives plc

British Library Cataloguing in Publication Data
A CIP catalogue record for this book is available from the British Library

ISBN: 978-0-141-33255-0

www.greenpenguin.co.uk

MIX
Paper from
responsible sources
FSC
www.fsc.org   FSC® C018179

Penguin Books is committed to a sustainable future for our business, our readers and our planet. This book is made from Forest Stewardship Council™ certified paper.

ALWAYS LEARNING   PEARSON

For my son, Zach,
the fire in our lives

CONTENTS

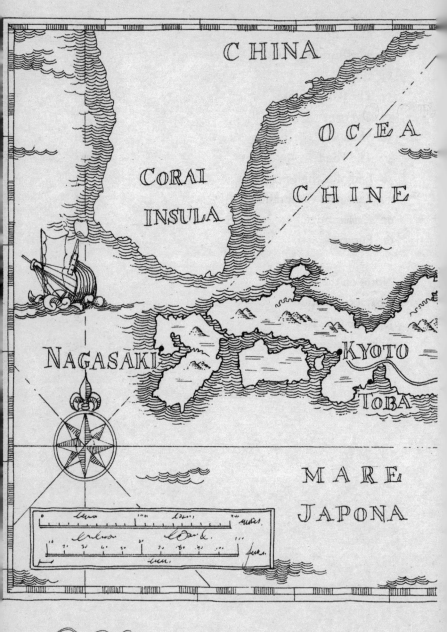

CHINA

OCEA
CHINE

CORAI
INSULA

NAGASAKI

KYOTO

TOBA

MARE
JAPONA

TOKAIDO ROAD

TERRA DE
IESSO

NUS

NSIS

EDO

THE
JAPANS
17 TH
CENTURY

THE LETTER

Japan, 1614

My dearest Jess,

I hope this letter reaches you one day. You must believe I've been lost at sea all these years. But you'll be glad to know that I am alive and in good health.

Father and I reached the Japans in August 1611, but I am sad to tell you he was killed in an attack upon our ship, the Alexandria. I alone survived.

For these past three years, I've been living in the care of a Japanese warrior, Masamoto Takeshi, at his samurai school in Kyoto. He has been very kind to me, but life has not been easy.

An assassin, a ninja known as Dragon Eye, was hired to steal our father's rutter (you no doubt remember how

1

important this navigational logbook was to our father?).
The ninja was successful in his mission. However, with the
help of my samurai friends, I've managed to get it back.

This same ninja was the one who murdered our father.
And, while it may not bring you much comfort, I can
assure you the assassin is now dead. Justice has been delivered. But the ninja's death doesn't bring back our father —
I miss him so much and could do with his guidance and
protection at this time.

Japan has been split by civil war and foreigners like
myself are no longer welcome. I am a fugitive. On the run
for my life. I now journey south through this strange and
exotic land to the port of Nagasaki in the hope that I may
find a ship bound for England.

The Tokaido Road upon which I travel, however, is
fraught with danger and I have many enemies on my trail.
But do not fear for my safety. Masamoto has trained me as
a samurai warrior and I will fight to return home to you.

One day I do hope I can tell you about my adventures
in person . . .

Until then, dear sister, may God keep you safe.

Your brother, Jack

P.S. Since first writing this letter at the end of spring, I've been kidnapped by ninja. But I discovered that they were not the enemy I thought they were. In fact, they saved my life and taught me about the Five Rings: the five great elements of the universe – Earth, Water, Fire, Wind and Sky. I now know ninjutsu skills that go beyond anything I learnt as a samurai. But, because of the circumstances of our father's death, I still struggle to fully embrace the Way of the Ninja . . .

1

FROZEN

Japan, winter 1614

Jack's limbs were frozen solid. He was so cold he could no longer even shiver. Only sheer willpower kept him putting one foot in front of the other as he battled through the blizzard.

He seriously regretted his decision to take the mountain route. He may have evaded the Shogun's samurai, but he'd barely made it over Funasaka Pass alive. During the night the weather had turned harsh, battering him into submission and forcing him down the mountainside.

The icy gusts cut through his silk kimono straight to the bone like knives. Jack clasped his body for warmth, his head down to the wind, his thin straw hat offering poor protection against the stinging snow. Upon his hip rattled the two red-handled samurai swords his best friend, Akiko, had given him. Slung across his back was the pack that contained her black pearl, five *shuriken* stars and, most importantly, his father's *rutter* – the priceless navigational logbook he'd fought tooth and nail to keep safe. Yet, however precious these items were to him, they were now like lead weights round his neck.

Cold, tired and hungry, Jack felt the last of his strength ebbing away.

Glancing up to get his bearings, there was nothing to see. The landscape was shrouded in a thick blanket of white, the sky swallowed up by endless grey clouds. Behind him, his lone track of footprints was already disappearing beneath a new veil of snow.

At least I'm off the mountain, he thought, taking in the vast featureless expanse of the Okayama Plain. *Perhaps I should rest awhile. Let the snow cover my body. No one would find me, not even Kazuki –*

Jack shook himself. He couldn't allow such self-defeating thoughts to overwhelm him. Fighting his exhaustion, he focused on the burning hope in his heart: of returning home to his sister Jess.

Since leaving his friends – the samurai Ronin and the girl thief Hana – he'd been making good progress with his escape to Nagasaki, the southern port where he hoped to find a ship bound for England. Miraculously, he'd passed unscathed through the outskirts of Osaka. He'd then followed the coastal road, avoiding all the samurai checkpoints, to reach the castle town of Himeji. Here Jack made his first mistake. Having run short of supplies, he'd risked buying some rice in a market with the last of his coins. But the Shogun's samurai were everywhere – on the lookout for foreigners, in particular a *gaijin* samurai. Although he'd tried to keep his face hidden, Jack was spotted and forced to flee. For the next three days, troops of samurai were hard on his trail. He only managed to lose them when, using his ninja stealth skills, he broke from the coastal road and headed deep into the mountains.

But that decision now looked to be the end of him.

Praying for shelter, Jack stumbled on blindly through the snowstorm. Twice he fell to the ground and got back up again. On the third time, his body simply gave in – the lack of food, sleep and warmth finally taking its toll.

The snow quickly began to settle upon his frozen form.

As the ground consumed him, Jack heard the faint voice of his friend Yori in his head . . . *Seven times down, eight times up!*

The mantra, which had been his saving two years before in the *Taryu-Jiai* interschool martial arts contest, repeated itself, growing louder and louder.

Seven times down, eight times UP! Seven times down, EIGHT TIMES UP! SEVEN TIMES DOWN, EIGHT TIMES UP!

The lesson of never giving up was burnt so deep into his soul that Jack overruled his body's failure. Summoning up the last of his energy, he dragged himself to his feet, snow tumbling from his shoulders. In his determination to rise, he thought he saw the flickering orange flame of an oil lamp in the distance. Staggering towards the light, more lanterns came into view until an entire town materialized out of the storm.

Although Jack avoided civilization whenever he could, desperation now drove him forward. In a final burst, he fell into the shelter of the nearest building, huddling from the bitter wind in the corner of its veranda.

Once he'd recovered slightly, Jack took in his new surroundings.

Lights spilt on to the main street in welcoming arcs and the warm glow of fires beckoned the weary traveller inside the numerous inns and eating establishments lining the road. The noise of laughter and drunken singing greeted Jack's ears as small groups of samurai, *geisha*, merchants and townsfolk hurried between the wooden slatted premises in search of entertainment and refuge from the storm.

Slumped where he was, Jack realized he was in full view of these people and would soon draw attention to himself. Gathering his wits, he pulled his straw hat further over his face and entered the town, acting like any other samurai.

The smell of cooked rice, soy sauce and steamed fish assaulted his senses. To his right, a *shoji* door was partially open. Three samurai warriors sat round a roaring hearth fire, knocking back *saké* and scooping generous portions of steamed rice into their mouths. Jack couldn't remember the last time he'd eaten a proper meal. For the past week, he'd been forced to forage. But winter was a meagre time. Early on he'd managed to kill a squirrel with his *shuriken*; otherwise in the mountains he'd found nothing, the snow having driven all animals to ground.

As one of the samurai closed the *shoji*, blocking his view, Jack knew food had to be his priority. But with no money to his name, he'd have to beg, barter or steal in order to survive.

All of a sudden he collided with something solid, the impact almost bowling him over.

'Watch it!' snarled a burly samurai, accompanied by a white-faced *geisha* girl who began to giggle incessantly.

'*Sumimasen*,' said Jack, apologizing in Japanese and bowing respectfully. The last thing he wanted was trouble.

But he needn't have worried. The samurai was drunk and more intent on reaching the next inn to care any further about Jack.

Up ahead a *shoji* flew open and three men were ejected from the hostelry. A roar of laughter followed as they landed face first in the snow.

'And don't come back!' shouted the innkeeper, wiping his hands of them before slamming the door shut.

The three men picked themselves up and despondently dusted themselves down. Dressed in threadbare smocks and trousers, they looked like beggars or impoverished farmers. Whoever they were, it was clear to Jack that this town had no sympathy for vagrants.

While Jack considered the few options he had left, the three men headed towards him. Although they didn't look like fighters, they outnumbered him and, given his weakened condition, posed a threat. As they drew closer, Jack's hand instinctively went to his swords. His frozen fingers could barely grip the handle of his *katana* and Jack wondered if he'd even have the strength to fight them off.

'Go on!' said the apparent leader of the group, a sour-faced man with hollow cheeks and thin weathered lips. He shoved the youngest forward.

Jack stood his ground.

The young man, a nervous individual with a missing front tooth and jug-like ears, asked, 'Are you a . . . *ronin*?'

Jack simply nodded that he was a masterless samurai and made to walk on. But the young man stepped into his path. Jack tensed in readiness as his challenger summoned up the courage to make his next move.

Taking a deep breath, the young man blurted, 'Do you want a job?'

2

RICE

Jack was dumbfounded at the suggestion.

'We can pay you,' said the third and eldest man, who possessed only a few strands of hair on his otherwise bald head.

Jack hesitated. He certainly needed the money. But looking at their dishevelled appearance, he wondered how they could afford to pay *anyone*. Even if they could, taking a job was too much of a risk. How could he trust them? His identity was bound to be discovered. His journey would be delayed. Besides, their offer was most probably a trap.

Shaking his head, he walked away.

'*Please* . . . hear us out,' the old man insisted, an imploring hangdog expression on his wrinkled face. 'At least join us for supper. We've freshly cooked rice.'

Jack's stomach growled at the thought. And the old man's desperation appeared genuine. What had he to lose simply by listening? His need for food outweighing his better judgement, Jack agreed. 'But I'm not making any promises,' he added.

'We understand,' said their leader, bowing in acknowledgement. 'Come this way.'

Jack followed the three men down a side street to a

dilapidated storehouse at the edge of town. His senses on high alert, he glanced around for telltale signs of an ambush – footprints leading to a darkened alley, snow disturbed from a rooftop, a building that could conceal a surprise attack. But if there were enemies around, they were well hidden.

The sour-faced man pushed open a rickety door and entered first. Jack paused at the threshold, trying to assess the danger within. But it was pitch-black inside and all he detected was the stench of rotting straw.

'My apologies,' said the old man, ushering him meekly in. 'But this is the only lodging we can afford.'

A stub of a candle flickered into life, its weak flame illuminating a spartan room with a hard-packed earthen floor and a rough wooden deck for sleeping.

The young man closed the door behind them as Jack was invited by the leader to be seated upon the raised platform. Unshouldering his pack, Jack removed his swords and placed them, close at hand, by his side. The three men knelt before him on the dirt floor.

'My name is Toge,' said the leader, bowing his head. 'We're farmers from Tamagashi village. This here is Sora –' the old man bowed – 'and the boy is Kunio.'

Offering a gap-toothed grin, Kunio prostrated himself before Jack. Peering from beneath the brim of his hat, Jack now saw Kunio wasn't much older than he was. Sixteen or seventeen, at most.

Jack nodded his head in acknowledgement, deciding not to reveal his own name. Until he knew these people's intentions, he had to be cautious, but he didn't wish to lie to them either. An awkward silence fell and the three farmers began to fidget uncomfortably as their anxiety grew at this mysterious samurai.

'Your rice is just coming,' said Sora quickly, gesturing towards the far corner of the storehouse.

Only then did Jack notice a fourth person in the room; his fatigue had clearly impaired his warrior awareness. He reached for his *wakizashi*, then, on closer inspection, checked himself. Hidden in the shadows, a girl crouched over the dying embers of a small fire. Scooping out a portion of rice from a battered pot, she scurried over to Jack and presented him with the bowl.

Little more than a waif in a tattered kimono, the fourteen-year-old girl had a tangled bob of black hair and a round pale face that appeared pretty beneath the many layers of grime. As she looked to Jack, he noticed her cat-like eyes constantly flitting between him and the farmers, revealing a lively spirit behind her unkempt condition.

Toge batted his hand impatiently at the girl and she returned to the pot. Working silently, she served out three more bowls of rice and handed these to the farmers.

'Please enjoy,' said Toge through tight unsmiling lips.

'Thank you,' replied Jack, trying not to wolf down the food in one go. He couldn't appear too desperate. No chopsticks were offered, so he used his fingers. As soon as the rice touched his tongue, however, Jack let out a grateful sigh and dug in.

'You like?' said Sora, his expression genuinely pleased.

Jack nodded. Unable to hold back, he stuffed the rest into his mouth, the food disappearing in several ravenous gulps. The nourishing rice warmed his stomach and revived him a little.

'Have some more,' insisted Sora, ignoring the vexed look from Toge. The old man gestured to the girl, who collected Jack's bowl and refilled it.

With his immediate craving satisfied, Jack took his time with the second serving. He didn't want to gorge himself and end up being sick.

'So why do you need the services of a samurai?' asked Jack, aware that he had to uphold his end of the bargain.

'To guard our rice store,' explained Toge, chewing steadily on his food as if each grain was his last.

'That doesn't seem like a task for a samurai warrior.'

Quickly swallowing his rice, Toge replied, 'Oh, I can assure you it is.'

'Our rice is very valuable to us,' added Sora. 'It's vital to our village's survival and we can't be too careful, especially during winter.'

'Do you get many thieves then?' asked Jack.

'Once in a black moon,' Toge replied, putting down his empty bowl.

Jack considered this for a moment. 'Is your village far from here?'

While Toge explained its remote location upon the edge of the Okayama Plain, Jack noticed the farmers only had a few tiny mouthfuls of rice left, while his own bowl was still more than half full. He glanced over at the girl to see her picking at the dried scrapings from the pot. All of a sudden a wave of guilt consumed Jack as he realized he was eating *all* their provisions.

Though he could have devoured another five bowls at least, Jack stood up and offered the girl his meal. She looked worried and confused. Lifting up the pot, she showed him it was empty and shook her head to say there was no more.

'For you,' said Jack, presenting her with his rice.

The girl didn't seem to understand his Japanese and Jack had to force the bowl into her hands. Now realizing his intention, she glanced towards Toge but didn't wait for his permission. Flashing Jack a smile, she scampered off into the corner. The three farmers exchanged surprised looks, astonished at his gesture of generosity.

'*See! I knew he had a good heart for a samurai,*' whispered Sora behind his hand to the open-mouthed Kunio.

'He could have given it to *us*, though,' Kunio muttered under his breath.

Jack caught all of this but pretended not to hear. He sat back down and pondered his options. The farmers had been honest with him and had sacrificed everything they had in the vague hope he might help them. As a samurai, bound by the code of *bushido*, Jack felt compelled to honour their sacrifice by at least considering their proposition.

The job seemed simple and he was certainly skilled enough to deal with a few thieves. Moreover, with it being mid-winter and no provisions of his own, Jack had little chance of progressing any further on his trek to Nagasaki. He needed to recover his strength first. Yet this had to be weighed against the risk of delay and the Shogun's samurai catching up with him – Kazuki and his gang couldn't be too far behind either.

'I'm on an important pilgrimage,' Jack explained. 'I wouldn't be able to stay very long.'

'No, that's fine!' replied Toge, seizing upon this slightest of hopes. 'A month is all we need . . . until the next new moon.'

Jack thought about this. The village was off the beaten track, so it was unlikely his enemies would discover him during that time. And there was nothing to stop him leaving as soon as the bad weather had passed and the roads were clear again.

'What pay are you offering?'

The three farmers looked sheepishly at one another. Toge coughed, then mumbled, 'We're farmers, so can only pay you in rice. Two meals a day, plus lodging.'

Jack realized this would allow him to recover, but the pitiful pay didn't solve his provision problems.

When Toge saw their potential recruit wavering, he added quickly, 'Three meals a day. And whatever supplies you need for your journey.'

Sora, keen to seal the agreement, suggested, 'Why not visit our village first? Then you can make your decision.'

The offer had become very tempting. Although Jack knew the sensible decision was *not* to get involved at all, the practical solution to his predicament was to take the work. The question was whether Jack could entrust the farmers with his identity. But this matter could be dealt with when the issue arose. If they reacted badly, he stood a better chance of escaping a remote village than a bustling town.

Besides, did he *really* have a choice? The only alternative to the farmers' offer was fighting for his survival in Okayama, a hostile place swarming with samurai where he was guaranteed to be discovered and reported.

Turning to the farmers, Jack announced, 'I accept your offer.'

3

NEKO

Sora and Kunio were delighted at the news. Toge was more subdued, but Jack put that down to his dour personality.

'We'll leave in the morning,' said Toge, pulling a large straw mat from beneath the decking. He placed it beside Jack along with a bundle of straw.

The three farmers huddled together by the opposite wall for warmth, leaving the entire deck to Jack. Since he was a samurai, the hierarchy of Japanese society meant Jack was given the best position and the greatest comfort.

As he arranged the loose straw into a mattress, Jack spotted the girl out at the back, scrubbing away at the cooking pot in a trough of ice-encrusted water. Though she worked without complaint, Jack didn't envy her lowly position.

Pulling the mat over his weary body and his hat on to his face, Jack settled down to sleep. The three farmers began whispering to one another, but Jack was too exhausted to follow the conversation. With his hunger satisfied, he quickly drifted off . . .

Jack snapped awake as he sensed someone removing his hat. His *taijutsu* training was instinctive – he grabbed the offending hand and twisted it into a lock. But his hat fell to the floor and he came face to face with the girl. She made no sound, despite the painful wristlock Jack had put her in. She merely gawped in utter amazement at his blond hair, blue eyes and white skin.

Hoping he hadn't hurt the girl, Jack released her from his grip.

'Sorry, but you shouldn't have done that,' he whispered as she rubbed her wrist in the darkness.

But she was more taken by his blond locks. Reaching out, she touched a stray curl and grinned in delight at its softness. Jack smiled back, relieved by her friendly reaction to his foreignness. Glancing over his shoulder, he saw the three farmers were still fast asleep, Kunio snoring as loudly as a pig.

The girl returned his hat with a respectful bow, then silently padded over to her corner and curled up on the floor, her eyes never leaving his face. She didn't appear afraid and, to Jack's surprise, didn't alert the farmers to her discovery.

Perhaps she doesn't know about the Shogun's decree banishing all foreigners from Japan, thought Jack. *Or the reward for capturing me, dead or alive.*

This gave Jack cause for hope. Maybe the farmers hadn't heard the news either. If that was the case, then their village would make the perfect safe haven. Covering his head to go back to sleep, Jack prayed the farmers' reaction to finding out he was a *gaijin* samurai would be as welcoming as hers.

Bleary-eyed and stiff with cold, Jack emerged from the store-house. The storm of the previous night had passed and the snow-covered landscape now glistened crystal-white in the early dawn sun. Breakfast that morning had been meagre – a thin miso soup with a cup of weak green tea – but at least it had been warming. Sora, apologetic as ever, had promised a hearty supper on arrival at their village.

The three farmers were treating him with the same wary respect as the night before and Jack could only assume that the girl had kept quiet about their encounter. She now trailed behind, having been burdened with all the cooking utensils, as the five of them trekked out of town and across the Okayama Plain.

With the snow knee-deep, their going was slow and arduous. Jack envied the farmers' thick straw boots, since the socks and sandals he wore provided little protection from the icy conditions. He stamped his feet as he walked, trying to force some blood back into them, before noticing that the poor girl was barefoot. She trudged on through the snow, bent over with the pack's weight, her breath puffing out in little white clouds. No longer did Jack feel quite so sorry for himself.

'Are you *sure* we can trust him?' whispered Toge, who forged ahead with Sora. In the still winter air, his voice carried. And Jack, whose hearing was acute thanks to his sensitivity training at the *Niten Ichi Ryū*, had no trouble eavesdropping on their conversation.

'We have to,' replied Sora, his tone despondent. 'He's our only choice.'

'We don't even know his name,' Toge hissed.

'Samurai can be rude like that. They think all farmers are beneath them. Yet where would they be without us, I ask?'

'But he won't *even* show his face. There's something odd about him –'

At this point, Kunio shuffled up to Jack's side, interrupting his concentration.

'Winter's harsh this year,' he said, rubbing his hands for warmth.

Nodding, Jack tried to catch the rest of the farmers' conversation, but Kunio continued chatting.

'Where have you come from?' he asked.

'Kyoto,' Jack replied.

'Is it as beautiful as they say? I hear the temples are made of gold and silver!'

'It's true,' said Jack.

Kunio's eyes went wide with delight and Jack recalled his own amazement when Akiko had shown him the Silver and Golden Pavilions of Ginkaku-ji and Kinkaku-ji.

'So are you on a *musha . . . musha . . .*' The boy sought for the correct phrase.

'*Musha shugyō,*' Jack prompted, referring to the warrior pilgrimage that many samurai embarked upon to test their sword skills in life-and-death duels.

'That's it! Have you fought anyone yet?'

Jack thought about the time he'd been tricked into a duel with Sasaki Bishamon, a fearsome samurai on a quest for glory. He'd almost been impaled on the man's sword.

'Yes, I have,' replied Jack, an involuntary shiver running through him at the memory.

Kunio stared in awe of him. 'I've never met a *real* warrior before.' He glanced down at the swords on Jack's hip and became mesmerized by the red silk handles. 'They're beautiful,' he said, reaching out to touch them.

'And deadly,' added Jack, grasping the hilt of his *katana* in warning.

'Yes, they must be *very* sharp,' agreed Kunio, smiling awkwardly as he snatched his hand back.

Wanting to change the topic from himself, Jack asked, 'Tell me, who's the girl?'

Kunio glanced over his shoulder as if he'd forgotten she was there. 'Her name's Neko. We call her that because she acts like a cat.'

Jack observed Neko struggling on valiantly through the snow. He wanted to help her with her load, but he realized his status as a samurai prevented him taking on such menial tasks. He had to act according to his role and couldn't risk raising any further suspicion among the farmers.

Nonetheless, Jack demanded of Kunio, 'Why aren't you helping her?'

Kunio's face creased in bafflement. 'Why should I?'

'Because you're stronger than her.'

Grinning, Kunio puffed his chest out at the compliment. 'True, but I wouldn't want to tire myself out. It's a long way to Tamagashi.'

Jack shook his head in disbelief. He wondered if the girl had any say in this. 'Neko doesn't talk much, does she?'

Kunio laughed. 'Of course not. She's a deaf-mute and stupid.'

Jack's heart went out to the girl. Now he knew why she hadn't told the farmers about him. But she still could have woken them. Neko had proved herself an unlikely ally.

Neko looked up and caught Jack's eye. She grinned slyly at him, then tapped her nose as if to say his identity was her little secret. Jack realized the girl might not have all her senses, but she was tough, tenacious and certainly not stupid.

4

BLACK MOON

Tamagashi village was a ramshackle collection of thatched houses perched on the edge of the Okayama Plain. To its north rose an immense mountain range that dominated the skyline and seemed to squash the settlement by its very size. Fanning out to the west was a sprawling cedar forest, while to the south a patchwork of paddy fields, barely visible beneath the snow, traced their way on to the plain. As they approached from the flatlands of the east, Jack couldn't see anyone working the fields and the village appeared to be abandoned.

Passing a couple of rundown farmhouses and an old mill, they came to a wide fast-flowing river. The wooden bridge creaked uneasily as the five of them made their way across, following the main track beside some paddy fields and into the village itself. Skirting a large pond, they entered the central square. Here, Jack had an even greater sense of a ghost town. No one greeted their arrival, but he noticed shutters and doors opening a crack, eyes peeking fearfully out at the mysterious samurai.

'What's everyone afraid of?' asked Jack.

'Nothing,' replied Toge, a little too quickly.

Smiling awkwardly, Sora explained, 'They're busy preparing their supper, that's all.'

Before Jack could ask any more, Toge hurried them on. 'The head of the village is waiting to welcome you.'

Striding up a muddy slope to the largest house, the three farmers took off their boots and stepped on to the veranda. Jack slipped off his sandals and joined them, but Neko was waved away by Toge to return the cooking pots to Sora's wife.

'One moment please,' said Toge, bowing to Jack.

Knocking on the farmhouse door, he then entered with Sora, leaving Jack and Kunio to wait outside.

'What do you think?' asked Kunio, gesturing with pride at his village.

'Very . . . peaceful,' replied Jack. Though in truth, the depressing silence unnerved him.

Compared to the ninja village, Tamagashi was clearly a lot poorer and far less organized. The farmers' homes were dotted haphazardly around, most needed re-thatching and some even looked to be on the verge of collapse. Although the head farmer's house was the grandest in the village, it was still no palace. The wooden decking was rough and warped, its walls uneven and gapped.

'My family's house is that one by the pond,' said Kunio, pointing to a small lopsided building.

As he went on explaining who lived in each of the houses, Jack was more drawn to what was occurring within the farmhouse.

'You've been gone three weeks and come back with just *one* samurai!' exclaimed a man's voice in outrage.

'No other samurai agreed to our request,' replied Toge.

'So where's all the rice we gave you?'

'Any *ronin* we did attract simply ate our food and left,' he explained bitterly. 'As soon as we told them about the job and what it paid, they scorned us for wasting their time. Or else were too scared.'

'But you took enough rice to feed a small army!'

'Okayama isn't a safe place,' a grieved Sora admitted. 'Much of our rice was stolen. That deaf Neko makes a useless guard.'

'You idiots! What are we going to do now?'

The rasping voice of an old man cut in. 'We have one. That is a start.'

'Yoshi, with all due respect, what use is *one* samurai?'

'Let's meet the man and we shall find out.'

The door creaked open and Sora's hangdog face appeared.

'Come in!' he said with forced cheerfulness. 'Our village head and elder are pleased you're here.'

Wondering what he'd got himself into, Jack stepped through the doorway. The room was dim, the tang of woodsmoke heavy in the air. There was no furniture, just a few clay pots for storage and a water butt in one corner. Hanging from a chain, a pot of rice boiled over an open-hearth fire in the centre of the room. Although the place was austere, the warmth of the hearth was welcoming, and Jack was invited to take prime position next to it.

Toge sat opposite him beside two men. In the gloom, Jack's face was heavily in shadow beneath his hat, so he risked a glance up. One of the men was middle-aged, with a permanent frown and stubble like a harvested field left untended. The other was ancient, a wizened old man with spidery white hair and eyes screwed up so tight they were barely visible. The faces of all three farmers appeared gaunt and haunted in the flickering light of the fire.

'I'm Junichi, the head of this village,' announced the middle-aged man, with a bow of his head. 'This is Yoshi, the elder.'

The old man grunted, but being stiff with age he couldn't bow.

Jack returned Junichi's greeting with his own bow. As he rose, he caught sight of Neko peering through a gap in the rear wall, her eyes avidly following the proceedings.

'We thank you for coming to our rescue in our time of plight,' continued Junichi. 'The village is in need of a brave samurai such as yourself. I can only apologize the reward is so little, but the glory and honour will be great – and *worthy* of a samurai.'

The farmer's grave tone gave Jack an uneasy feeling in the pit of his stomach. 'Surely, it's just a matter of guarding your rice store from a thief or two . . .'

The old man, Yoshi, cleared his throat. 'You're aware of Black Moon?'

Jack nodded, familiar with the Japanese term for a new moon. He was willing to stay the month, as agreed.

'Yet he doesn't scare you?'

'*He?*'

Yoshi squinted at Jack, then turned on Toge. 'You didn't tell him?'

'I . . . I was going to,' stammered Toge. 'But the moment never arose.'

The knot in Jack's stomach tightened.

Sucking on his gums, Yoshi shook his head woefully. 'Black Moon is the name we call the mountain bandit Akuma.'

The room seemed to darken at the very mention of his name, the farmers visibly trembling and looking to the shadows.

'For this is the time he strikes,' explained Yoshi. 'On the first black moon of winter, when the night is at its darkest, he attacks our village and steals all our rice. We're left starving and foraging for scraps.'

'One man does all this?' asked Jack. 'But there's a whole village of you.'

'He rides with others.'

'How many?'

'Forty or so bandits.'

5

SEVEN SAMURAI

Jack didn't know whether to laugh or run for his life. 'Even the greatest samurai couldn't defeat so many!'

'I told you, Yoshi,' said Junichi. 'It's futile. We should just hand our rice to Akuma. Get it over and done with.'

Yoshi ignored him, asking Jack, 'Then how many *do* you need?'

'Against *forty*?' Jack couldn't believe he was even contemplating the prospect. He thought back to his warrior training and the Battle of Osaka Castle. He'd witnessed the best samurai swordsmen handle five or six adversaries at once. Even more, if the enemy was disorganized or poorly trained, which was likely the case with bandits. 'If the recruits are skilful and experienced, then perhaps . . . seven samurai.'

'Seven!' exclaimed Toge. 'It took us weeks to find one. Where on earth will we get seven samurai?'

'What about your *daimyo*?' asked Jack, who knew that samurai lords were charged with protecting the citizens of their domains.

The farmers all snorted in derision.

'*Daimyo* Ikeda doesn't care about us,' spat Junichi. 'As long as he gets his rice tax that two-faced lord wouldn't lift a finger to come to our aid.'

'But if your rice has been stolen, how can you pay him?'

'Akuma's crafty,' explained Yoshi. 'He only raids us *after* the tax has been collected.'

'This'll be the third year in a row,' stated a despondent Junichi. 'We've had no option but to look for our own samurai. But it's all been in vain. Our situation is hopeless.'

Jack had to agree. Outnumbered forty to one, the battle was lost before it had even begun. 'I'm sorry,' he admitted reluctantly. 'But I can't help you.'

Fury born out of despair seized Toge. He shook an angry fist at Jack and bawled, 'You samurai are *all* the same! We work the fields, till the soil, grow the rice to fill your stomachs. So that you can go to war over your lords' domains. Then the day we need you, where are *you*?'

'What do you expect me to do?' said Jack in his defence. 'Fight off forty bandits on my own!'

'Aren't samurai meant to be courageous?' snapped Toge.

'Yes, but not suicidal.'

'How I despise –'

'Enough, Toge!' interrupted Yoshi. 'That's no way to treat our guest. He came of his own free will. We must respect his decision to leave.'

The room fell into a sullen silence, leaving only the crackle of the fire and the bubble of the boiling rice.

Jack's conscience was torn. He dearly wanted to help the farmers. As a samurai, he felt honour bound to defend them. But the stark truth was that, against so many enemies, he'd only get himself killed – and for nothing. The bandits would still seize the rice.

Tears welled up in Sora's eyes and he began to sob. Wiping a dirty hand across his nose, he snivelled, 'How will we feed our little ones?'

No one answered him. The farmers merely stared in wretched misery at the floor, wringing their hands.

All of a sudden Kunio looked up, his face bright with an idea. 'We can recruit *more* samurai!' he blurted.

Toge shook his head in disbelief at the boy's stupidity. 'Think how long it took us to get *one* samurai! We've less than a month before the black moon.'

'But it'll be easier for *him*,' said Kunio, indicating Jack.

'Yes, yes!' agreed Sora, his eyes sparkling with promise. 'Samurai won't listen to a farmer, but they will to another samurai.'

The farmers turned expectantly to Jack.

'I don't know . . .' began Jack, fully aware that a *gaijin* would have even less chance than a farmer.

'I beg you!' cried Sora, prostrating himself before Jack. 'You're our *only* hope.'

Kunio threw himself down too, followed by Junichi and Toge. Trembling like a leaf, Yoshi held his hands out in prayer. Their abject deference made Jack uncomfortable. But these poor farmers were so desperate. And their local *daimyo* clearly wouldn't be coming to their rescue.

Perhaps I can train them to fight, considered Jack. *Or at least improve the village defences. Still,* forty *bandits!*

Whatever the odds, he had to do something for them. When he'd first arrived in Japan, the great samurai swordsman

– Masamoto Takeshi – had rescued him from certain death. With no parents and no way home, Jack had been adopted by the man, trained in martial arts at his samurai school in Kyoto, and given a fighting chance. It was time to repay that debt, for him to become that samurai saviour. He knew he'd be risking all, but his late friend and Japanese brother Yamato had shown him what it meant to be a samurai of the Masamoto clan – selfless sacrifice.

'I'll help you,' Jack announced.

Sora now wept with joy. He scurried over to the fire and began to heap piles of steaming rice into a bowl. Bowing, he presented the meal to Jack.

'*Arigatō gozaimasu, arigatō gozaimasu*,' he repeated in thanks.

He then shared out the remainder of the rice, while Kunio poured everyone a cup of *sencha*. With great ceremony, Junichi raised his green tea in a toast.

'For your service, we honour you. May I ask your name, samurai?'

Jack realized the time had come to reveal his identity. This was the perfect moment. The farmers were in his debt and in need of his services and, judging by Neko's reaction, there was no reason to hide any more.

'Jack Fletcher,' he replied, boldly taking off his hat.

6

FIRE

Sora fell backwards on to his rear. Kunio's mouth dropped open in shock. Junichi cried out in amazement, while Yoshi squinted even harder, disbelieving his old eyes.

'A *gaijin*!' exclaimed Toge.

'And a boy at that! Get out!' yelled Junichi, pointing to the door.

'But I'm here to help you,' Jack protested, as Toge snatched the bowl of rice from his hands.

Jack stared at the farmers, thunderstruck by their response. A moment ago, they were crying out for him. Now they couldn't wait to be rid of him.

Junichi turned on Toge. 'Is this some sort of joke? A foreign boy pretending to be a samurai!'

'We were deceived!' said Toge, glaring at Jack.

'No more than you not mentioning Black Moon,' replied Jack. 'I may not be Japanese, but I *am* samurai.'

'And I'm a *daimyo*!' shot back Toge with a mocking laugh. 'Now you heard Junichi: leave our village – you're not welcome.'

Sora, who'd recovered from his initial shock, stepped to

Jack's defence. 'B-b-but he agreed to stop Black Moon. We *need* him.'

Junichi gave Sora a withering look. 'Do you really think a *boy* can defeat a devil like Akuma?'

Sora opened his mouth then closed it, stumped for an answer.

'Sometimes it takes a devil to beat a devil,' said Yoshi, siding with Sora.

'He's an ill omen,' argued Junichi. 'We should get rid of the *gaijin* before any more bad luck befalls our village.'

'No samurai has come to our defence, yet this foreigner has,' Yoshi pointed out.

'We cannot take such a risk,' said Toge. 'When we were in Okayama, I heard that the Shogun had banished all foreigners. Anyone caught harbouring a *gaijin* is to be punished with death!'

'That settles it,' said Junichi. 'As head of this village, I declare the boy be cast out immediately.'

He indicated for Kunio to open the door. Before Jack could object, Toge ushered him on to the veranda and slammed the door shut behind him. A moment later, the door opened again and his straw hat came flying out.

There's gratitude, thought Jack, bending down to pick it up.

Gazing round at the decrepit village, all doors closed to him, and at the stark snow-laden landscape, Jack knew his future survival looked bleak. He had no shelter, no food and was stranded in the middle of nowhere. Once more he stood in the cold, alone and friendless.

Well, not quite. He sensed eyes upon him. At the end of the veranda, Neko was observing him with a mixture of confusion and sadness on her grimy face. Her eyes silently pleaded with him not to leave, as he put on his sandals and stepped on to the muddy road.

Tracks led off in all four directions and Jack wondered which one to take. He was miles off his route and the sun was close to setting, so he wouldn't get far tonight. He could retrace his steps back to Okayama, or cut south-west to the main coastal road. But from what he'd seen, the plain was desolate and exposed. He'd more than likely perish. The mountains to the north would be too harsh and dangerous, and anyway took him the wrong way. The forest appeared to offer the best hope. It provided protection against the elements, with the possibility of scavenging for food, and was more or less the direction he needed to head in. Hoisting his pack over his shoulder, Jack gave the despondent Neko a sorrowful wave, then trudged west out of the village.

As he passed each farmhouse, Jack caught glimpses of the villagers' haggard faces watching him. He no longer felt so much pity for them. They had the warmth of a fire and the benefit of food. Already there was a sharp bite to the chill air and Jack shivered. He wasn't looking forward to another frosty night out in the open. The rice of the previous day was now a distant memory and hunger began to gnaw at his insides. The churlish Toge hadn't even allowed him to eat that final meal!

Jack was at the village border when Neko jumped out from behind the last building. Breathless from running, she presented a small bag to him. Inside were a few hastily snatched handfuls of rice.

'Thank you, Neko,' said Jack, bowing gratefully as he accepted her charity.

Putting the precious food inside his pack, Jack walked on

into the forest. The last he saw of Neko was her bowing him goodbye, a light snow falling around her. Jack just hoped she wouldn't be in trouble for helping him.

As he trekked west, the sun dropped behind the horizon and the evening light began to fade fast. The forest grew cold and threatening. He hadn't gone far when he heard the sound of hurried footsteps.

Immediately, Jack diverted off the main track and hid behind a tree. He unsheathed his sword, ready to defend himself. Had the farmers changed their minds? Or was it the dreaded Akuma and his bandits?

His pursuer drew closer.

Blending himself with the tree, Jack held his breath and became still as a stone. Practised in *gotonpo*, the ninja Art of Concealment, Jack would be virtually invisible to his enemy.

A figure ran past and came to a stop where the track forked.

Jack peered round the trunk and saw Neko, a look of desperation on her face, her eyes searching the forest. She was about to set off again, when Jack stepped out from his hiding place.

'What do you want?' he demanded.

Neko gestured wildly, but Jack couldn't make head or tail of what she was saying. Shrugging, he shook his head.

Giving up on signing, Neko grabbed Jack's arm and pulled him off the road and into the forest. She led him up a rise to a small clearing, where she urgently pointed to Tamagashi village below.

In the gathering gloom of dusk, Jack saw a bright red fire burning out of control in the square. To his horror, one of the farmhouses was ablaze.

7

BABY

Jack sprinted down the track, hard on Neko's heels. For such a small thing, she was as fast as a fox. And she had also proved very persuasive – she'd mutely entreated him to return to the village, unwilling to let go of his arm until he agreed. Jack could only presume that Akuma was raiding the farmers' rice store, the harsh snows having encouraged him to seize provisions early.

The two of them burst from the forest and ran along the muddy track into the village centre. All the farmers had gathered in the square and were now staring in horror at the inferno before them. The thatched roof of the farmhouse was alive with flames. A few men were trying to douse the blaze with buckets of icy water from the pond, but their efforts were making little impact and the fire continued to spread.

A woman wailed, struggling in the arms of a round-faced man with thinning hair, who appeared just as tormented. She seemed desperate to throw herself inside the burning building.

Neko and Jack came to a halt beside Sora, whose face was more anguished than ever.

'Where's Akuma?' demanded Jack, looking around for the bandits.

'Akuma?' gasped Sora, shocked by the name almost as much as by seeing Jack again. 'No . . . no bandits. A cooking pot full of oil spilt and set the house on fire.'

Jack sheathed his *katana*, annoyed that Neko had dragged him back just for this. Tragic as it was, it was of no concern to him. He turned to resume his journey.

'B-b-but their baby's still inside,' Sora exclaimed.

Above the roar of the flames and the mother's own cries, Jack now heard the screams of a small child. The farmhouse was close to collapsing, but the farmers still stood doing nothing. It was clear they were all too scared to risk their lives.

Jack lost no time. Passing Neko his swords and pack, he ran over to a nearby shed and ripped away the cloth sacking that hung from a window. He then seized a full bucket from one of the farmers and threw it over himself. Shuddering with the cold, he grabbed a second bucket and soaked the sack too. Wrapping himself in the sodden cloth, he took a deep breath and charged into the blazing farmhouse.

Jack was hit by a wave of heat so intense it almost knocked him off his feet. The air was scorching and burnt all the way into his lungs. Hacking violently, he peeked from beneath the sacking. The room was a swirl of smoke, ash and flames. To his right, one wall was engulfed in fire, the kitchen area a brimstone hell in which no one could survive. To his left, the raised wooden sleeping area smouldered but had yet to catch alight.

In the far corner he caught a glimpse of a makeshift cot and heard the high-pitched screams of the abandoned baby. The infant began to wheeze and choke as smoke descended over the cot.

Pulling the wet sacking closer round his face, Jack dashed across the room. Even through the soles of his sandals, he could feel the blistering heat of the wooden deck. It wouldn't be long before the whole floor burst into flames.

Reaching the baby, he was amazed to find it unharmed, its face protected beneath an old shawl. Snatching it from the cot, he wrapped the little infant protectively within the sacking. But the cloth was almost dry and would soon be useless. He started to run back outside when all of a sudden an almighty *crack* sounded. Looking up, he saw a flaming roof beam split in half.

At the last second Jack dived out of the way, rolling across the decking with the baby in his arms as the beam crashed to the ground. The infant screamed even louder as its world was turned upside-down. Jack flipped to his feet, only to discover they were now encircled by a ring of fire.

He could see the doorway tantalizingly close, but he would have to run a gauntlet of flame to reach it.

The sacking on his back, now dry as tinder, ignited and he was given no other choice. Shrugging the cloth from his shoulders, he clasped the baby to his chest and threw himself towards the only exit. Flames licked at him as he ran, his soaked kimono his last defence.

The farmhouse creaked and groaned, then caved in on itself as Jack tumbled out into the square. Coughing and spluttering, he collapsed in the snow, for once grateful for its cold embrace.

'*My baby! My baby!*' cried the mother, breaking free from her anxious husband's grasp.

Jack handed her the screaming child. As soon as it was in her arms, the baby fell quiet, comforted by the mother's embrace. The woman inspected her child with relief, then looked to Jack, her eyes filled with tears of gratitude.

'*Arigatō gozaimasu*,' she sobbed, bowing her head low.

The man now approached and Jack prepared himself to be run out of town once again. But the farmer dropped to his knees, throwing his arms out and placing his head to the ground in total respect.

'Young samurai, our family is forever in your debt,' he said. 'My name is Yuto. I'm the father of this child and now your humble servant.'

8

ABDUCTED

Jack tucked into the biggest bowl of rice he'd ever seen. All the village women had come together to bring him gifts of food. Jack didn't wait on ceremony this time. Deftly using his chopsticks, he polished off the meal and moved on to the miso soup, steamed vegetables and even some smoked mackerel. Given his last experience with the farmers, he had to make the most of being in their favour while he could.

He sat in Junichi's house, warming by the fire in a fresh kimono, the baby's mother having insisted on washing his dirty blue one. Neko had crept in and now knelt beside him, proudly guarding his swords and pack. Junichi, Yoshi and Toge sat opposite and joined Jack in his meal with freshly brewed cups of *sencha*. Behind them knelt Sora and Kunio, the boy transfixed by the new hero in their village.

'Please accept my apologies for our previous ill manners,' said Junichi, bowing his head. 'I only had the village's safety at heart. It was a shock to discover you were a foreigner. And we have no wish to defy the Shogun's orders.'

'I understand,' replied Jack, knowing the power of life and death that the Shogun held over his subjects.

'We would like you to stay. At least for a few days until you're fully rested,' continued Junichi. 'Of course, if you wish to stay longer . . .'

'I'll have to think about it,' said Jack. The farmers had shown their fickle nature and Jack wasn't willing to commit to anything, although he would take them up on their offer to stay a couple of nights.

'A great fire burns within you,' observed Yoshi. 'You saw for yourself our feeble-hearted men. We *need* a person of your courage.'

'The boy may be brave,' muttered Toge, moodily sipping his green tea, 'but that doesn't make him a samurai.'

Fed up with Toge's scepticism, Jack put down his chopsticks and, without warning, whipped out his *katana*. The razor-sharp blade sliced clean through Toge's cup, spilling hot tea into the farmer's lap.

Too stunned to move, Toge could only let out a pitiful whimper as the steaming *sencha* seeped through the cloth of his kimono. Recovering his wits, he examined his fingers in panic to check they were all still there.

Neko clapped her hands in delight at the farmer's hysteria, while Kunio rolled with laughter on the floor. Even Yoshi gave a toothless grin at this fine display of swordsmanship.

'If that doesn't convince you,' chortled Yoshi, 'why don't you challenge the boy to a duel?'

'Yes, a duel!' Kunio blurted eagerly. 'Jack's on his *musha shugyō* – his swords are deadly!'

Shamefaced, Toge sullenly crossed his arms and shut up.

Junichi, hastily putting down his own cup, declared, 'I have *no* doubt in your abilities, young samurai.' With a nervous smile, he added, 'Sora has offered his house for as long as you wish to stay. And you may use my bathtub at any time.'

Jack acknowledged their hospitality. His point having been made, he sheathed his *katana* and returned to his meal.

Rested, bathed and fed, Jack felt like a new person as he stepped out of Sora's house and into the morning sun. Last night was the first time he'd enjoyed an undisturbed sleep in weeks. At this rate, it would only take him a few days to recover his full strength.

Neko, now his constant companion, was waiting outside. Sora also joined him on his stroll down to the village pond. As Jack passed other homes, he was greeted with respectful bows and kindly looks, and it was clear the farmers had accepted him into their community. Although he could never truly be a part of Japanese society, there were moments like this when the barriers dropped and Jack felt like he belonged – just as he always did at Akiko's side. His thoughts went out to his closest friend and Jack prayed she was safe and well. Kazuki had vowed revenge on Akiko for disabling his sword hand with an arrow during the Battle of Osaka Castle. Yet despite having recently saved his rival's life in return for the promise of her safety, Jack didn't trust Kazuki. That's why he'd sent his friend Hana to warn Akiko, while Jack left clues along his route, so that his arch-rival would track *him* down instead.

'Are you all right?' enquired Sora, noticing the frown on Jack's face.

Jack nodded. 'I'm concerned for my friends.'

'Aren't we all?' he replied mournfully.

Jack studied Sora's despairing expression and sensed an inconsolable loss in the old man's heart. But it wasn't just him. On reflection, Jack realized that all the farmers bore a similar air of grief. He'd put this down to the impending threat posed by Akuma, but even the children in the square were solemn and unusually subdued.

It was then Jack noticed there were hardly any young girls – only mothers and their smallest children.

'Where are the girls of your village?'

Sora sniffed. 'All gone.'

'You mean, to market?'

'No, abducted.'

Jack was stopped in his tracks. 'Who abducted them?'

'Akuma! Who else?' spat Sora, clenching his fists in futile rage. 'He took my only daughter.'

Sora began to sob uncontrollably at the memory.

'The first two years . . . Akuma only stole our rice . . . leaving us barely enough to survive . . . But last winter . . . he kidnapped our girls to become the bandits' slaves!'

'Do you know where they took them?' asked Jack, appalled at this news.

'No. We searched for months, but the bandits' camp is hidden somewhere deep in the mountains. Our girls are lost forever!'

Sora wiped the tears from his eyes and fell into a shuddering silence.

For the first time, Jack truly appreciated the suffering Akuma and his bandits had delivered upon this innocent community. Not only had they taken the food out of the farmers' mouths but the life and soul from the village itself.

'Perhaps Akuma won't come this year,' said Jack, trying to console the old farmer.

'He will,' replied Sora. 'Black Moon always does.'

9

RECRUITMENT

'So what's the story with Neko?' asked Jack as the three of them walked round the pond, its rim encrusted with ice and snow. 'She's still here.'

Neko looked up expectantly at Jack, somehow aware that he was talking about her.

'The bandits didn't want *her*,' replied Sora, with uncharacteristic bitterness.

'Neko's parents must be thankful.'

Sighing heavily, Sora revealed, 'Her parents were killed in the first raid.'

'So who looks after her now?'

'No one. She's an orphan of the village. We all take care of her, but Neko remains a painful reminder of our loss.'

Jack felt his outrage boil over. Neko had lost all that was dear to her, just as he had. But at least he'd been fortunate enough to have friends like Akiko, Yamato and Yori to turn to. She had no one to comfort her. Knowing the torment she would have suffered alone, Jack felt his resolve harden. This Akuma was cruel and merciless – worse than a devil.

'I must return to Okayama,' stated Jack, much to Sora's alarm.

'B-b-but you can't go yet!'

'Don't worry, I'll be back,' he replied. 'With more samurai!'

News of Jack's decision spread like wildfire and he was heralded as the village's saviour. In spite of his determination earlier that morning, Jack was beginning to question his ability to deliver on the promise. He might be able to convince other warriors to join the cause. But once they discovered he was a *gaijin*, what then?

The villagers in their excitement seemed to have forgotten this.

Yoshi, the elder, hadn't.

'Take Toge with you,' he instructed as they discussed his departure over lunch at Junichi's house. 'He can act as your servant. It'll lend you more status.'

Toge's expression soured at the idea, but he was given no choice.

'You go too, Sora, as representative of the village.'

'And me!' volunteered Kunio.

'If you must,' replied Junichi wearily. Though his expression suggested relief that he'd be rid of the boy for another few days.

'Neko comes too,' said Jack.

'What for? She's a terrible cook,' muttered Toge.

'Are *you* going to cook for me?' challenged Jack. To which Toge didn't answer.

By the time all the travel preparations had been made, it was late.

'We'll leave tomorrow morning,' said Jack.

★

Jack awoke at first light, fresh and more positive about his forthcoming mission. The weather also appeared to be in their favour. A bright winter sun shimmered across the crisp white carpet of the Okayama Plain and the main road was clearly visible, snaking its way towards the horizon.

All the villagers gathered in the square to wave them off. As the provisions were divided up between the party of five, Jack ensured Neko wasn't overburdened this time.

'Kunio!' he called as the boy went for the smallest load. 'This rice sack and cooking pot should be no trouble for a strong farmer like you.'

Not wanting to lose face in front of the other boys, Kunio smiled gamely.

'No problem,' he grunted, hauling the heavy iron pot along with the cumbersome sack on to his back. He staggered slightly, then followed Jack and the others out of the village.

Working their way past the snow-laden fields, the group crossed the bridge by the mill and soon left Tamagashi behind. Neko skipped merrily at Jack's side, clearly delighted not to be treated as the village slave for once.

With the route clear, they made good time and by mid-afternoon the outskirts of Okayama came into view. Toge managed to acquire the same rundown accommodation as before and they left Neko and an exhausted Kunio to guard the provisions. Okayama's main square was bustling with people and there was a buzz of excitement in the air.

'Market day,' explained Toge as he led Jack through the crowds and past stalls of fish goods, silk traders, spice merchants and vendors selling everything from oil and wood to farm tools and pottery.

'That's good news,' said Jack, keeping his hat low over his eyes. 'There'll be more samurai to choose from.'

They decided the marketplace itself was too hectic to make a personal appeal to anyone, so Jack chose a small tea house at one corner of the square. As well as providing good views across the market, it was an appropriate meeting place for *ronin*. More importantly, it offered Jack the best escape route should his identity be exposed.

Acting according to his role, Toge ordered a pot of *sencha* for his master, poured out a cup, then knelt to one side with Sora. The three of them surveyed the market for suitable samurai.

Jack spotted one almost immediately. He wore a plain black kimono and had a neatly trimmed beard. On his hip were a pair of well-maintained swords and he walked with an air of confidence, but not arrogance.

'Try him.'

Toge jumped to his feet and hurried over to the man. Jack and Sora watched as, bowing profusely, Toge introduced himself and invited the samurai for tea. The warrior appeared to ask a question, to which Toge answered. The samurai then shook his head and walked on. Toge returned to the tea house, a glum expression on his face.

'He said to thank you for your offer, but he wasn't in need of a job.'

They resumed their search.

'What about him?' suggested Sora, pointing to a well-dressed samurai with a long moustache, plump jowls and a visible paunch.

'No,' said Jack, realizing the man was too affluent to be a *ronin*. 'We need to find *hungry* masterless samurai.'

'How about that one?' said Toge.

A stick-thin warrior with pinched cheeks and a shabby brown kimono wandered through the market.

'Possibly,' replied Jack, taking a sip of tea while he considered the man.

The samurai drew closer. As he passed a fruit stall, he slipped an apple into his kimono sleeve.

'He's definitely hungry,' said Sora.

'He's also a *thief*!' muttered Toge.

Jack was inclined to agree with Toge's disapproval. They needed honourable trustworthy samurai. But under the circumstances, they couldn't be too choosy.

All of a sudden there was a commotion in the crowd and an old woman barged her way through. Raising a gnarled walking-stick aloft, she began to beat the hungry samurai around the head.

'You pathetic excuse of a samurai!' she shrieked. 'Hand back my apple!'

'I . . . I . . . was going to pay,' protested the samurai feebly, scrabbling for his purse.

'You'll pay all right!' she crowed, thumping him again and again.

The samurai cowered under her blows. Dropping the apple, he ran as if his life depended upon it. The surrounding shoppers burst into laughter at the sight of the warrior fleeing an old woman half his size.

'No good,' said Jack. 'Any recruit has to be brave, at the very least.'

With potential candidates few and far between, their quest was proving even more difficult than he'd expected.

Then a tough, battle-hardened samurai strolled past the tea house. Judging by his frayed kimono with no affiliating *mon*, the warrior was a *ronin* seeking work. Furthermore, his *sayas* displayed the scars of numerous fights.

'He's our man,' said Jack.

Toge hurried over and bowed to get his attention.

'May my master have a word?' asked Toge, directing the *ronin* to Jack, his face shielded beneath the straw hat.

Intrigued, the *ronin* curtly nodded his agreement. He sat down at Jack's table, placing his swords close by his side. Sora immediately poured out some *sencha*.

'Thank you for taking the time to join me,' said Jack, toasting the *ronin* with his cup. Adopting his guardian's name, Jack introduced himself. 'My name's Takeshi.'

The samurai bowed his head. 'I'm Honen. How can I be of service?'

'I'm seeking samurai on behalf of Tamagashi village – to defend them against bandit raids during the winter.'

'An honourable if inglorious cause.'

'But a worthy one,' countered Jack. And, guessing the *ronin* would appreciate directness as well as a challenge, he added, 'The bandits' leader is the notorious Akuma, the man they call Black Moon.'

'He's a fearsome warrior. Killed hundreds of men, I hear.'

'What sort of courage does it take to defeat unarmed farmers?' said Jack. 'Such a bandit wouldn't stand a chance against a samurai like you. Are you willing to join us in our campaign?'

Taking a long draught of *sencha*, Honen considered the proposition.

'And if I was to accept, what would my reward be for such *dangerous* work?'

'As poor farmers, they can offer three meals a day and lodging.'

The expression on the samurai's face turned from sympathy to indignation.

'How dare you, a fellow samurai, offend me with such a paltry offer!' he growled, slamming his cup on the table. 'I may be a *ronin*, but that doesn't make me a beggar!'

Grabbing his swords, the samurai stormed off.

'This is hopeless,' moaned Sora.

'We can't give up yet,' said Jack, though he was beginning to doubt their chances.

With the light fading, the market grew quieter. Still they managed to attract the attention of two more samurai. The first had also heard of Akuma and hurriedly made his excuses to leave; the second balked at the lack of glory in dying for lowly farmers.

'I'm sure we'll have better luck tomorrow,' said Jack, hiding his own disappointment.

Dispirited, Toge paid the bill and the three of them headed back to the storehouse. As they crossed the street, Jack sensed someone following them. Without looking round, he indicated for Toge to take the next alley.

But their pursuer wasn't far behind.

Weaving through the backstreets, Jack urged the farmers to quicken their pace. Still they couldn't shake him off. Signing for Toge and Sora to continue, Jack ducked into a narrow passageway. Footsteps crunched in the snow. Jack tightened the grip on his sword. A shadowy figure passed by.

Then stopped.

'Do you always hide from friends?'

10

AN OLD FRIEND

A round-faced boy with thick bushy eyebrows and an ample belly grinned down the passageway at Jack.

'SABURO!' exclaimed Jack, recognizing his old friend at once. 'What are *you* doing here?'

'I was about to ask you the same question.'

Toge and Sora shuffled back, bemused expressions on their faces.

'You know this samurai?' queried Toge, eyeing the swords on Saburo's hip.

'*Know* him? I trained with him for three years!' Jack exclaimed, as he abandoned Japanese etiquette and embraced his friend warmly. 'We were at the *Niten Ichi Ryū* together in Kyoto.'

'And Jack was the teacher's pet,' teased Saburo, elbowing his friend in the ribs.

'Yes, the one that was kicked and punched around the *dojo* by Sensei Kyuzo.'

Saburo laughed. 'Well, you needed toughening up!'

'How did you *ever* find me?'

'I was watching you for ages in the market,' explained

Saburo. 'I couldn't be certain it was you, so I waited until you left the main square.'

'Does your samurai friend want to join us for supper?' interjected Sora.

Saburo beamed at the suggestion of food. 'I'd be delighted.'

The four of them made their way back to the dilapidated storehouse.

'You're living the life of a lord!' mocked Saburo as he inspected the decaying wooden walls and dirt floor.

'I have to keep a low profile,' explained Jack, noticing the shame on Sora's face at his friend's offhand comment.

The farmer manically tried to clean the raised platform before inviting both of them to sit.

'So, what are you doing in Okayama?' asked Jack.

'I'm on my *musha shugyō*.'

'You!' said Jack, surprised. His friend was a loyal and occasionally brave samurai, but he wasn't a born fighter or a glory seeker.

Saburo gave a weary nod of the head. 'My father's idea. After my brother's legendary sacrifice at the Battle of Osaka Castle, my arrow wound for saving your life during the school attack was no longer so impressive. You know how my father is – not satisfied with one heroic son, he wants to brag about my duelling exploits. He even presented me with this new *daishō*.'

Saburo passed Jack two impressive-looking swords. 'As a good-luck gift.'

Jack admired the honed blade of the *katana*. 'So, how many duels have you won with this?'

'All of them,' replied Saburo.

'Really!' said Jack, handing back the weapons with respect. 'You've certainly become a mighty swordsman.'

Leaning in, Saburo lowered his voice. 'That's because I haven't fought any yet,' he admitted with a canny grin. 'But I won't be telling Father that.'

Jack laughed. *Same old Saburo!*

'And what about you?' asked Saburo. 'The last I heard, you'd left Akiko in Toba some time back in spring. What have you been doing all this time?'

While Jack recounted the events of his last six months, the farmers huddled in the far corner, discussing the new arrival and leaving Neko to tend to the rice. Saburo was amazed and appalled in turn to learn of Jack's exploits and hardships: his escape from Osaka Castle with the wounded Akiko; the pursuit of the Shogun's samurai through the Iga mountains; the intervention of the ninja and how they helped him; the violent robbery with the loss of all his possessions and his memory; and the relentless hunt by Kazuki and his Scorpion Gang across Japan.

Although Jack trusted his friend completely, he was careful not to go into too much detail about his encounter with the ninja. He wasn't sure how Saburo would react to the news that he'd become a fully trained *shinobi*.

'That Kazuki's a bully and a thug!' exclaimed Saburo, upon hearing of the boy's intention to go after Akiko. 'I knew his father had been made *daimyo* of Kyoto Province, but the power's gone to Kazuki's head too.'

'I'm just praying Hana's reached Akiko first,' said Jack.

'Don't worry,' consoled Saburo, laying a hand upon Jack's shoulder. 'We both know Akiko was one of the best samurai at our school. Even if Kazuki does find her, she'll make him regret he ever did!'

Jack took comfort from Saburo's confidence. It was good to have a friend by his side again – one he could rely on while being himself, without fear of prejudice.

Neko padded over and presented Jack and Saburo with two heaped bowls of rice. They tucked in, while the farmers ate their share in the corner.

'Good rice,' said Saburo, through a mouthful of food.

'Enjoy it while you can,' replied Jack. 'The farmers don't have much to go round.'

Saburo looked up and saw the meagre portions the others had.

'Glad I wasn't born a farmer,' commented Saburo and resumed eating.

Jack realized his friend wasn't being purposefully hard-hearted. Having been brought up a samurai, he was simply indifferent to the lower social castes.

'What are you doing with these farmers anyway?' asked Saburo.

'I'm helping them to recruit samurai.'

Saburo almost spat his food out. '*You!* What on earth for?'

Jack explained about Akuma and his forthcoming raid at the next black moon.

'Just one bandit?' queried Saburo.

'No, forty.'

Saburo whistled in awe. 'Those farmers don't stand a chance!'

'That's why I'm going to fight for them.'

Saburo's jaw dropped open and he stopped eating. 'You're

not serious, are you? You have to leave Japan before the Shogun or Kazuki find you.'

Jack nodded his intent to stay. 'If we don't help the farmers, no one else will.'

'*We?*' spluttered Saburo, his high-pitched exclamation drawing the farmers' attention.

'Yes, I was hoping you'd join me.'

'You're worse than my father!' said Saburo, his eyes widening in alarm. 'You're *both* trying to get me killed.'

'It won't just be us,' countered Jack. 'We'll recruit another five samurai.'

'That's still only *seven* samurai against forty bandits!'

'*Please*, Saburo. These people are desperate and we don't have much time left.'

Sighing heavily, Saburo considered Jack's proposal. The farmers had stopped talking and were now transfixed, awaiting Saburo's answer. Jack realized he may have asked too much of his friend.

'You'll be the death of me, Jack,' Saburo said finally.

'You'll help me then?' replied Jack, both amazed and relieved. 'We'll be rewarded with food.'

'Well, why didn't you say so?' said Saburo, grinning. 'That's all the incentive I need!'

The farmers threw themselves to the ground in gratitude.

'But I'm only agreeing to this,' added Saburo quietly, 'because it's *you* who asked. I expect that I'll be needed to save your miserable life again!'

A HELPFUL MONK

'Pester someone else with your childish games!' growled the samurai, irritably waving Saburo away.

'But this is a *real* mission,' insisted Saburo, pursuing the *ronin* across the square.

'Don't take me for a fool. If there was a serious problem, the farmers wouldn't be hiring *young* samurai like you.'

'That's why they need your help.'

'*You're* the one needing help. Now leave me alone before I'm forced to end your very short life!'

At that, Saburo stopped in his tracks and let the *ronin* walk away. Returning to the entrance of Okayama's main Buddhist temple, he slumped on the steps next to Jack.

'That's the sixth *ronin* to say no,' complained Saburo. 'They just won't take me seriously.'

Peering from beneath the rim of his hat, Jack surveyed the square. They'd been trying all morning to recruit samurai. But with market day over, Okayama was no longer as busy and the choice of *ronin* was limited.

'I can't believe there isn't a single samurai willing to help,' said Jack.

Saburo shrugged. 'Everyone's out for themselves since the Shogun came to power.'

'Then why not look to yourselves for salvation?' advised a small monk descending the steps of the temple.

Dressed in white robes with a saffron-coloured mantle, he wasn't much bigger than a child and carried a *shakujō* – a ringed staff – its pointed iron tip and six metal bands jangling with each step. The monk's face was in shadow beneath a large conical straw hat. Jack had come across similar monks on his travels. They often hid their faces as a symbol of their detachment from the outside world.

'We're not the ones who need help,' explained Jack, bowing his head respectfully. He pointed to Toge and Sora, glumly crouching on their haunches nearby. 'The farmers need samurai to protect their rice harvest. But no *ronin* will help them.'

'And no *ronin* will listen to us,' said Saburo, sighing.

'Then why not approach *young* samurai?' suggested the monk. 'They can be just as brave.'

Jack considered this. 'They might still be training and won't have the sword skills. It's too risky against a bandit like Akuma. We need warriors with battle experience.'

'Do *you* lack such experience?'

'Not entirely,' Jack admitted, his mind returning to the attack on the *Niten Ichi Ryū* and the Battle of Osaka Castle.

'Have you not duelled adult samurai . . . and won?'

'Errr . . . yes,' replied Jack, taken off-guard by such a knowing question.

'Then who's to say there aren't more warriors like you?'

'Because I'm . . .' Jack trailed off. *Because I'm a* gaijin, he'd almost said.

Yet maybe the monk was right. *He*, Jack, was willing to tackle the bandits. And if the *Niten Ichi Ryū* could produce warriors like Akiko, Yamato and himself, then why couldn't there be other young samurai of equal skill?

'But this isn't Kyoto,' argued Saburo. 'There won't be many sword schools here – if any! Where will we find young samurai?'

'Sometimes what you seek is right in front of your eyes,' the monk replied, lifting the hat from his face.

Dumbstruck, Jack and Saburo could only stare open-mouthed at the little monk with bright eyes and a smooth shaven head.

'B-b-but you're supposed to be at the Tendai Temple in Iga Ueno . . . with Sensei Yamada,' Jack finally managed to gasp.

'And *you're* supposed to be on a ship bound for England,' replied Yori.

Back at the storehouse, Neko brewed a pot of *sencha* while Jack, Saburo and Yori caught up on each other's news. Yori couldn't believe all the trials and tribulations Jack had suffered; and Saburo was stunned to learn of Yori's gruesome escape from the Red Devils at the Battle of Osaka Castle. All three of them mourned the tragic closure of their school, but Jack and Yori were pleased to learn from Saburo that Sensei Kano, their blind *bōjutsu* master, had safely returned the surviving young samurai to Kyoto before going into hiding himself. To Jack's disappointment, there was no further word of his guardian Masamoto's fate, following his banishment to a remote temple on Mount Iawo. But sorrow turned to laughter when Yori learnt of Saburo's uneventful *musha shugyō*.

'No point taking unnecessary risks!' explained Saburo,

archly raising his eyebrows. 'What brings *you* to Okayama anyway?'

'Sensei Yamada sent me on a pilgrimage too,' replied Yori. 'But a religious one.'

'Is Sensei Yamada here?' Jack asked, eager to see the Zen philosophy master who'd been his closest mentor at the *Niten Ichi Ryū*.

Shaking his head, Yori gave a sad smile. 'I think something died in him during that last battle in Osaka. Sensei Yamada's been teaching me everything he knows, as if he expects to depart this world soon.'

Jack and Saburo exchanged worried glances.

'Then why aren't you with him now?' asked Saburo.

'*Life is the greatest teacher*, he told me. That's why he sent me on this pilgrimage, asking that I deliver a message to an old friend at the Okayama Temple.'

Neko, a steaming teapot in hand, approached the raised platform with deference and poured out three cups of *sencha*. Saburo raised his cup in a toast.

'To the *Niten Ichi Ryū*!' he said, hoping to lift their spirits.

'To friends!' said Jack, still reeling from the fortuity of meeting both Saburo and Yori but overwhelmingly grateful to have them once more at his side.

'To friends, gone but not forgotten,' agreed Yori, his eyes reddening with tears.

The reunited young samurai drank in their friends' honour. A moment of respectful silence settled between them, Saburo choking up at the memory of his brave brother Taro, and Jack mourning the loss of Yamato, who'd sacrificed himself to save him and Akiko from the ninja Dragon Eye.

Neko looked shocked, thinking her tea was to blame. But Yori signed to her that the *sencha* tasted good. She bowed at the compliment before scampering back to her corner to prepare their lunch.

As ever, Jack was amazed at Yori's sensitivity to people – without even being told, his friend was aware of Neko's condition. He was just the same as Jack remembered. Although small of stature, Yori possessed a great heart and a warmth of spirit that made him the perfect monk. Such virtues hadn't always helped him during his training to become a samurai warrior. Nonetheless, Yori had demonstrated surprising resilience and extraordinary skills that belied his mild-mannered appearance.

'I still can't believe I ran into you *and* Saburo,' said Jack.

Yori smiled warmly at him. 'Coincidence is a deity's way of staying anonymous. Perhaps Hotei the Laughing Buddha, one of our seven lucky gods, was looking favourably upon you.'

'I must thank him for his kindness,' said Jack, smiling too. 'So when do you go back to Iga Ueno?'

'When my good friend is safely home,' replied Yori, bowing his head.

'You're as loyal as ever,' said Jack, returning his bow. 'But before I can go anywhere, I've promised to help these farmers.'

Yori nodded sagely, as if expecting this answer. In the true spirit of a Buddhist monk, he replied, 'In helping others, we shall help ourselves.'

'You don't have to stay,' insisted Jack. 'This mission will be dangerous.'

So far he hadn't directly asked Yori to join them, since he

knew his friend avoided violence wherever he could. But Jack couldn't deny Yori's wisdom and sound advice would be useful in the forthcoming battle against Akuma.

'Where there are friends, there's hope,' said Yori. '*You* told me that.'

'Wise words, Yori,' remarked Saburo. 'But where do we find more young samurai to help *us*?'

'You've such little faith, Saburo!' chastised Yori, with a shrewd look in his eyes that was reminiscent of Sensei Yamada. 'The priest at the Okayama Temple told me about an archery contest down by the riverside. That's where they'll be.'

12

SPLITTING ARROWS

A large crowd had gathered along the eastern bank of the Asahi River. The area itself was the thriving centre of Okayama's merchant quarter. Several flat-keel riverboats with single square sails were moored at the dock. Porters rushed around lugging bales of rice or transporting barrels of *saké*, stacked by the dozen, upon rickety wooden carts. Goods of all descriptions were being unloaded into the vast wooden warehouses that lined the riverbank, while empty vessels awaited their loads for distribution to other parts of Japan.

Upon the opposite shore, a five-tiered castle dominated the skyline, its all-black exterior casting an oppressive shadow over the proceedings.

'That's Crow Castle,' said Toge, as they worked their way through the throng. 'The home of *daimyo* Ikeda.'

Jack realized that a lord who lived in such an imposing structure would have little sympathy for *any* of his subjects, especially lowly farmers.

The archery contest was taking place on the broad veranda of the largest of the warehouses. Six small targets had been set up at one end and the archers were lined up at the other, some sixty metres away. The competing samurai were dressed in winter kimono, their left arms pulled out of the sleeve and laid bare to the elements so that they could draw their bows and shoot cleanly.

Arrows flew through the air like flights of startled sparrows, followed by a percussive thunder of steel tips striking hard wooden targets. As soon as one round was complete, another hail of arrows was unleashed.

'Every year Okayama holds a *Tōshiya* contest,' explained Toge. 'The archer who hits their target the most out of a hundred arrows is declared the winner.'

Another pepper of bolts struck home, the shafts quivering upon impact. Those that missed either fell short into the veranda's decking or embedded themselves in the warehouse wall behind.

Saburo spotted several young samurai among the spectators. 'Which one shall we ask first?'

Jack followed his gaze. The group were a mix of boys and girls, but none were anywhere near their coming-of-age ceremony. He shook his head. 'Far too young.'

'How about those two?' suggested Sora.

An older boy and a girl, who appeared to be his sister, stood at the front, transfixed by the ongoing contest. Scanning the crowd, Jack considered they were the only likely candidates.

'What do you think, Yori?'

'I need to have a closer look,' he replied, unable to see over the crowd's shoulders.

'Follow me,' said Saburo, leading the way.

Just as they reached the front row, a great shout went up.

The archers had ceased firing and the judging now began. The spectators fell silent in anticipation, while a white-robed official inspected the targets in turn, counting the successful hits of each archer.

'Fifty-two,' he announced to respectful applause, and the first samurai gave a humble bow.

'Sixty-four.' To which the second archer allowed himself a smug grin as he was greeted with enthusiastic cheering.

'Twenty-one.' A polite yet half-hearted clapping couldn't hide the crowd's sniggering, or the shame burning on the third samurai's face. But he didn't have to suffer their ridicule for long. A collective gasp of amazement sounded when the fourth competitor's score was revealed.

'*Ninety-eight!*' declared the official, clearly astonished himself. 'A new record!'

Dressed in a crisp white *gi* and all-white *hakama*, a severe-looking samurai with a thin moustache gave a victorious shout and thrust his bow into the air.

'Why not him?' said Yori, nodding towards the veranda as the official called out a disappointing 'Forty-seven' for the fifth samurai.

'Make your mind up, Yori,' said Saburo. 'I thought we were looking for young samurai.'

'We *are*,' said Yori, directing their attention to the sixth and final archer.

A lone boy stood among the other competitors. Wearing a plain black kimono, his hair tied up into a topknot, the boy appeared unexceptional. Yet his face was sharp and attentive, and his demeanour cool and collected.

The official had completed his count of the boy's target,

but he seemed uncertain of the result and checked again. The excitement among the crowd grew. Then the official turned to them and announced, 'Ninety-nine!'

For a moment, no one could believe the result – in particular, the samurai with the thin moustache, who stared in fury at the boy's target as if trying to re-count the forest of arrows from a distance. Then the spectators burst into amazed applause.

When the initial cheering had subsided, the official approached the boy and began, 'I declare the winner to be –'

'No, *I'm* the champion!' cut in the other samurai, striding angrily over. 'Tell us how old you are,' he demanded of the boy.

'Fifteen . . . and a half.'

'See! He's not yet of age.'

'What does age have to do with it?' argued the boy. 'I beat you.'

The samurai looked ready to explode. 'You arrogant child! I'll teach you your place,' he said, waving a fist in the boy's face.

The boy didn't flinch. 'I welcome a challenge.'

'Then we'll double the target distance *and* put it on water,' snapped the samurai. 'Best of two arrows.'

The boy coolly bowed his acceptance and the crowd buzzed with excitement at this unprecedented development. The official ordered a porter to move a target on to a boat and row it out into the middle of the river. A path was cleared from the veranda to the dock, allowing a clear line of sight for the two archers.

'Now we'll prove who is the *true* champion,' said the

samurai, lining himself up to take his first shot. 'Prepare to be humiliated.'

With practised ease, he raised his bow, pulled back on the string and released the arrow. It soared through the air, arcing high above the crowd and towards the distant bobbing boat. They all strained to see where it would land upon the target. But, even without the porter raising a black flag in confirmation, it was clear that the arrow had struck dead centre – a bullseye.

The crowd went wild – no one had ever witnessed such an incredible feat before.

Caught up in his own conceit, the samurai shot the boy a superior look before taking his next shot. This was his mistake. The tiny break in his concentration sent the second shot a fraction off-course. The porter, his eyes wide with alarm, leapt from the boat and into the river as the stray arrow struck the wooden seat he'd just been sitting on.

This time the crowd broke into laughter.

'It was *meant* to test his reactions,' muttered the samurai, trying to cover up his error as the bedraggled porter clambered back in. 'You'll be lucky to even hit the boat, boy!'

Ignoring the samurai's jibes, the boy positioned himself side-on to the target, forming a perfect A-shape with his body. Jack recognized the motions the boy was going through from his own *kyujutsu* training – the perfect balance, the unwavering focus, and the combining of the spirit, bow and body as one.

The boy moved with the fluidity of a single breath and, upon release, the arrow cut through the cold air like a knife.

The eyes of the crowd followed it across the sky and towards the constantly shifting target. As it landed, a splintering sound travelled back across the waters to the dock.

Raising a soggy black flag with a trembling hand, the porter cried out, 'The boy split the samurai's arrow in half!'

More amazed applause burst forth from the crowd.

'I think we've found our first young samurai,' said Jack, grinning at the others.

The boy placed his second arrow back into his quiver and stepped off the veranda.

'Where do you think you're going?' demanded the samurai.

'I've nothing else to prove,' replied the boy.

'Come back here! I'm not finished with you.'

But the boy continued to walk away. The applauding crowd parted to let him through. Utterly humiliated, the samurai reached for an arrow with which to kill his opponent. Jack was about to shout a warning, when the boy spun round with lightning speed, drew his own arrow and shot at the samurai first.

But the arrow flew clear past the man's shoulder and disappeared into the depths of the warehouse.

With a sorry shake of his head, Saburo leant close to Jack. 'Are you *sure* we want him?'

Laughing, the samurai nocked an arrow and slowly drew back on his bow. 'Now you'll pay for your insolence.'

The boy stood his ground.

He merely watched as the warehouse's *saké* barrels tumbled off their cart, bounced across the wooden dock and hurtled into the samurai. The impact knocked the man clean over the side. With the boy's arrow having sliced through the cart's binding rope, several more heavy barrels rapidly followed their victim into the murky depths of the river.

By the time the battered and half-drowned samurai was rescued, the boy had disappeared into the crowd.

13

HAYATO

'Any luck?' asked Jack, returning to the storehouse with Toge. Having lost sight of the archer boy, the five of them had split up to find him.

Slumped on his haunches, Sora woefully shook his head.

'Are Yori or Saburo back yet?'

'What do *you* think?' Kunio sulked, waving a hand at the empty room.

Toge clipped the boy round the ear. 'Show some respect!'

'*Ow!*' cried Kunio, rubbing his head and bowing an apology to Jack. 'But why did *I* have to miss the *Tōshiya* contest? Sora could have guarded the rice.'

'We weren't there for the show! Need I remind you our village is at stake –'

The door opened and Yori stepped through, a flurry of snow following in his wake. They all looked expectantly in his direction.

Yori shook his head as he dusted himself down and put his *shakujō* in the corner. 'I asked everyone I met, but no one saw the boy cross the bridge or head west out of town.'

Jack sighed wearily. 'He would have been perfect for this mission.'

'There will be others,' consoled Yori.

'Will there?' snapped Toge, his cheeks hollower than ever in his despair. 'As poor farmers, we can't afford proper *ronin*! All we can persuade are children! And I didn't see that many *young* samurai at the contest!'

'There were at least two others,' countered Jack.

'And how are we supposed to find *them* now? We're running out of time. The black moon is only three weeks away!'

'Have faith,' said Yori.

'Faith?' spat Toge. 'Every year I pray to the gods. I pray for rain. I pray for sun. I pray for a good harvest. I pray that we can feed the village. I *pray* that Akuma won't come! And do the gods answer?'

'They will,' assured Yori.

'For you, they might. But not for us farmers!' shouted Toge.

Consumed with frustrated rage, he stomped out through the back of the storehouse, leaving Jack and the others to stare at one another in shocked silence.

Neko appeared a moment later, her eyes panicking. But once she spotted Jack, she breathed a sigh of relief and went back to preparing dinner.

'Please don't take his words to heart,' said Sora meekly. 'He's upset, that's all. He always is when Black Moon nears.'

Nodding their understanding, Jack and Yori settled upon the wooden platform and waited for Saburo to return.

'Do you think he's all right?' asked Yori, peering out at the darkening sky.

'He's probably eating!' quipped Jack, in an attempt to mask his own unease.

Another hour went by and Neko served up a meal of plain rice and a few steamed vegetables. They ate in silence, Yori and Jack's concern for Saburo growing with each passing moment.

All of a sudden, the door flew open. Jack leapt to his feet, sword in hand.

'I found him!' cried Saburo, wind and snow swirling into the room.

Sheathing his blade, Jack hurriedly put on his hat to cover his face as Saburo ushered a shadow in from the cold.

The archer boy entered, his falcon-brown eyes darting round the room for any threats.

'Please sit with us,' said Saburo, inviting him to join Yori and Jack on the raised platform.

The boy's gaze lingered on Jack, noting his concealed face, but he made no comment. Seemingly satisfied with his safety, he laid down his bow and knelt in a half-seated position. He wasn't taking any chances – with one knee still raised and a *katana* on his hip, the boy could react instantly to any surprise attack.

Neko rushed over with two bowls of steaming rice. Saburo tucked in, but the boy politely waved his meal away.

'I've already eaten, with Saburo,' he said. 'You may have it.'

Neko looked to Jack for an explanation. Jack clumsily signed that the meal was hers. Delighted, she beamed at Jack, then bowed gratefully to the boy.

'This is Hayato,' announced Saburo through a mouthful of rice. 'I found him practising in the fields.'

Hayato gave a humble bow, then glanced to where Toge, Sora and Kunio crouched in the corner. 'I understand these farmers have a problem with bandits.'

'Yes,' Jack replied, returning the boy's greeting. 'Has Saburo explained about the enemy we're facing?'

Hayato nodded, apparently unfazed by the prospect of such a dangerous foe.

'And that the farmers can only offer food and lodging as payment?'

Again, Hayato nodded. 'That's more than enough. As a samurai, it's my duty and honour to protect the rice that feeds our nation.'

Jack, Saburo and Yori looked at one another. The boy was pure *bushido*: the ideal that Masamoto always drove his students to attain. They couldn't wish for a better ally. But there was one more hurdle to overcome.

Turning back to Hayato, Jack said, 'If you are to join us, there's something you should know first.'

Taking a deep breath and preparing for the worst, Jack removed his hat.

Hayato's eyes widened momentarily and his hand edged towards his *katana*, but his demeanour did not change.

'I presume you're the infamous *gaijin* samurai.'

Jack's own hand now twitched for his sword. *Was the boy intending to kill him for the reward?*

'Are there any *more* surprises?' asked Hayato, eyeing the three of them warily.

Saburo and Yori shifted closer to protect Jack. The farmers shrank back into the corner as the tension between the four samurai increased.

'No,' said Jack.

Letting his sword hand relax, Hayato smiled. 'Don't worry, I'm not seeking you out. In fact, we fought on the same side at the Battle of Osaka Castle. My father was *daimyo* Yukimura.'

Jack remembered the man. The samurai lord had been assassinated by ninja during an attack organized by the Shogun himself.

'My father . . . he talked of you,' revealed Hayato, a crack of emotion in his voice. 'You saved his friend's life, the great *daimyo* Takatomi. I admire any samurai who confronts a ninja, especially one as deadly as Dragon Eye.'

'I was in the right place at the right time, that's all,' replied Jack.

'You're too humble,' said Hayato. 'I like that. I'd be proud to fight at your side against this bandit Akuma.'

Overcoming their fear, the farmers shuffled forward and bowed their gratitude. Even Toge's mood seemed improved at the news and he signed impatiently to Neko to brew some fresh *sencha*.

As the four samurai sipped their tea, Jack admitted to Hayato, 'We've struggled to find willing volunteers. Do you know anyone else who might join us?'

Putting down his cup, Hayato pondered this for a moment, then raised a single finger in the air. 'One boy may be worth recruiting.'

14

YUUDAI

'What do you think?' asked Hayato, the following morning down by the docks.

Jack and the others were momentarily speechless. The young samurai in question was lugging *saké* barrels two at a time into a warehouse – other porters could barely manage one cask between two.

'He's the size of a mountain!' gasped Yori, who didn't even measure up to the boy's hip.

Jack was equally astonished. This young samurai possessed a broad chest, legs like tree trunks and arms rippling with muscles. His hair, swept up into a topknot, was slick and black as tar, and his face seemed to be chiselled out of granite.

'Yuudai is big for his age,' granted Hayato. 'But that's what makes him such a formidable warrior.'

A stick-thin woman with narrow eyes and grey papery skin marched out of the warehouse.

'What's taking you so long?' she demanded, waving a slim bamboo cane threateningly in the air. 'We've three more shipments to unload. Get moving!'

She chased Yuudai and the other porters into the warehouse, barking orders and abuse as if she was the Shogun herself. One porter was apparently too slow for her liking and she whipped him across the legs.

'That woman's worse than my mother!' commented Saburo as her victim limped rapidly inside.

All of a sudden a high-pitched scream pierced the air.

'Sounds like the samurai's had enough of her?' said Jack, and they ran to see what was causing the commotion.

They found the woman standing upon an empty cart, her face greyer than ever and her kimono held tight to her skeletal body.

'Kill it! Kill it!' she screeched, pointing a gnarled finger at a tiny brown mouse on the floor.

A porter grabbed a broom and tried to beat the creature over the head. But the mouse was too quick. It darted up the cart's wheel and the woman became hysterical as the mouse scurried about her feet. She jumped around like a maniacal puppet, while the porters struggled to stifle their laughter.

'*You*, samurai boy!' squawked the woman, her eyes bulging with terror. 'Help me!'

Cornering the little creature, Yuudai bent down and scooped it up in his huge hands.

'Squash it!' she cried.

Yuudai, ignoring the frenzied woman, strode out of the warehouse. Going over to the far side of the dock, he released the mouse on to the riverbank and watched it scamper safely away.

The woman stood at the warehouse door, fuming at him.

'I ordered you to *kill* the wretched creature!'

'What harm did the mouse ever do to you?' asked Yuudai, his voice low and gentle.

The woman's lips appeared to chew themselves as she sought for a suitably vicious reply. Eventually, she spat, 'How dare you disobey me! You get half-rations today. Now back to work, all of you!'

Resuming her tyrannical abuse, the woman lashed out with her cane and the porters scattered to their posts, their moment of amusement over.

With a weary sigh, Yuudai followed the woman inside.

'A bit soft for a samurai, isn't he?' commented Saburo.

'But very strong!' said Jack.

'I like him,' said Yori. 'He respects life.'

'What good is *that* if he's facing a bloodthirsty bandit like Akuma?' argued Toge.

'He's trustworthy and loyal,' replied Hayato. 'That counts for a great deal.'

Toge still wasn't convinced. 'If he's samurai, then what's he doing working as a porter?'

'Yuudai has no family left,' revealed Hayato. 'He must fend for himself – any way he can. And not many lords are hiring *young* samurai.'

'Do you think he'd be willing to join us?' asked Jack.

Hayato nodded confidently. 'It doesn't look as if he's enjoying his current position. And he needs food to keep his strength up.'

Turning to Yori, Jack whispered, 'Remind you of anyone?'

Yori glanced at Saburo and smothered a giggle.

They waited until midday when the porters took a short break for lunch. Yuudai sat by himself at the end of the dock, his long legs dangling over the edge, his feet almost touching the water. Hayato made the approach, since he knew the boy.

Jack and the others watched from a distance as the two of them conversed. Hayato pointed to the farmers, then to the three samurai. Yuudai slowly chewed his food as he listened. Hayato finished and, bowing, awaited his reply.

Everyone craned their necks, anxious for Yuudai's response.

The boy mountain wiped his hands on a cloth and stood – then walked slowly back along the dock, the wooden planks creaking under his weight. When he reached Jack, he stopped.

Yuudai looked down at him and smiled. 'Your offer sounds worthy.'

Bowing in appreciation of his acceptance, Jack asked, 'When can you join us?'

'Now,' he replied, collecting his *nodachi* sword from inside the warehouse door. He slung it across his back. In spite of its extra-long blade, the *nodachi* looked like a child's toy in his hands.

Striding over to her workforce, the withered woman snapped, 'Stop idling! Get back to work!'

The porters wearily hauled themselves to their feet.

'Where are you going, samurai boy?' she demanded.

Yuudai gave a respectful bow of his head. 'I have another job.'

Her face became taut with indignation. 'If you leave now, you'll never work here again!'

'That must be a relief,' said Saburo, grinning at their new friend as they all walked away.

Staring in rage as her workhorse departed, the woman slammed her cane upon a *saké* barrel so hard that it snapped in half.

'That's your fault!' she squawked, shaking a bony fist at Yuudai. 'You owe me a new cane!'

15

OUT OF TIME

'We only need *two* more,' said Jack, as they split up and scoured the town for young samurai. Despite the odds, he was so close to fulfilling his promise to the village. But with market day and the *Tōshiya* contest over, Okayama had seemingly emptied of potential recruits.

A whole afternoon went by and they spotted just one young samurai worth approaching. She quickly rejected their offer, saying her parents wouldn't allow it. But they'd seen the fear in her eyes at the mention of Akuma. Jack didn't blame the girl, though. Defending the village was no game; it would be a *real* battle and Akuma wouldn't take any prisoners.

'Perhaps Saburo and Hayato have had more luck?' Yori suggested.

The two of them had gone in search of the brother and sister who'd been at the archery competition the previous day.

'I hope so,' said Jack.

A disheartened Sora led them back to the storehouse, Jack and Yori walking beside the mammoth Yuudai. As they wound their way through the side streets, no one dared approach them and, for the first time in many months, Jack almost felt safe.

Even when Jack had shown his face, Yuudai had bowed courteously, offering a warm smile and stating, 'Any friend of Hayato is a friend of mine.'

A bored Kunio was slouched by the storehouse door, waiting for everyone to return. He almost fell over himself when he saw Yuudai enter. Unable to tear his eyes away, he simply gawped at the new arrival.

'Don't stare!' hissed Toge.

But Kunio remained open-mouthed and in awe of the mighty young samurai. Toge shoved him out of the back of the storehouse, ordering him to fetch some logs for a fire. A few minutes later, Neko appeared with freshly brewed *sencha*. She almost dropped the kettle when she caught sight of Yuudai.

Bowing shyly, she poured tea for the samurai with a trembling hand. In her haste, she spilt some on the floor. Her dark eyes widened into massive moons and her face flushed red.

'She's deaf and mute,' apologized Toge, pushing Neko to one side in shame at her mistake.

'Let her be,' growled Yuudai, fixing him with a stern gaze. 'Most people with ears don't listen anyway.'

Chastened, Toge retreated into the corner. Yuudai smiled kindly at Neko and beckoned her to repour his cup. He bowed his appreciation for the *sencha* and, once Neko had served Jack and Yori, she backed out of the room. As they drank their tea, Jack noticed Neko peeking through the gap in the wall as she washed the rice for dinner.

Saburo and Hayato returned soon after, appearing weary.

'We found them,' announced Saburo.

'But unfortunately we were too late,' explained Hayato.

'They were already on a boat heading south to Imaban.'

'It's all over then,' said Sora, his face downcast. 'Our village is doomed.'

'Don't despair,' said Yori. 'We'll look again tomorrow.'

'What's the point?' said Toge. 'We must go back and prepare. We're running out of time!'

'And we don't have *seven* samurai yet,' stated Jack.

'But you're great warriors!' interrupted Kunio. 'Surely five is all we need.'

Jack stared into his half-empty cup. The tea matched their own situation – some, but not enough. The wretched desperation on the farmers' faces was almost too much to bear, but Jack couldn't be reckless with his friends' lives. This was a dangerous mission with seven. Being only five samurai, the risk was even greater.

Coming to a difficult decision, he announced, 'If anyone wants to leave now, then they should do so.'

No one moved.

'Why seven?' asked Hayato.

'There are at least forty bandits. I calculate a skilful samurai could handle up to six enemies at most.'

'Well, Yuudai counts for at least two people,' responded Hayato. 'With my bow, I can bring down several bandits before they get within fighting distance. And we haven't yet allowed for your skills.'

Jack looked to the others. Yori seemed nervous but resolved. Saburo was surprisingly committed too, and Yuudai appeared as indestructible as rock.

He nodded his reluctant agreement. 'Five it is then.'

★

The next morning the five samurai, three farmers and Neko left for Tamagashi village. The winter wind blew a bitter chill as the group trekked across the snow-covered plain. Their going was slow and when the drifts became too deep, Yuudai carried Yori on his shoulders.

Hayato marched alongside Jack. 'How much further?' he asked, studying the bleak terrain ahead.

'Last time we arrived around dusk.'

Noticing Jack glance over his shoulder, Hayato leant in close. 'Do you sense what I do?'

'Yes,' said Jack, glad he wasn't the only one to feel it. He scanned the vast open landscape. 'Nowhere to hide, but some-one *is* following us.'

16

WHITE SHADOW

Entering a patch of sparse woodland, the sense of being watched grew. Jack kept his hand upon his sword and Hayato unslung his bow. The others remained oblivious to the threat and Jack wondered if the two of them were being over-cautious. There was *still* no sign of pursuit. And their remote location begged the question, who would be following them in the first place?

The tactics of the Shogun's samurai were usually direct and unsubtle. If they'd planned to ambush him, the ideal place would have been Okayama. It could be Kazuki and his Scorpion Gang. They often proved more devious and might be laying a trap. But it seemed odd to wait this long and the isolation meant no chance of reinforcements.

'Bandits?' whispered Hayato, his eyes darting from tree to tree.

'Maybe,' agreed Jack.

There was a strong possibility Akuma had got word of their plan to help the farmers – any of the samurai they'd approached in Okayama might have talked. If that was the case, the best opportunity Akuma had to attack the young samurai was *now*.

The five of them were at their most vulnerable – before they reached the village and before they could prepare any defence.

The three farmers were slightly ahead and Jack urged everyone to catch up. It would be fatal if the group was split during a fight. They crunched on through the snow, their crisp footsteps the only sound.

Out of the corner of his eye, Jack caught a movement. Snapping his head round, he saw . . . nothing but the frozen skeletons of trees, their branches laden with ice and snow. The sole sign of life was a deer track that wound its way through the woodland.

'Why are you both so edgy?' asked Saburo.

'Bandits may be stalking us,' replied Hayato, under his breath.

Saburo looked around and laughed. 'Well, if they are, they must be snowmen!'

In the space of a heartbeat, Hayato drew his bow and shot at Saburo. He yelped in surprise as the arrow flew past his ear and struck a snowdrift.

A fraction before it did, a white shadow flitted away. Camouflaged to the surroundings, the figure immediately disappeared into the snow-shrouded landscape.

'You could be right!' said Hayato, hurriedly nocking another arrow.

Jack withdrew his sword, but the attack happened so fast, it took them all by surprise.

Out of nowhere, a *manriki* whirled through the air towards Hayato. He ducked, but the short weighted chain wrapped itself around his bow, incapacitating it. A moment later, a white shadow materialized from behind a tree and kicked Saburo in the gut. He collapsed to the ground, winded. Hearing his cry, the farmers fled in panic. But Yori quickly rallied them back into a group, holding out his *shakujō*'s pointed iron tip as a weapon.

Jack turned to pursue Saburo's assailant, but once again the white shadow had vanished. As Hayato disentangled his bow, Jack scanned the woodland for their invisible enemy. But it was like hunting for a needle in a haystack.

He felt a tug on his sleeve and Neko was by his side, indicating with her eyes to a nearby tree. He saw nothing. Yet Neko was insistent.

Staring more intently, he noticed a slight bulge on the topside of a lower bough. Yuudai spotted it too. Being closest, he rushed to grab the hidden form. But it flew from the bough, kicking out as it launched itself over Yuudai's head. A mountain of snow cascaded from the branches, engulfing the boy up to his waist.

The white-clad assassin landed cat-like in front of Jack.

Before his opponent could attack, Jack brought his *katana* slicing downwards. Pulling a white-handled blade from the *saya* on its back, the shadow deflected the lethal strike and locked eyes with Jack.

'*What a way to welcome a friend!*' hissed the assassin.

Jack almost dropped his *katana*.

'Miyuki?' he said, recognizing the voice behind the mask.

'Who else could sneak up on you so easily?'

Miyuki was dressed head-to-toe in a pure white *shinobi shozoku*, the customary winter garb of a ninja. Sheathing his *katana*, Jack burst into a grin at being reunited with his ninja training partner.

Hotei the Laughing Buddha is certainly on my side, thought Jack.

Although to begin with Miyuki had despised him for being a samurai – a ruthless samurai warrior having murdered her parents and baby brother – over time their respect and trust for one another had grown until they became firm friends. He was over the moon to see her again.

'NO!' shouted Jack, as Hayato freed his bow and aimed an arrow at her back.

In the blink of an eye, Miyuki spun to throw a *shuriken* in retaliation. Jack grabbed her arm before she could release the deadly throwing star. Hayato and Miyuki glared at one another, a fierce battle of wills in play.

Yuudai, shaking off the snow, advanced on her too.

'Miyuki's a *friend*!' insisted Jack, holding up a hand in a vain attempt to stop the massive boy.

'She's a ninja!' said Hayato coldly, keeping the bow in tension.

'And you're a samurai!' replied Miyuki with equal contempt. Her free hand now held a throwing knife targeted at Hayato's throat.

Jack stepped between them, trying to break the tension. 'Her ninja clan once saved me. She's on our side.'

Groaning, Saburo struggled to his feet with the help of Neko.

'If she's a friend of yours,' he wheezed, rubbing his belly, 'why did she have to kick me so hard?'

'I didn't know if *you* were friend or foe,' replied Miyuki, offering no sympathy.

Yori, leaving the bewildered farmers huddled at a safe distance, placed himself in the middle of the confrontation.

'I'm Yori,' he said, bowing respectfully to Miyuki. 'I'm a friend of Jack's – which must make us friends too!'

His smile was both genuine and disarming, and Miyuki lowered her knife in acknowledgement. With the situation defused, Hayato released the tension on his bow and retreated with Yuudai. But he didn't take his eyes off the ninja.

'What are you doing *here*?' asked Jack.

Miyuki stared at him as if the answer was obvious.

'To rescue you, of course!' she replied, pulling off her hood to reveal a striking girl of sixteen with spiky black hair and eyes as black as midnight.

'But I'm not in trouble.'

'That's not what Hana said.'

'*Hana?*' exclaimed Jack, surprised Miyuki knew the girl.

'Don't worry, she's fine. She got lost in the Iga mountains, but Hanzo's guiding her to Akiko as we speak.'

Jack was reassured by this news. He was also delighted for Akiko and for her mother, Hiroko, who would be seeing her long-lost son – Hanzo, originally named Kiyoshi – for the first time since his kidnap by Dragon Eye at the age of five.

'We didn't believe Hana to begin with,' continued Miyuki. 'We suspected she'd stolen your *inro*. But her detailed knowledge of you convinced us. She was very worried about Ronin and your safety.'

'Did you find Ronin on your travels?' Jack asked hopefully.

Miyuki shook her head, much to Jack's dismay. 'But *you* were easy to track! Didn't you learn anything from the Grandmaster?' she scolded.

'I left a trail on purpose. So that Kazuki would follow me, instead of Akiko.'

Miyuki rolled her eyes in disbelief. 'Well, it worked. Not

only are his Scorpion Gang after you but half the Shogun's samurai!'

Jack blanched and felt an icy shiver run down his spine. 'How close are they?'

'The last storm closed the Funasaka Pass. No one will be getting through there for a month or so.'

Jack breathed a sigh of relief, knowing his enemies couldn't follow his trail for a while at least. Miyuki glanced round at his travelling companions, her brow wrinkling in puzzlement at the odd mix of farmers, samurai and the tiny monk.

'What are you doing with these people anyway?' she asked.

'I made a promise to help these farmers,' he replied, and explained why they were heading to Tamagashi village.

'Now I remember why I like you so much, Jack,' said Miyuki, her usual cool demeanour breaking into a dazzling smile. 'Looks as if you could do with some help, though.'

'A ninja wasn't part of the agreement,' spat Hayato, his expression fierce.

'But we do need another warrior,' argued Jack, who was delighted at her offer. 'Miyuki's one of the best ninja I know. Her skills will be invaluable.'

'She's the *enemy*,' said Hayato with a clenched jaw.

'And samurai are *my* enemy,' shot back Miyuki.

The two of them reached for their weapons.

Yori raised his hands for peace and cut in, 'Our *only* enemy is Akuma.'

17

ARMY OF CHILDREN

'So that's our castle!' laughed Saburo as they approached the run-down village of Tamagashi. 'It's more like a dung-hill!'

'Samurai are so arrogant,' said Miyuki, shooting him a reproachful look. 'This is their home. Show some respect.'

Chastened, Saburo became ashamed at his insensitive comment, but Hayato glared at Miyuki for having the auda-city as a ninja to criticize a samurai. He barely managed to keep his hostility in check.

Jack thought he may have to step in again. He'd explained about his relationship to Miyuki and tried to convince Hayato that the ninja were misrepresented as a whole. Hayato had acknowledged that Jack as a foreigner might be able to bridge the gap, but that he would *never* trust a ninja. This suited Miyuki just fine, since she wouldn't ever trust a samurai. Thankfully, Yori managed to negotiate a truce between Hayato and Miyuki – the differences of the samurai and the ninja were to be set aside for the common goal of defeating Akuma.

But Jack realized this was a fragile alliance.

'Tamagashi may not be much to look at,' he said, ushering the two of them over the mill's rickety bridge. 'But I can assure you its people deserve defending.'

They followed the farmers along the muddy track and into the square. As they passed the ramshackle homes, the villagers came out to greet them. But upon seeing the tender age of their saviours, they could only gawp in disbelief.

'Not much of a welcome!' remarked Hayato.

'They're probably just nervous,' suggested Yori, although he too sensed the growing awkwardness of their arrival.

Entering the square, they made for the main farmhouse where Junichi was waiting on the veranda. He bowed low at their approach, keeping his eyes respectfully to the ground.

'As the head of this village, I welcome you and offer our undying gratitude for helping us in our hour of need. Please consider Tamagashi your home –'

Standing up, Junichi took a double take and became lost for words. He stared aghast at the four young samurai, one tiny monk and the lone ninja before him.

Jack and his recruits bowed back, all made uneasy by Junichi's horrified expression.

'*What's the meaning of this, Toge?*' demanded Junichi, out of the corner of his mouth.

Toge stared blankly back, while Sora piped up in their defence, 'We couldn't get any more samurai.'

'That's not what I mean,' hissed Junichi. 'You've hired *children* to do men's work!'

'They're the best we could do,' replied Toge grimly.

An air of desperate disappointment consumed the villagers gathering in the square.

'We might as well give up now!' shouted a farmer to Junichi.

'Akuma will slaughter them,' cried an old woman, her face pitying the young warriors.

'Where are the *real* samurai?' shouted another man.

The calls of outrage, frustration and despair grew louder and Junichi's pleas for calm went unheeded. The farmhouse door opened and Yoshi the elder came tottering out. He thumped the wooden veranda with his walking-stick and fixed the villagers with a furious glare.

'What right have you to judge these young samurai? When you can't even fight as men yourselves! This village doesn't deserve to be saved.'

The crowd fell into a disgraced silence.

Then the old woman cried, 'You can't allow children to fight our battles!'

'Who else has stepped to our defence?' challenged Yoshi.

No one answered.

'These young samurai have skills we don't. They are brave and willing to make a stand for us. We should respect them.'

'I can really see Akuma respecting them,' shouted a farmer sarcastically. 'He might just laugh himself to death!'

At this the crowd began to disperse, realizing the futility of battling bandits with a pitiful army of children.

'It appears we're *not* wanted, after all,' said Hayato, turning angrily to leave.

'This is simply a misunderstanding,' said Jack, exasperated by the farmers' short-sightedness. Unwilling to give up on them, he added, 'Let me explain the plan to them.'

'No, the situation is perfectly understood. The farmers don't want *our* help. Come on, Yuudai.'

Bowing farewell to Jack, Yuudai followed Hayato back in the direction of Okayama.

'I have to agree, Jack,' said Miyuki. 'We're wasting our time here.'

'But how will the farmers survive without us?' said Jack, thinking of poor Neko and the fate of her parents.

'You can't help those who won't be helped,' responded Yori with a reluctant sigh.

Heading back down the track, Saburo asked, 'What about food and lodgings tonight?'

Jack was about to answer, when an alarm suddenly clanged.

The faces of the villagers became taut with terror. 'Bandits!' cried a farmer and everyone fled in wild panic. A few desperately gathered their belongings, others ran for their lives, but most rushed after the departing young samurai.

'Save us! Save us! You must help us!' they implored.

'*Now* they want our services,' called back Hayato. Nonetheless, he unslung his bow and dashed into the square, Yuudai at his side.

Jack, Saburo and Miyuki unsheathed their swords and prepared for the surprise attack. Yori gripped his staff, his hands trembling at the thought of the forthcoming battle.

'Which direction is Akuma coming from?' demanded Hayato, running up to the main farmhouse.

'I don't know,' cried Junichi, his eyes darting fearfully in all directions.

'Well, who rang the alarm?'

'It wasn't *me*,' he said, as if the raid was his fault.

'Then who did?'

'It was her!' shouted Kunio, pointing to the roof of the blacksmith's hut.

Neko was standing upon its ridge, an iron bar and hammer in hand. She pummelled it again and grinned in delight as the villagers scattered like startled mice.

'So where are the bandits?' questioned Miyuki, scanning the deserted horizon.

It was then Jack realized Neko's ploy. 'There are no bandits!'

Smiling with relief, Yori said, 'She's just proving to the farmers they really do need us.'

'There's more to that girl than meets the eye!' said Yuudai, letting loose a great booming laugh at the chaos she'd caused.

Neko, seeing Yuudai applaud her, rang the alarm again. Yoshi shuffled over to the edge of the veranda and addressed the young samurai.

'Please help our village,' he beseeched. 'We're all children when it comes to fear.'

18

THE RELUCTANT LEADER

That evening, the young warriors received a proper welcome. Sora and his wife gave over their entire house to them, Junichi arranged for straw beds and the contrite villagers brought offerings of rice, fish and steamed vegetables. A roaring hearth fire was built, before Jack and the others were left alone to eat and recover from their journey.

'This is more like it!' said Saburo, digging into a bowl of sticky rice.

The six of them ate in contented silence, Neko pouring out tea and water whenever required. Once they'd had their fill, they sat back and listened to the crackle of the fire. Staring into the flames, Jack became lost in his own thoughts – of Akiko, of his sister, Jess, in England, and how one day he'd find his way home.

For a moment, everyone appeared to have forgotten why they were there.

'So what's the plan?' asked Hayato, breaking their reverie.

Jack blinked. 'I . . . don't have one.'

'But you said earlier you did.'

He smiled sheepishly. 'That was to convince the farmers.'

There was an exchange of concerned looks all round.

'Well, you must have *some* idea,' said Saburo, abandoning his meal.

Jack shook his head. 'I really hadn't thought that far.'

'Every good leader has a plan,' observed Hayato.

'Leader?' queried Jack.

The five recruits looked unwaveringly at him.

'This is your crusade,' said Hayato. 'You brought us together, so *you* should lead us.'

Jack felt his mouth go dry and his stomach tighten into a knot. He hadn't considered the consequence of his actions. He'd simply been driven by a desire to help. Now he found himself unwittingly positioned as their leader – responsible not only for the mission's success, but for their lives too.

'I . . . I think we need to discuss this first.'

'We could just put it to a vote,' suggested Yori.

'Well, I'm for Jack,' said Miyuki, raising her hand.

'Me too,' said Saburo, his hand joining hers.

Hayato's hand also went up, soon followed by Yuudai's. Figuring out what was occurring, Neko raised her hand too.

Yori smiled artfully at Jack. 'You have my vote – so it's unanimous.'

Jack couldn't sleep, his mind whirling with worries. The black moon was less than three weeks away and he had no idea how to prevent forty bandits raiding the village with only six warriors.

Getting out of bed, he crept over to the door, slipped on a ragged overcoat and stepped outside. The night air was chill and his breath blew out in ghostly clouds as he made his way along the deserted street. Shuddering against the cold, he walked down to the pond and gazed across the desolate paddy fields. The sky was crystal clear, its stars gleaming brighter than diamonds. And under the silvery moonlight, the snow-clad land looked like a shimmering white sea.

Jack could almost fool himself that he was back on the *Alexandria*, sailing the oceans with his father. But he knew that life was long gone. He just wished his father was with him now. As always, Jack looked to the stars in hope of guidance from him. Along with the precious *rutter* that he'd stowed carefully beneath the floorboards in Sora's farmhouse, the constellations were the only other connection to his late father. As a pilot, his father had spent many a night teaching him how to navigate by their positions. But tonight Jack felt well and truly lost, with no guiding star.

As he stared into the blackness, Jack became aware of someone approaching.

'When it is dark enough, you can see the stars,' observed Yori.

Jack laughed at this. It was one of Sensei Yamada's sayings, meaning there was always hope even in the worst of times.

'My father used to say, *a clear sky makes a clear mind*,' replied Jack. 'But I still can't think of a plan.'

'Give it time – it'll come.'

'How can you be so certain? I don't know the first thing about battle tactics or strategy.'

'Of course you do,' replied Yori, his conviction taking Jack by surprise. 'Masamoto taught you the Two Heavens.'

Jack was a little bemused. The Two Heavens was his guardian's secret double-sword technique.

'But *that's* for duelling with swords, one-on-one,' he argued. 'Won't a strategy that works against one enemy work against ten . . . twenty . . . a thousand?'

As Jack considered the possibility of Yori's suggestion, Masamoto's teachings from his final lessons came to mind. *The true Way of this style is not solely about handling two swords. The essence of the Two Heavens is the spirit of winning – to obtain victory by any means and with any weapon.*

'It might work,' Jack admitted, a few ideas from his samurai training already taking hold. 'But I'm no leader.'

'You're a natural, Jack,' insisted Yori. 'A leader guides by example, whether he intends to or not. Your courage and determination to protect this village inspire the rest of us.'

Jack had an overwhelming sense that Yori, while not much older, was definitely wiser since he last knew him. It was like talking with a younger version of Sensei Yamada.

'But no one else was given the chance to be leader,' Jack argued, thinking Hayato might have been a better choice.

Yori looked up at Jack. 'There was no need. The vote proved we *all* believe in you. You're the only one who can lead us.'

19

A NINJA'S INSPIRATION

'What are you doing up here?' asked Miyuki, finding Jack the next morning on a rise overlooking the village. 'Everyone's waiting for you.'

She handed him a cup of green tea, which he gratefully accepted, its warmth taking the chill from his bones. He'd managed to get some sleep during the night, but had risen early, his mind still churning with thoughts.

'Every battle strategy I've come up with has major flaws,' explained Jack. 'Either not enough samurai, not enough time or simply too risky.'

'Why not ask the others for suggestions?'

'But as leader *I'm* expected to come up with the plan,' said Jack, a hint of desperation entering his voice.

'Just because you're the leader doesn't mean you have to decide everything,' reassured Miyuki. 'In our clan, Shonin often asks the Grandmaster and the family heads for their ideas.'

'Really?' said Jack, feeling the weight of responsibility lift a little from his shoulders. He'd considered the others would think him weak to do so.

Miyuki nodded. 'The Grandmaster always says *to lead people, you should walk beside them.*'

Familiar with such pearls of wisdom from his time at the *Niten Ichi Ryū*, Jack instantly grasped the old ninja's lesson. He'd been so wrapped up in the idea of *being* leader that he'd forgotten the importance of working as a team.

Prompted by her mention of the Grandmaster, he asked, 'How is Soke now?'

'He's strong-willed, but the cold is getting to him,' Miyuki replied, her eyes betraying a deep-rooted concern. 'He's concentrating on preparing Hanzo to be the next Grandmaster.'

Jack nodded sympathetically, knowing Soke hadn't looked forward to their clan's enforced relocation even deeper into the Iga mountains. He was saddened to hear of the old man's fading health. The Grandmaster had been his *ninjutsu* mentor, saving him from the Shogun's samurai and teaching him the necessary skills to help survive the perilous journey to Nagasaki.

'And what about you?' asked Jack.

Miyuki forced a smile. 'The refuge is fine, but not like our last home. Life's tougher the higher up you are. The weather's more severe and the land not so fertile.' She gazed at the farm-houses below with a wistful smile. 'Tamagashi reminds me of our old village. The square, the pond, the open fields – although our houses were in far better condition and the paddies set out more efficiently.'

'That's because you're ninja as well as farmers,' Jack reminded her.

'True, but it doesn't take much thought to organize things.

I mean, look at their paddy fields. If ninja had plotted them, they'd be –'

'*A defence!*' interrupted Jack, his face suddenly lighting up. 'Miyuki, what would I do without you?'

Miyuki looked bashfully at the ground, then glanced up at him. 'I missed you too, Jack.'

But Jack was too inspired by her observation to notice the tender look that passed across her face.

'Why didn't I think of it before?' he exclaimed. 'The Five Rings!'

During his *ninjutsu* training, Jack had been taught about the Five Rings by the Grandmaster. These five great elements of the universe – Earth, Water, Fire, Wind and Sky – formed the basis of a ninja's fighting techniques and tactics. In fact, the Five Rings influenced their whole approach to life – including how they built their villages.

To the uninitiated eye, a ninja village looked like a simple farming community. In truth, it was a cleverly constructed fortress. By applying the Ring of Earth, the ninja exploited their natural surroundings – flooding paddy fields to form moats, building paths into confusing mazes, growing hedges into barriers, and using the hills and steep slopes as battlements.

'We need to *ninja* this village!' said Jack, a triumphant grin on his face.

He ran back down to the square, Miyuki hot on his heels, to find the others waiting by the pond.

'You look pleased with yourself,' remarked Saburo.

'I have a plan!' announced Jack.

The young samurai hurriedly gathered round in anticipation. Neko, eager to be a part of the action too, pushed her way to the front beside Yuudai. Emerging from the main farm-house, Junichi, Toge and Sora watched from a respectful distance.

'Our priority is to stop the bandits reaching the rice store,' stated Jack, indicating the large barn overlooking the square. 'So we need to turn this village into a fortress.'

'In three weeks!' exclaimed Saburo. 'This isn't exactly Osaka Castle!'

'With teamwork and the help of the farmers, we can do it,' replied Jack confidently.

'I must agree with Saburo,' said Hayato. 'Defence is more difficult than attack, and this village is wide open to any assault. Where would we even start?'

'That's what I was going to ask *you*!' said Jack.

Understanding that a combination of ninja and samurai tactics would offer the best chance of success, he recited one of Masamoto's strategies. '*In order to know your enemy, you must become your enemy*. So how would *you* attack this village?'

20

THROUGH THE EYES OF THE ENEMY

'Coming from the mountains,' said Hayato, 'the most obvious raiding route would be the northern road. Akuma won't expect resistance, so why make any detours?'

'Agreed,' said Jack. 'That's where our first defence must be.'

Leaving the square, they walked to the outskirts of the village, where the main track petered out at the mouth of a narrow valley. A dirt road snaked its way up the slope and disappeared over a rocky ridge.

'There's nothing to stop the bandits here,' observed Hayato grimly.

'Then we need a barricade,' suggested Jack. He scored a line in the snow with his foot, marking the boundary of the village. 'At this point.'

'I can build one,' offered Yuudai, 'with the help of some farmers.'

'Great!' replied Jack, pleased the boy was so willing to volunteer. 'Toge says the bandits have horses. So it'll have to be high enough to stop them jumping over and strong enough to resist a charge.'

'Don't worry,' said Yuudai. 'When I've finished, even a dragon couldn't get past!'

'Still, we won't have much warning of an attack,' Miyuki noted, eyeing the closeness of the valley ridge.

Jack recalled the Grandmaster's Ring of Fire lesson. This element represented energy and motivation for a ninja and was closely aligned to weapon work. Its key influence was in *kajutsu* – the Art of Fire – which included explosives, gunpowder and the use of fire for diversion and destruction. But Jack had also learnt that it could be more subtle, acting as a ninja's first line of defence.

Jack pointed to a nearby hill. 'We need a smoke beacon up there, to give us advance warning.'

'I'll ask the villagers to make a woodpile,' said Yori, 'and organize a lookout rota.'

'Thank you, Yori,' said Jack, already feeling more confident in his role as leader.

'But what if they attack from a different direction?' questioned Saburo.

'Good point. We should also build a watchtower in the square. That way we can keep an eye on all approaches to the village. I'll take charge of that.' He turned to Saburo. 'So, looking through the eyes of the enemy, where's our next weak point?'

Saburo's brow crinkled in thought. 'Probably the road from Okayama.'

The band of young samurai headed back into the village and down to the river, where the icy waters churned and flowed freely from the mountains.

'This is easier to defend,' said Hayato with relief, noting

the opposite bank was some ten metres away and the river too deep for horses to ford it. 'Akuma can't cross here if we dismantle the bridge.'

'No, we must keep it,' said Miyuki.

They all looked at her, Hayato glaring with annoyance at being contradicted.

'We leave it as a trap,' she explained. 'Like fish to a cat, the bandits will want to cross here. As they do, we blow it up!'

'That's dishonourable!' said Hayato. 'A samurai doesn't fight like that.'

'Do you think Akuma cares anything for honour?' countered Miyuki.

Clenching his jaw, Hayato conceded, 'Probably not. But *what* will you blow the bridge up with?'

'Gunpowder.'

Hayato eyed Miyuki dubiously. 'Do you have any?'

'A little,' she said, patting a small tube attached to her *obi*, along with various other pouches.

Hayato laughed. 'That wouldn't be enough for a firework!'

Now it was Miyuki's turn to look annoyed. 'We could make more. All we need is charcoal, sulphur and saltpetre.'

'Do you think these poor farmers have *all* that?' mocked Hayato.

Miyuki glared at him and Jack intervened before the quarrel got out of hand.

'Both ideas are strong,' he said. 'If the farmers have what Miyuki needs, then we can go with her plan. If not, we proceed with Hayato's. Whatever, we'll have to sacrifice the two houses on the far side and the mill.'

'You can't do that!' said Toge, walking up behind them.

'Junichi owns the mill. His mother, Natsuko, still lives there.'

'But we can't protect everything,' explained Hayato.

'Natsuko's a stubborn old woman.'

'She'll be less stubborn when Akuma's at her door.'

Toge shrugged. 'I'm telling you she won't like it.'

21

LOCKED HORNS

As the farmer headed over to deliver the message, Jack asked him, 'Where's the next crossing point on this river?'

'There's a ford, a few miles to the south,' Toge replied, pointing towards the paddy fields. 'That track over there eventually leads to it.'

'Then that'll be Akuma's next route of attack.'

The young samurai trekked across the fields. They followed the network of paths, many only visible as a slight ridge in the snow.

'Open land is hard to defend,' muttered Hayato, biting his lip pensively.

'At least we'll be able to see them,' said Jack. 'And with your bow, you could pick off bandits as they ride in.'

Hayato nodded. 'But we still need to slow them down. They'll overrun us otherwise.'

'We could flood the fields,' suggested Miyuki.

'That should work,' agreed Jack. Such a strategy was part of the ninja's Ring of Water techniques and he remembered how effective it had been against the army of samurai invading Miyuki's village.

'But that won't stop them,' argued Hayato. 'They'll just use the paths.'

Jack studied the walkways bordering the fields. The ninja would have made them narrow so only one person could pass at a time, and their arrangement would form a maze to slow down intruders. But the farmers' paths were wide and led directly to the village.

'How about a ditch?' suggested Saburo. 'We could fill it to become a moat.'

'A far better idea!' said Hayato, clapping him on the back.

'It'll have to encircle the *whole* village,' noted Miyuki. 'That's a lot of work.'

'Well, I bet Saburo's the very man to lead the digging!' said Hayato, dismissing Miyuki's objection.

Saburo smiled awkwardly, not sure how he'd volunteered for the task but nonetheless pleased with the praise. Yori saw the frustration on Miyuki's face at being cold-shouldered again, and stepped forward.

'Hayato, it may be wise to do both,' he said.

'Of course,' replied Hayato heartily. 'There can never be enough defences.'

'Which leaves us with the last approach – the forest to the west,' said Jack, and led the way.

As they walked out of the paddy fields, Jack felt a tug on his sleeve. Neko was beckoning him to follow her.

'Hold on!' said Jack to the others, as she steered him over to the pond.

Once there, she gestured to the ice now covering its surface. Jack wondered what her point was, until she stepped out on to the pond and walked straight across it.

'Neko's spotted a problem!' shouted Jack, waving the others over and giving Neko a thumbs-up in recognition. 'The bandits could circle the paddy fields and cross *here*.'

'Not if the ice breaks,' said Miyuki.

'Who says it will?' countered Hayato, pulling an arrow from his quiver and tapping the surface. 'It sounds pretty thick to me. And Neko just walked on it.'

'We *weaken* the ice first,' said Miyuki condescendingly. 'It makes the perfect natural deception.'

'Are *you* volunteering to go out there and break the ice?' challenged Hayato.

As the two of them once again locked horns, Yuudai picked up a nearby rock and hurled it high into the air. It landed in the centre of the pond with an almighty crack, smashing through the icy surface and sinking without trace. Tiny fracture lines spidered out from the hole.

'That should do it,' said Yuudai, grinning.

Jack laughed. He liked this boy's attitude. Yuudai took no sides; he simply wanted to get the job done. With the pond's threat now turned to a defensive advantage and with three angles of attack covered, Jack was beginning to feel more confident about their chances against Akuma.

That was until they entered the forest.

'This is our greatest weakness,' declared Hayato, studying the path before them. 'Lots of cover, little advance warning and countless gullies to bypass any barricade we build.'

Jack and the others fell silent as they all sought a solution. But none was forthcoming. The forest simply provided too many opportunities for an attacking enemy.

'Leave it to me,' announced Miyuki.

'But what *exactly* do you plan to do?' demanded Hayato.

'I have a few ideas.'

Hayato was about to protest, but Jack, wishing to avoid another clash of opinion, interjected first. 'I trust your judgement, Miyuki.'

'And I won't let you down,' she replied, bowing.

Before anyone could challenge her further, Jack went on. 'Now we've a lot of work to do, so you're each responsible for an approach. Yuudai, north at the barricade; Hayato, east at the bridge; Saburo, south at the paddy fields; Miyuki, west in the forest. Yori, you're organizing the smoke beacon and can also act as runner between the four posts. I'll be in the square coordinating the defences and the building of the watchtower. Any questions?'

Yuudai raised a hand. 'Our plan's good, as far as it goes. But we'll still need an army of men to defend each post.'

Saburo nodded in agreement. 'But we can't even get samurai to join us. Where will we find an army?'

To everyone's shock, Hayato and Miyuki replied in unison, 'We'll train one!'

22

DEFENCES

For the next week, the village became a whirlwind of activity. Toge helped rally the farmers and Jack split them into four units of eight men, each with their young samurai commander. Miyuki handpicked just three helpers, including Neko, before offering her remaining men to Jack for the construction of the watchtower. One of them was an able carpenter and Jack left him in charge whenever he went to check on progress of the other defences.

Yuudai proved to be a tireless worker and his barricade soon began to take shape.

'Good work!' said Jack, testing one of the spiked tree trunks rammed into the ground.

Dropping another beam into a foundation hole, Yuudai wiped the sweat from his brow. 'We're halfway done!' he announced. 'But we still need to reinforce these pillars, build a wall between them with thorn bushes and add bamboo spikes to prevent charging.'

'That should keep Akuma out,' said Jack, impressed with the scale of his fortifications, and they both grinned.

Noticing four farmers struggle with a felled tree, they

hurried over. Between the six of them, they managed to manhandle it to the log pile, where two villagers were cutting and shaping the wood for use. The four farmers then collapsed with exhaustion.

'Well done!' Yuudai shouted, clapping them on the backs enthusiastically. 'But no sleep till bedtime!'

Hauling another spiked tree trunk on to his shoulder, Yuudai headed back to the barricade where two men were digging the next foundation hole. Despite their fatigue, the team of farmers dragged themselves to their feet and obediently followed. Jack noted Yuudai's work ethic and constant encouragement kept everyone motivated and in good spirits.

'Do you need anything else?' Jack called to Yuudai.

The boy thought for a moment, the beam still slung across his shoulder as if it weighed no more than a spear. 'We could do with some hay bales to hide behind as a secondary defence line.'

'Good thinking,' agreed Jack. 'I'll put Yori on to it.'

Leaving Yuudai and his farmers to their work, Jack headed into the village to see how Saburo was getting on. He found his friend sitting beneath a tree overlooking a pile of earth.

'Put your backs into it!' he ordered as he sipped from a cup of green tea.

Kunio's muddy face popped out of the hole. 'Can't we take a break yet?'

'Do you think Akuma takes a break when raiding?' asked Saburo.

Kunio scratched at his ear. 'No.'

'Then we can't stop either!'

Sighing wearily, Kunio resumed shovelling with the rest of the men.

'How's it going?' asked Jack.

'Honestly?' replied Saburo. 'Pretty slow. The ground's frozen solid.'

Jack inspected the shallow ditch that ran part-way along the village's southern boundary. 'Any chance you'll finish this before the black moon?'

'At this rate, unlikely,' Saburo admitted. 'We're using the excess dirt to shore up the bank on this side, but I can't see us digging all the way round the village.'

'We need *every* advantage we can get over Akuma,' insisted Jack. 'We must complete this moat. I'll ask Hayato to put his men on to the task as well. They've already finished preparing the fields for flooding.'

'But what about the bridge?' asked Saburo.

Although Junichi had been able to provide Miyuki with charcoal and suggest a nearby hot spring for sulphur, the village had no saltpetre and their dunghill was too poorly maintained to produce any. Miyuki's plan, therefore, had been set aside in favour of Hayato's strategy, much to his gratification.

'Junichi insists on access to the mill, and his mother still hasn't moved out,' sighed Jack. 'So we'll have to take it down nearer the time.'

Saburo raised his eyebrows in concern. 'Let's hope Akuma doesn't decide to attack early then.'

'Let's pray he doesn't attack at all!'

Skirting the village, Jack worked his way up to the forest. Compared to the feverish activity in the village, there was no sign of Miyuki or her team. Apart from a wooden barrier on either side of the main track, she appeared to have done nothing. Jack stepped through the narrow gap in the barrier and went to look for them.

'Stop!' came a cry.

Halted in his tracks, Jack looked up to see Miyuki hanging from a tree branch.

'What are you doing?' asked Jack.

She smiled teasingly at him. 'If I told you, it would spoil the surprise.'

Neko appeared out of the bushes. She weaved between the trees, taking a circuitous route to them. Grinning up at Miyuki, she nodded.

'Good work, Neko!' said Miyuki, signing to her.

'You can communicate?' asked Jack, pleased to see Neko looking so content.

'Easily,' Miyuki replied. 'She has her own signs, but I taught her some of the ninja hand signs we use on missions. I can teach you a few tonight, if you want.'

Miyuki made some more gestures and Neko ran off eagerly into the forest. Working alongside Miyuki, Jack saw she was clearly in her element.

'Neko *would* make a perfect ninja,' agreed Miyuki, reading Jack's thoughts. 'She's silent, quick and, with training, she'd be deadly.'

Jack laughed. 'Well, let's survive Black Moon before you recruit her into your clan!'

Hearing footsteps in the snow, Jack turned to see Hayato walking up the track.

'So while everyone's slogging their guts out, our ninja is hanging about in the trees!'

Miyuki dropped to the ground. 'We're working just as hard as you.'

'But where are your defences?' Hayato demanded, inspecting the undisturbed forest.

'That's *exactly* the point!' Miyuki shot back and turned away from him.

Her blatant show of disrespect maddened Hayato and he went to challenge her. Once again Jack was caught in the middle. He was beginning to think it would be easier to defeat Akuma than keep these two from each other's throats.

Leading Hayato away, Jack tried to distract him with questions.

'Saburo needs your help with the ditch. Can you spare some men?'

Seething, Hayato nodded wordlessly.

'Have you managed to make enough spears?'

'Almost,' he grunted. 'It'd be better if we had real ones, but we'll have to make do with bamboo.'

'So when can you start training our army?'

'This afternoon.'

'Excellent!' said Jack, ushering him ahead through the barrier's gap. He'd put Hayato in charge of organizing the army – not only because he thought Hayato would do the best job, but to show fairness in his dealings between him and Miyuki.

Hayato glanced back in her direction. 'Do you *really* trust that ninja?'

'With my life,' replied Jack.

Hayato looked at him dubiously. 'I don't understand. How can you forgive any ninja after what I hear they did to your father?'

Jack felt his heart constrict at the memory. The sudden and brutal attack on the *Alexandria*. His first fateful glimpse of the shadow warrior, Dragon Eye. The vindictive pleasure the ninja had shown, thrusting the sword through his father's chest. The blood that had stained his own hands as he clung desperately to his dying father . . .

Hayato saw the pain in Jack's eyes. 'My father meant the world to me too. I *know* what it feels like to have those ninja rip the soul from your family.'

Swallowing back his sorrow, Jack repeated the phrase the Grandmaster had told him. '*A single tree doesn't make a forest.*'

'That may be true,' replied Hayato. 'But they're all made from the same wood! It's only because I respect you, Jack, that I've agreed to tolerate her presence. But, after we've saved these farmers, I can't promise the forgiveness you've shown her kind.'

23

A SAMURAI'S SWORD

'Line up!' ordered Hayato.

Chaos reigned in the village square as the farmers shuffled to and fro. Confused about where to stand, many bumped into one another, some clustered with their friends, while others simply stood looking bewildered.

Hayato shook his head in despair and Yuudai stepped forward.

'STOP!' he bellowed.

The whole square ground to a halt.

'*My barricade unit in three rows here!*' he commanded, pointing to the left of the veranda upon which he and the other young samurai stood. '*Digging unit in front. Bridge unit to their right. Forest unit in one line, far right.* MOVE!'

The startled farmers ran to their positions, Yuudai's barricade unit being the first to get in line. The others eventually followed suit.

'That's more like it,' acknowledged Hayato.

He stepped from the veranda to inspect the rabble of farmers before him. Some carried roughly hewn bamboo spears, while others brandished rusting or broken farm tools as makeshift weapons. Walking the line with Jack, Hayato assessed each of the recruits. Although toughened from their working lives in the fields, the past three years of raids had taken their toll and many were malnourished and gaunt. Barely half the men appeared strong enough to fight. The other half of this peasant army consisted of young boys or old men – neither group fit for the bloody battle ahead.

Turning to Jack, Hayato whispered, 'If this is our army, we'll need a miracle!'

'What we've *got* is less than two weeks,' replied Jack.

Hayato and Jack came to Sora, who was trembling so much he could hardly hold his spear.

'What are you afraid of?' asked Hayato.

'F-f-fighting Akuma,' said Sora feebly.

Hayato looked at the rest of the men. 'Is anyone else afraid of Akuma?'

Countless heads bobbed up and down.

'ME TOO!' Hayato declared, much to the men's surprise. 'But remember this, when the bandits see us next, they'll also be scared – of *us*!'

Hearing this, Sora's shaking subsided – until a farmer from the back shouted, 'Nothing frightens Akuma!'

Hayato glared at the man. 'Everyone's afraid of something.'

'Not Akuma. He's evil itself.'

A murmur of nervous agreement rose among the farmers. Keen to stamp out such demoralizing talk, Hayato unslung his bow and fired an arrow directly at the dissenting farmer. The man screamed in panic, terror etching his face at his imminent demise. But the arrow missed him by a whisker and pierced the wooden handle of his scythe instead.

'Akuma's a man like any other,' said Hayato. 'He'll fear death, if nothing else.'

His deadly shot silenced the farmer, along with the rest of the peasant army who gazed in awe at the young samurai's expert archery skills. Hayato continued to work the line, adjusting the men's grip on their weapons, showing basic techniques and offering advice. Jack had to admire the boy – he had the gift of military command and of making a point!

When they came to the last row, they found Neko standing proudly to attention, one of the few recruits seemingly ready to be a soldier.

'This is the courage we're looking for!' said Hayato.

'I think we've found our seventh samurai,' exclaimed Jack with a smile, pointing to the *katana* on Neko's hip.

Hayato's expression turned from approval to quiet outrage.

'Hand it over,' he said, gesturing to the weapon.

Neko wrinkled her brow, unwilling to relinquish her prize possession. But Hayato was insistent and took the sword from her. 'You can carry a spear like the others.'

Miyuki came over, a thunderous expression on her face. 'Why can't she have it?'

'She's *not* a samurai,' said Hayato matter-of-factly.

'What difference does that make?'

Hayato held up the sword. '*This* is the weapon of a samurai. She's a farmer.'

'Of course,' said Miyuki, her voice dripping with sarcasm. 'There must be a clear hierarchy. We *can't* have the samurai losing their *only* authority over the masses.'

'Farmers don't have the right to carry a sword.'

'Neko has the right to defend herself!'

'I don't make the laws. I only uphold them,' countered Hayato. 'And that's why we samurai are here – to fight for the farmers.'

Yuudai now stepped to Neko's defence. 'Hayato, you can't deny she has the spirit of a warrior.'

'And the stealth of a ninja,' added Miyuki quickly.

'I have to agree,' said Yori, joining the debate as he noticed the disagreement drawing the attention of the other villagers and causing a stir. 'Neko has proven her worth on a number of occasions. Perhaps we can make a temporary exception in her case?'

Yori bowed respectfully to Hayato. 'If you agree, of course.'

Finding himself in the minority, Hayato reluctantly handed back the weapon.

Neko grinned as she took the sword and attempted to slip it into her *obi*.

Hayato rolled his eyes at her fumbling. 'Someone teach her how to use it, at least before she cuts off her fingers!'

24

A DARK SECRET

The afternoon was filled with displays of out-of-step marching, clattering weapon drills and shambolic defence formations. Despite the aid of Yuudai's booming voice, Hayato's attempt to transform the rabble into an organized military battalion was proving an impossible task.

The farmers weren't used to the discipline and coordination required to be an effective soldier. They often forgot which unit they were in. Multiple commands confused them. The weapons in their hands were wielded with little or no skill, the spears being twice their height and cumbersome. And the mere idea of fighting and killing someone daunted many of them.

At one point, the Digging unit charged the Bridge unit and there was a near-fatal collision of sides, the tragedy only averted by the quick-thinking Yori. By then, dusk was approaching and Hayato decided to call it a day. Demoralized and exhausted, the farmers trudged back to their homes. Equally dispirited, the young samurai returned to Sora's farmhouse for much-needed food and rest.

'That was a nightmare!' sighed Miyuki, as they slumped round the hearth and waited for Neko to cook their rice.

'It is *only* their first day,' reminded Yori with forced optimism.

'It was anarchy,' said Saburo, holding his head in his hands. His unit had been the hardest to control and he'd almost been trampled by them during a marching exercise.

'Remember, the Way of the Warrior is unfamiliar to the farmers.'

'Well, it certainly doesn't come naturally to them!' Saburo exclaimed. 'That Kunio boy had his spear upside-down!'

Jack was dismayed with the training session too. He tried to convince himself the farmers had made some progress. But if they continued at their present rate, their army would be little more than a chaotic mob. And with the black moon fast approaching, they didn't have time for individual tuition.

'What do you think we should do, Hayato?' he asked, aware the boy had been unusually quiet since their return.

Hayato didn't reply, his brow knitted, deep in thought.

Then, glancing round at the others, he said, 'Neko's sword is bothering me.'

'We've already discussed this,' said Miyuki wearily.

'I'm not disputing the decision,' replied Hayato, glaring at her. 'I'm simply wondering *whose* sword it is.'

'Well, it's not mine.'

'And my *nodachi*'s on the bed,' said Yuudai, pointing to the massive blade lying across his straw mattress.

'As a monk, I don't carry one,' Yori explained with a smile.

Jack patted the *daishō* on his hip. 'Both my swords are here.'

'I've got mine too,' said Saburo, holding up his shiny untested blades.

'My point exactly!' said Hayato. 'We all have our weapons

and the farmers aren't supposed to have swords, so where did she get hers?'

They all turned to Neko, who was merrily preparing their dinner, her mystery *katana* propped up in the corner.

'I'll ask her,' Miyuki offered. She came back a moment later. 'Neko says she found it.'

'But *where* did she find it?' demanded Hayato.

'She'll show us after dinner.'

They dug into their usual meal of plain white rice and steamed vegetables. Once finished, everyone put on overcoats against the night chill and followed Neko outside. She led them across the square and, to their surprise, came to a halt in front of the rice store. Pulling back the large wooden doors, Neko held up an oil lamp she'd taken from the farmhouse. Its flickering light illuminated a cavernous barn with a hard-packed earthen floor. Bales of rice, wrapped in their own straw, were stacked five high upon rough wooden planks down each side.

'Appears to be plenty of rice,' remarked Saburo.

'For you, maybe!' Miyuki snorted. 'The store's half empty and this stock has to last the *entire* village until spring!'

Beckoning them inside, Neko headed for a large mound of hay by the back wall. Walking round it, they were shocked to discover Kunio amid a pile of weaponry and armour. Caught in the act, his face flushed with shame. On his head a horned helmet sat askew, far too big for him. He wore a bloodied breastplate and held a battleworn *katana* aloft, as if pretending to be some legendary warrior.

'Put that sword down!' ordered Hayato, staring aghast at the ominous collection of weaponry.

'Neko's got one,' moaned Kunio petulantly. 'Why can't I?'

Hayato turned on Miyuki. 'This is just what I feared would happen!'

He bent down and picked up one of the spears. As he did so, he dislodged some hay to reveal a trapdoor in the wooden planking. Through the opening, they could see a hoard of spears, swords and armour.

Hayato grabbed Kunio and shook the boy violently.

'*Where did all this come from?*' he demanded, but Kunio was too petrified to reply.

Toge appeared out of the darkness and answered for him. 'From dead samurai.'

25

DIVISIONS

'These farmers are all thieves and murderers!' exclaimed Hayato, pushing Kunio away and glaring at Toge with contempt.

Saburo, Yori and Yuudai exchanged looks of equal disgust at the revelation.

'There must be some other explanation,' said Jack, struggling to come to terms with the farmers' dark secret.

'No, there isn't!' snapped Hayato, picking up a helmet and brandishing it in their faces. 'This is plunder from vanquished samurai. After a battle, such farmers as *him* swoop on to the field like vultures, hunting the wounded and defeated, and stealing all they can!'

Turning on his heel, Hayato strode towards the door.

'Where are you going?' asked Jack.

'I'm leaving,' he announced.

'But what about Akuma?'

Hayato laughed coldly. 'Are we to risk our lives, only for the farmers to kill and rob us? Not me.'

'Toge, this can't be true,' Jack begged, as Yuudai went to follow his friend.

'Hayato's right,' replied Toge matter-of-factly. 'We've ransacked battlefields. Stolen from dead samurai. Ignored the pleas of dying warriors.'

Jack was astounded at the lack of remorse shown by the farmer.

'But we've done no more than his kind do to us!'

Hayato halted in his tracks and stared in outrage at Toge. 'Samurai lay down their lives to protect this land from invaders, tyrants and bandits, so that you're safe to grow your rice. And *this* is how you reward our services?'

'*Services?*' spat Toge, snatching up a spear and shaking it furiously. 'Wherever samurai fight, they burn and destroy our crops, kill our women, hurt our children and destroy our homes! As farmers, we must fight for survival *every* day!' Toge lashed out, kicking a pile of armour with his foot. 'You accuse us of being thieves and murderers! But *who* made us so?'

He pointed the spear tip defiantly at them, his face contorted with anger.

'*Your parents did!*'

Throwing the weapon to the ground, Toge stormed out of the storehouse, leaving the young samurai shamed into silence. Jack too was lost for words. He hadn't been fully aware of the bitter division between farmer and samurai. He now understood why the *ronin* were reluctant to help the farmers; but, even more, why the farmers were so mistrusting of the samurai. Their lives were ruled and ruined by the actions of the warrior class.

'Do you still intend to leave?' asked Jack of Hayato.

He shrugged noncommittally. 'After dishonouring our

dead in such a way, they've only themselves to blame for their situation.'

'Fix the problem – not the blame,' said Yori.

Everyone turned to him. His quiet voice had become the word of wisdom among the group.

'That's what Sensei Yamada always says,' he explained. 'If our parents are the cause of the farmers' problems, can we not be the solution?'

'I don't see how,' said Saburo bitterly.

'By working together. If we make a stand and defeat Akuma, we can regain the farmers' respect for samurai that our elders lost.'

'And we could certainly do with this weaponry,' added Miyuki, picking up a sharpened *naginata* and giving it an admiring look.

'Yes,' agreed Jack. 'That way, at least we'd be putting their bad deeds to good use.'

Hayato nodded with stoic acceptance. 'I suppose, their shame is our shame. As samurai, we're duty-bound to make amends.'

Junichi appeared at the storehouse door with Yoshi, shuffling in behind.

'We heard shouting. Is anything wrong?' he asked, glancing between the strained faces of the young samurai. Then he saw the weapons and his own guilt-ridden expression said it all.

'I-I-I can explain . . .' he stuttered.

'There's no need,' replied Yori. 'Whatever the past has been, it need not be the future.'

Junichi smiled with awkward relief. 'Of course not.'

Yoshi squinted at Yori with genuine respect. 'For such a

young monk, you possess an old soul,' he croaked. 'In my life, I've learnt that there is no future without forgiveness. Our village is grateful for the mercy you've shown us.'

'Does that mean I can keep this?' asked Kunio, holding up the sword he'd found.

'By all means,' replied Hayato with a sly grin. 'We'll even send you in *first* to fight Akuma.'

Kunio's face went pale at the thought and he hurriedly put down the sword. 'On second thoughts, I think I prefer a bamboo spear.'

26

SAMURAI SCHOOL

Shouts of fighting assaulted Jack's ears before he'd even turned the corner. In front of him, a group of farmers stood in three rows, their fists held up, feet planted in a defensive stance.

'*Ichi, ni, san . . .*' shouted Saburo, counting off each of their punches.

The farmers cried '*KIAI!*' with every strike, their bursts of breath fogging in the chill air. What they lacked in coordination and timing, they made up for in enthusiasm.

Since the discovery of the weapon hoard, the villagers had been repentant, humbled by the forgiveness shown by the young samurai. They now worked without complaint, trained like dedicated warriors, and saw the young samurai as allies rather than oppressors – a preconception they'd found hard to shake off in light of their experiences with *daimyo* Ikeda and his samurai.

The outrage felt by the young samurai themselves had been buried in order to focus on Akuma's forthcoming raid. They'd all agreed to honour the fallen by using their stolen weapons and armour to defend the village and, in doing so, atone for the villagers' suffering caused by previous samurai wars.

Jack had gone so far as to suggest that they train the farmers in basic martial arts and sword skills. If the bandits made it through their outer defences, they would need every available hand to fight. Although it broke the law and further blurred the social boundaries, Hayato saw the sense in such a strategy and had even agreed to lead one of the sword classes himself. Time wasn't on their side, but they hoped the training would improve *everyone's* chances of survival.

In the field adjacent to Saburo's, Yuudai was instructing his Barricade unit in the Art of the Spear. He was drilling them in thrusts, charges and various attack and defence manoeuvres. His camaraderie with the men, established during the construction of the barricade, was proving invaluable and his unit quickly fell into line to become the most disciplined and capable of all the groups.

Next to him, Miyuki was with Neko, demonstrating basic self-defence for the women of the village to use against the bandits. Neko was relishing her new status as a trainee ninja and, with her falls cushioned by the thick snow, she literally threw herself into every move.

As Jack approached the group, he heard one woman say, 'But Neko's no bandit. We wouldn't stand a chance against a fully grown man.'

At this, Miyuki invited Yuudai to join them. He towered over the women, who all shrank back in trepidation. Miyuki signed some instructions to Neko, then turned to Yuudai.

'Grab her,' she ordered. 'Then hit her.'

Yuudai's broad brow creased with concern. 'I don't fight women, let alone young ladies half my size.'

'You won't hurt her, I promise.'

Grudgingly, Yuudai seized Neko by the lapel of her kimono and, with an apologetic smile, raised his fist. Before he could take a swing at her, she grabbed his hand and compressed his thumb into a lock. Strong as he was, the pain crippled Yuudai. As he tried to strike, Neko stamped on his lead foot and drove the tip of her own thumb into the side of his ribs – just as Miyuki had taught her to. *Boshi-ken*, Finger Sword Fist, was one of the ninja's Sixteen Secret Fist techniques and was devastatingly effective. Grunting with more pain, Yuudai doubled over and lost his balance. Still holding on to his hand, Neko gave Yuudai's wrist a sharp twist and he was thrown backwards. She then pinned him to the ground with an arm lock.

'Even the smallest ant can bring down the biggest tree,' said Miyuki proudly, as the women stared in awe of Neko's effortless defeat of the muscular boy. '*Ninjutsu* isn't about size or strength; it's about skill and technique. You're *all* capable of this.'

Empowered by the demonstration, the women couldn't wait to attempt it themselves. Miyuki partnered them up and began to instruct her eager students. Meanwhile, Neko, mortified at hurting Yuudai, offered her hand to help him up. Yuudai readily accepted, only to pull her to the ground and playfully shove a handful of snow in her face. Rolling away, Neko burst into silent giggles. She hurriedly gathered snow for a retaliation attack. But Yuudai had already scooped up a huge ball and was about to launch it, when a hail of snowballs pummelled him from behind.

'Teamwork helps too!' Miyuki cried, catching Yuudai full in the face.

Laughing, Yuudai begged for mercy as the women villagers drove him back with snowball after snowball. His loyal Barricade unit dropped their spears and joined in the fight, sending a barrage of snowballs in a counter-attack at the women.

Jack left them to their antics, pleased to see some light-hearted fun in the village for once.

In the far corner of the field, Hayato had begun the training in *kenjutsu*, the Art of the Sword. Jack hurried over to his half of the students, who were waiting patiently for his instruction. As there hadn't been enough swords for every man in the village, a small group of farmers had been selected to become the Sword unit. Each of them had been given either a *katana* or a shorter *wakizashi*. Jack would have preferred them all to start with a *bokken*, a wooden sword being far safer for a beginner than a live blade. But with little more than ten days before the black moon, there simply wasn't time. So he decided to instil in his students a healthy respect for the samurai sword from the very beginning. Picking up a length of bamboo, Jack said, 'This is as tough as the bones in your body.'

He rammed the stem into the ground so that it stood upright. Within the blink of an eye, Jack drew his *katana*, its steel blade flashing through the air in three lightning strikes. The whole display was over in a few seconds.

One of the farmers laughed. 'He missed it!'

The bamboo stem did appear untouched. Then the top segment slid slowly off, followed by two more surgically neat pieces. They fell to the ground like dismembered fingers.

Jack picked one up and showed the man the perfectly smooth slice his sword had made. 'That's how sharp these blades are,' he warned. 'Be extremely careful when training with your swords. You don't want your partner's arm – or your *own* – ending up like this!'

The farmers all held their weapons with a newfound reverence.

'But you need not be so respectful to a bandit!' added Jack.

A ripple of laughter greeted this and the farmers relaxed a little.

'As an extension of your arm, the samurai sword has no rival,' explained Jack, demonstrating the correct stance and grip – his *katana* in both hands, the tip pointing forward, in line with their faces. Having taught Akiko's brother Hanzo some *kenjutsu*, the role of teacher no longer daunted Jack and he already had a clear idea of what needed to be done. He realized only a few basic cuts and blocks could be learnt in the time. But his *taijutsu* master, Sensei Kyuzo, had ingrained in him that *the basics are for battle*, and Jack hoped this would be enough for the task ahead.

'By the time Akuma comes, you'll all be warriors,' promised Jack.

Cheered by this, the farmers copied Jack's stance and raised their swords. Once Jack had corrected their postures, he taught them their first cut – *kesagiri* – a simple yet deadly diagonal strike.

As the farmers swung their swords in unison and practised the technique, Yori came over.

'Any problems?' asked Jack, who'd left his friend in the half-finished watchtower to keep guard over the village.

Yori shook his head. 'The lookouts have spotted only a deer or two so far.'

'Let's hope it stays that way.'

Glancing around at the different classes going on, Yori remarked, 'This is like being back at the *Niten Ichi Ryū*!'

Jack nodded, feeling a pang at the memory. It seemed like only yesterday they were all together in Kyoto. He was amazed at how far they'd come since their own training days. 'Except now we're the sensei at this samurai school!'

Yori laughed. 'What's Sensei Saburo up to then?'

His group had gathered beside the woodpile at the back of a farmhouse and Saburo was laying a short plank of wood between two supporting beams at waist height.

'*Tamashiwari*, by the looks of it,' said Jack, intrigued.

He stopped his sword class so they all could watch the Trial by Wood.

'I'll prove how powerful these techniques are!' said an indignant Saburo to his students.

Raising his right hand, he clenched it into a hammerfist and, with an almighty *KIAI*, brought it smashing down on to the wood. His fist demolished the board in a single blow, splinters flying in all directions.

The gathered farmers burst into spontaneous applause.

'He's improved since last time!' remarked Yori.

Jack nodded his agreement, although he noticed the triumphant Saburo quietly massaging his hand behind his back.

As the applause faded, an old man muttered, 'That's easy.'

Saburo glared at the farmer, annoyed to have his impressive demonstration brought into question.

'Why don't *you* try then?' Saburo challenged, and set up another board.

Much to his and everyone else's surprise, the old man shuffled to the front. He was little more than skin and bone, and Jack wondered if the ageing farmer still had all his wits about him.

Standing in front of the board, the old man examined it briefly. Then, turning round, he picked up an axe. With one easy swing, he chopped straight through the wood.

The rest of the farmers fell about laughing, as did Jack and Yori.

'B-b-but that's cheating!' exclaimed an outraged Saburo.

The old man shrugged. 'You samurai make things so much harder than they need be!'

27

THORN BUSHES

The days passed quickly. Too quickly. With each setting of the sun, the threat of Black Moon drew nearer. No one spoke of Akuma out loud, but he was on everyone's mind. The earlier episodes of playfulness and light-hearted jesting disappeared, to be replaced by a grim determination. Alongside the daily training of the army, the defence preparations continued unabated. As the pressure grew, their labours stretched from dawn until late into the night.

On the sixth day before the black moon, Jack heard a great shout from the northern end of the village. Fearing the worst, he sprinted up the track, Yori following close behind.

'Why haven't the smoke beacons been lit?' he demanded, pulling out his *katana*.

'The bandits must have used a hidden route!' Yori panted, his staff in hand, its metal rings jangling as he ran.

Flying round the corner of the last farmhouse, they were met by a great wall of thorns and spikes. Twice the height of a man, the barricade blocked the entire northern approach. Stakes jutted outwards and the sharply pointed pillars threatened to impale anyone foolish enough to climb over.

Yuudai and his team were collapsed in a heap by the secondary wall of hay bales, admiring their construction.

'The barricade's finished!' declared Yuudai, to which the farmers gave another exhausted yet jubilant cry.

'*That* is worth shouting about!' said Jack, sheathing his sword with relief.

Crossing the wooden gangway Yuudai had built over Saburo's moat, he took a closer inspection of the barrier and could find no obvious weakness.

'With a unit of spearmen behind the barricade, Akuma should be unable to breach this,' explained Yuudai, patting it proudly.

'You beat us to it, Yuudai!' Miyuki called out, appearing from the direction of the forest with Neko and her two helpers. 'We're about finished too.'

Jack didn't bother asking her if they could have a look. He knew, apart from the narrow wooden barrier, there'd still be nothing to see.

Leaving a couple of farmers to stand guard, Jack and the others returned to the square. Positioned in the far corner, the watchtower was now twice the height of the rice store. On the top platform the last of the wooden protective screens was being hammered into place. Rough and ready in its construction, the tower nonetheless commanded views over the entire village and plain.

'I know it doesn't compare in strength to your barricade, Yuudai,' said Jack. 'But it serves its purpose.'

Jack stepped on to the rickety ladder to lead Miyuki and Yuudai up to inspect the finished tower.

'That won't take my weight,' excused Yuudai, indicating

he would stay on the ground with Yori. 'Besides, I'm no good with heights.'

Miyuki looked at him in amusement. 'How do you cope with being so tall?'

'I just don't look down!' replied Yuudai with a laugh.

Working their way up the ladder, Jack and Miyuki eventually reached the top and gazed across the Okayama Plain. Below, the paddy fields were filling with water, Hayato labouring with a team of farmers to redirect the river along pre-dug channels.

'You've done a great job, Jack,' said Miyuki, surveying the defences that the Five Rings had inspired.

'Thanks, but the carpenter did most of the work,' Jack admitted.

'I didn't mean the tower. I was talking about your leadership. Once the moat is complete and the bridge dismantled, the village will be the fortress you envisaged. No matter how powerful and dangerous Akuma is, he'll have second thoughts before raiding the farmers this year.'

'It's been a team effort,' reminded Jack.

'*To lead people, you should walk beside them*,' said Miyuki, smiling warmly at him. 'That's exactly what you've done. You should be proud of yourself.'

She looked into Jack's eyes with something more than admiration. 'I'm glad I came to rescue you,' she whispered, demurely lowering her gaze. 'The clan hasn't been the same since you left –'

'Jack! We've got a problem,' shouted Saburo, dashing into the square. He urgently beckoned them to join him on the eastern edge of the village.

'This doesn't sound good,' said Jack, making for the ladder.

Clambering back down, Jack and Miyuki joined the others and hurried after him. They discovered the ditch was still far from complete, more than a third remaining to be dug. Yet none of Saburo's team was working. Kunio sat morosely on a pile of fresh earth, his shovel discarded to one side, his head in his hands.

'It's been a total waste of time!' he moaned.

Walking over to the ditch, Saburo pointed to its muddy bottom. 'Hayato was flooding the paddy fields and I asked his team to divert a channel from the river, so we could test the moat. But as you can see, it doesn't work. Because the village lies on a slope, the water just drains away.'

Jack stared into the ditch and then at the other young samurai. They all realized the scale of the problem.

'It's my fault,' said Saburo, shaking his head with despair. 'It was a stupid idea in the first place.'

'No, it's still another defence,' consoled Jack, although he knew the immense effort made by the farmers had hardly been worth it.

'But without water, the bandits can *easily* cross.'

'Not if we fill it with thorn bushes instead,' Miyuki suggested.

There was a pause while this was considered. Then everyone began to nod their heads with approval.

'That's a great idea!' said Jack. He turned to Yuudai. 'Can your team collect more bushes?'

'Of course,' said Yuudai.

His ready agreement generated a groan of protest among his farmers.

'We've cut ourselves to shreds just building the barricade!' objected one man, raising his forearms to show the countless scratches he'd suffered.

'Akuma will cut far more than your arms,' said Yuudai, showing no sympathy. 'Come on, we've got work to do!'

As he led his group away for their painful mission, Hayato strode over.

'All the fields should be flooded by tonight,' he announced. 'Then we'll take down the bridge tomorrow.'

'Good work,' replied Jack. 'And we've found a solution to the moat – thorn bushes.'

Hayato regarded him with admiration. 'Brilliant idea, Jack!'

'Thanks,' said Miyuki, flashing him a smile, and Hayato winced at his unintended praise of her.

Concealing his amusement at their awkwardness, Jack handed them each a shovel. 'Let's start digging!' he said, jumping into the ditch.

28

A LOST CAUSE

The frozen earth was as hard as rock, hampering their progress to a snail's pace. Blisters formed on their hands and their muscles ached with the strain of digging. At the opposite end of the trench, repeated yelps and curses could be heard as Yuudai's team packed thorn bush after thorn bush into the ditch. After several hours of hard labour, Jack called a halt. Downing tools, the farmers headed wearily back to their homes.

'They can't leave yet,' said Hayato, wiping the sweat from his brow. 'We've still got army training.'

'Forget that!' Saburo exclaimed as he collapsed against a tree. 'Everyone's exhausted!'

'These farmers can either be dead tired – or dead. We *have* to practise our defence drills.'

'But it'll be dark soon,' countered Saburo, looking to the others to back him up.

'Even more reason to practise,' said Hayato. 'Akuma might launch his attack at night.'

'He's right,' said Miyuki, her ready agreement surprising Hayato. 'The farmers can rest once Akuma's dealt with for good.'

As tired as he was, Jack saw the necessity for the extra training. Only through constant repetition would the farmers have any chance of mastering the vital fighting skills in time.

Jack called after Toge. 'Gather everyone in the square for army training.'

'What?' he said, his face looking thinner and more gaunt than ever. 'If we keep this up, we won't have the strength to fight!'

'Well, you don't have the skill yet either,' said Hayato matter-of-factly.

Toge scowled. 'Whatever you command, young samurai.'

After several calls to assemble, the villagers eventually congregated in the square and wearily took up their positions. Standing on the veranda for a clear view, Hayato led them through their drills. The units shambled to and fro, their long spears rising and falling in disorganized waves. Their half-hearted efforts infuriated Hayato.

'No! An *arrow* formation!' he shouted at the Digging unit, holding his hands up in a V-shape. 'For attack.'

The Digging unit clumsily rearranged themselves on Saburo's instruction. At the same time, a farmer in the Bridge unit dropped his spear during a mock charge. A mass pile-up of bodies formed as several men tripped over it and went flying. Jack, who'd taken control of the unit for the drill session, began to feel Hayato's frustration.

'Stop!' cried Hayato in despair. 'All of you, STOP!'

The villagers stood where they were and stared glumly at their young commander.

'I've seen monkeys more coordinated than you! Have you learnt *nothing* in the past week?'

'We're trying our best,' said Toge indignantly.

'Well, your best isn't good enough! You must *focus*. Do I need to remind you the black moon is almost here?' A collective shiver ran through the villagers and they all bowed their heads submissively. 'Then back to your original positions. And this time, FOCUS!'

In the rush to reorganize themselves, even more chaos ensued.

Jack ran over. 'Maybe we should take a break?'

'We've not made enough progress yet.'

Yori joined the conversation. 'Perhaps you're being too hard on them?'

Hayato shook his head. 'Having attended the *Niten Ichi Ryū*, I thought you'd understand the importance of rigorous training.'

'I do,' said Yori. 'But they're not *that* bad.'

'Use your eyes, Yori. They're a lost cause! There's no fighting spirit. No *kiai*! No *bushido*!'

'I'm sure, when the time comes, they'll pull together.'

'I wish I had your faith,' said Hayato.

He strode over to the blacksmith's hut, found the iron bar and hammer, and began clanging it loudly.

'BANDITS! BANDITS!' he screamed at the top of his voice.

Startled by the sudden alarm, the villagers scrambled in all directions. Units collided with one another and spears became entangled as they ran in panic to their prearranged defensive positions.

Hayato walked back with a resigned expression. 'Not even close to being ready.'

The drill practice continued late into the evening. The light was almost gone, yet still they trained. The false alarm had proved to all the young samurai and their units that much more needed to be done. And they committed every last bit of energy to instructing and encouraging the exhausted farmers.

'Drill number one *again*!' ordered Hayato, his voice hoarse from shouting. 'The lines mustn't break like that. Remember, in a storm a single tree falls, but a forest still stands. How many times must I tell you?'

As the farmers dragged their worn-out bodies into formation for the umpteenth time, Toge threw his spear to the ground. 'I've had enough!'

He stomped off, but Hayato leapt from the veranda and seized his arm.

'*Never* desert your post!' growled Hayato.

Toge tried to shake Hayato off. 'Let me go! I'm *not* one of your samurai.'

'That's the problem,' replied Hayato, releasing him with disgust. 'You give in so easily. As samurai, we don't have that choice. We *must* fight. It's our fate.'

'Well, it wasn't *my* fate!' Toge shouted, his cheeks flushed with anger. 'I was born a farmer – not a samurai. This training is too little, too late. *All too late!*'

Stamping on his bamboo spear, he snapped it in half and stormed off.

'Toge's right,' mumbled an old man. 'We're fooling ourselves. We'll never be warriors.'

This was met with a murmur of defeated consent. As the despondency spread, more and more farmers lowered their spears and trudged back to their homes.

The young samurai watched helpless as their army disbanded.

Saburo shook his head regretfully. 'Now I understand why my father says the farmers need us more than we need them. They may grow the rice, but they don't have the will to protect it for our nation.'

With army training cut short, the young samurai drifted back to the farmhouse, Hayato kicking at the snow in frustration. As Jack started to follow, Sora shuffled over to him.

'I must apologize for Toge's behaviour,' he said, bowing low. 'He's always upset near the time of the black moon. His wife was killed by Akuma in last year's raid – for hiding a handful of rice to feed their little boy.'

Jack glanced at the shadowy figure of Toge, crouching on his own by the pond. 'He has a son?'

Sora woefully shook his head. 'Not any more.'

The old farmer then walked away, dragging his spear behind him.

The square had emptied of all people and Jack stood alone. His heart went out to Toge. The farmer seemed crushed by the weight of his grief, all the spirit beaten from him by a tragic life.

Yori returned from the farmhouse. 'Are you coming, Jack? Neko's got the fire started.'

Jack sighed. 'Perhaps Hayato's right. These farmers *are* a lost cause. They've been so trodden down, they can no longer make a stand, even if they want to.'

'Give a man a fish, and he'll eat for a day,' replied Yori. 'But teach him how to fish, and he'll never starve.'

'But they'll need a *lifetime* of teaching before they can defend the village,' argued Jack. 'We've only a few days. This crusade of ours is futile.'

'If you've nothing to lose, then nothing can be lost in the trying,' countered Yori. He paused, clearly pleased with his new proverb. 'Akuma will attack whether you help or not. But you're giving these farmers a fighting chance. That's more than they've ever had before.'

29

WANTED

'Jack! You'd best hear this for yourself,' said Miyuki, waking him the next morning.

She roused the others and led them quietly to the back of Junichi's farmhouse. Peering through the gap in the wall, they could see a crowd of villagers gathered before Junichi, Toge and Yoshi. A young farmer sat in the middle of the room, all eyes and ears fixed on him.

'And who told you this?' asked Junichi.

'A travelling merchant,' he replied. 'A sign's been posted in Okayama market.'

'How much is the reward?'

'Four *koban*!' he breathed, his eyes wide.

There was a collective gasp of amazement and the farmers began to whisper excitedly to one another.

'That's enough gold coin to feed the entire village for over a year,' said Junichi, rubbing his stubbled chin thoughtfully.

'Or we could pay off Akuma,' suggested one of the farmers. 'And we wouldn't need to fight.'

'It'd certainly be less painful than suffering the torture of any more army training!' said Toge.

Junichi held up his hand for silence. 'Are you suggesting we turn Jack Fletcher in?'

'Without question!' declared an elderly farmer. 'He's a wanted criminal. A traitor to the Shogun.'

'No!' cried Sora, pushing his way to the front. 'Jack's our saviour.'

'He's our downfall!' shot back the farmer. 'If we continue to protect him, the Shogun will raze our village to the ground and kill us all!'

The other farmers murmured their agreement.

'But without Jack, we're at the mercy of Akuma.'

The elderly farmer snorted. 'That *gaijin* doesn't know what he's doing. He's just a boy playing at being samurai! Desperation drove us to use him. But now we have a better option.'

'Have you forgotten Jack was the *only* samurai willing to help us?' interjected Yuto, pleading with the other villagers. 'He saved our baby and he can save this village too.'

'But Jack will *still* be saving us,' countered Toge. 'That four *koban* would solve a lot of our problems.'

Yoshi coughed for attention. 'And what will we do next year when Akuma returns? We won't have another *gaijin* samurai to betray.'

'We'll hire real samurai to get rid of Akuma!' argued the elderly farmer.

Yoshi laughed bitterly. 'Do you truly believe *daimyo* Ikeda will hand over the reward?'

'He'd have to! The money comes direct from the Shogun.'

'*Daimyo* Ikeda will want all the glory for capturing the *gaijin* samurai – and the money.'

'But we can't defy the Shogun!'

'We already have,' snapped Yoshi. He eyed the villagers with contempt. 'Is *this* how we repay those who risk their lives to help us?'

The young samurai watched as a heated argument broke out among the villagers, who were torn between fear, duty and a debt of gratitude.

Jack felt his stomach harden into a knot. Nowhere was safe for him to hide any more. And with such a large reward on offer, no one could be trusted either. He didn't blame the impoverished farmers for being tempted. But after everything he'd done for them, he couldn't believe they'd simply hand him over.

Miyuki turned to Jack. 'I think it's time you left.'

'But what about Akuma?' asked Jack.

'Your sense of honour is admirable,' said Hayato. 'But these farmers aren't worth it. I told you, they've no *bushido*, no sense of loyalty.'

'They won't turn me in,' insisted Jack.

'Farmers are as changeable as the seasons,' replied Hayato. 'You can't trust them.'

Jack looked to Neko, who was desperately trying to follow what was happening. He wished his faltering sign language was more advanced so he could explain.

'We can take her with us,' Miyuki suggested.

'Us?' said Jack.

Miyuki nodded, holding his gaze. 'You don't think I'll abandon you now!'

'You can count on me too,' said Yori faithfully. 'And Saburo.'

'Of course,' said Saburo. 'For that sort of money, I might hand you in myself!'

They all looked aghast at him.

'I'm only joking,' he added quickly. 'But the Shogun's clearly desperate to get his hands on you, Jack. That's the second time he's doubled the price on your head.'

'This is no time for jokes,' said Hayato sternly. 'Jack, you'd best gather your belongings and go. Yuudai and I will delay any attempt at pursuit.'

'But when Akuma discovers the farmers intended to put up a fight, he'll destroy the village,' argued Jack.

'It's the fate of farmers to suffer,' said Hayato. 'They've brought it on themselves. Now go!'

But as they went to leave, Yori beckoned them back to the wall.

'Wait!' he said. 'Junichi's called a vote.'

'All those in favour of turning the *gaijin* in, raise your hands,' instructed the village leader.

The elderly farmer's arm shot straight up, followed by several others.

From his restricted view through the rear wall, Jack couldn't see how all the villagers were voting. But there seemed to be a lot of hands.

'Those against.'

Yuto's hand went up, followed by Sora's, then the farmer's next to him. More arms were raised. Junichi began to count off the vote as Sora frantically encouraged others to follow his lead. Jack felt beads of sweat forming on his forehead. With his friends by his side, he didn't fear the farmers. But he did fear the Shogun's samurai. And their noose was once again tightening around him.

'That settles it,' declared Junichi. 'We agree to *ignore* the Shogun's order, whatever the consequences . . .'

Jack breathed a sigh of relief. His faith in the farmers had paid off.

'Well, there's a surprise!' said Hayato, raising his eyebrows. 'Farmers displaying honour and loyalty.'

As they returned to the farmhouse for breakfast, they spotted Kunio running up the road, waving his arms wildly. He stumbled in the snow, got up again and dashed over to them. He was breathing so hard he could barely speak.

'I . . . saw . . . them . . .' he panted. 'BANDITS!'

30

SCOUTS

'Black Moon's come early!' exclaimed Junichi, bursting from his farmhouse to see what all the commotion was about. The villagers around him began to panic.

'My moat's not finished,' said Saburo in alarm.

'Nor's the bridge,' added Hayato, pulling his bow off his back.

Jack noticed the metal rings on Yori's staff trembling. Although Yori put on a brave face, he knew his friend was not at heart a warrior. But he wasn't the only one to be nervous. All the young samurai looked tense. The moment of truth had come and there was no turning back. Ignoring his own fear, Jack attempted to reassure them.

'We've trained for this. We're samurai –' he glanced at Miyuki – 'and ninja! Now gather your units and take up your positions as planned. We still have the element of surprise on our side.'

Turning to Yori, he placed an encouraging hand upon his shoulder. 'Stay with me. I'll need your wisdom during the battle.'

Heartened by Jack's confidence in him, Yori held on tighter to his *shakujō*.

'Kunio, sound the alarm,' ordered Jack.

'But there's only . . . two of them,' explained the breathless farmboy.

Upon hearing this, Hayato halted in his tracks. 'Junichi, you said there'd be *forty*.'

Junichi nodded. 'Usually there are.'

'You can leave them to me then,' offered Yuudai with a grin, rolling up his sleeves. 'I'll have them for breakfast.'

'They could just be a scouting party,' said Miyuki. 'We don't want to forewarn Akuma of our presence.'

'I agree,' said Jack. 'Let's take a look at our enemy first. Kunio, where are they?'

Kunio pointed behind him. 'Down by the bridge.'

Sprinting to the village's eastern boundary, the young samurai ducked behind a defensive wall of hay bales beside the last house. Peering down the main track to the bridge, they spotted two figures on horses approaching the mill. Dressed in mismatched armour and loaded with weapons, they were the embodiment of lawless bandits.

'Definitely scouts,' said Miyuki, seeing them inspect the crossing point and scan the horizon.

'It's lucky we haven't dismantled the bridge yet,' said Hayato. 'That would have been a dead giveaway.'

'What about my moat?' asked Saburo.

'From their position, it should look like a drainage ditch,' Miyuki explained. 'Unless they're ninja, they won't realize its true purpose.'

'Do you recognize either of them?' Jack asked Kunio.

The boy nodded fearfully. 'The man on the right is Naka-mura Scarface.'

'A fitting name for such a handsome warrior!' remarked Saburo, swallowing uneasily at the sight of him.

The bandit in question boasted a large battleworn axe, thick leather armour and a crescent-moon helmet. His weather-beaten face was consumed with a ragged beard, sliced clean through on the left cheek by a thick red scar.

'The other bandit is Sayomi the Nightwoman.'

A mane of long black hair cascaded down the back of her blood-red armour. Strapped to her horse was a vicious double-edged *naginata* and she carried a bow and arrow as well as a *katana*. Her face was ghostly white, her eyes dark and shadowy, and her thin scarlet lips looked as poisonous as holly berries.

Jack shuddered at the sight of her. Only now did he appreciate why the villagers felt such abject terror at their coming. Any resistance to them would be met with a savage fight to the death. As the young samurai appraised their foe, an old woman tottered out of the mill, waving a stick at the two bandits.

'That's Natsuko!' exclaimed Kunio. 'Junichi's mother.'

Hayato stood up to fire an arrow, but Miyuki pulled him back down. 'You'll be seen.'

'They might kill her,' Hayato snarled, wrenching himself from her grip.

'Hold fire, unless you *have* to,' hissed Jack. 'If the scouts don't return alive, Akuma will be alerted to us. And we'd lose our greatest advantage.'

'You're the leader,' stated Hayato reluctantly, keeping his arrow primed in readiness.

The bandits were laughing at the woman's feeble attempts to shoo them away. Then she managed to catch Nakamura across the shin with her stick and he howled in pain. Sayomi laughed even harder at this display of weakness. Shock giving way to humiliation and rage, Nakamura kicked the old woman to the ground, then spat on her.

'See *you* on the black moon!' Nakamura yelled at the still-defiant Natsuko, who was shaking her fist at him.

Crouching low, Hayato kept his arrow trained on the bandit as the man turned his horse and rode off with Sayomi in the direction of the mountains.

'I'll follow them,' said Miyuki.

'Why on earth do that?' said Saburo, aghast. 'The further away from those two we are the better!'

'They'll lead me straight to Akuma's camp.'

'Do you need to take such a risk?' asked Yuudai. 'When the bridge is down, the village will be like a fortress.'

'*Know yourself, know your enemy. A thousand battles, a thousand victories*,' replied Miyuki. 'Our Grandmaster believed in a similar strategy to the honourable Masamoto. We must find out exactly how many enemy we're facing and what weaponry they'll be using. If all the bandits are like those two, we'll need every advantage we can get.'

'It's a good idea,' Jack agreed. 'But you can't go alone. It'll be too dangerous.'

'I'll go with her,' stated Hayato, to both Jack and Miyuki's astonishment.

'I should go too,' said Jack, not trusting them alone together. 'I need to see this Akuma for myself. It will help me decide our best tactics.'

'But we still need to protect the village,' Yori reminded him.

Jack smiled at his friend. 'That's why you'll be in charge while I'm gone.'

Yori blinked in shock at this unexpected responsibility. 'But –'

'I have every faith in you,' said Jack, not allowing his friend to doubt himself. 'Besides, Saburo will be here finishing the ditch with Neko and the rest of the villagers, and Yuudai will lead the army training.'

'But what if a snowstorm covers the bandits' trail?' asked Yuudai, glancing up at the sky.

Jack gave Miyuki a knowing look. 'Ninja are *excellent* trackers.'

31

TRACKING TRAILS

Gathering the minimum of supplies, Jack, Miyuki and Hayato prepared to leave.

'Wait!' said Junichi, hurrying over to them. 'You'll need a guide. The mountains are treacherous in winter.' He turned to the farmers behind him. 'Where's Toge?'

They looked around blankly and shrugged.

'We don't have time to wait,' said Miyuki, pulling on the hood of her white *shinobi shozoku*.

'I'll go,' volunteered Sora, clearly nervous at the prospect but determined to help.

Miyuki shook her head. 'Sorry, but I can't risk you slowing us down, especially if we need to make a quick escape.'

'We need local knowledge, though,' argued Hayato.

'True,' she agreed.

'And I'm faster than I look,' said Sora, grabbing a walking-stick from beside his door.

'Let's go then!' said Jack, putting on his *ronin*'s straw hat.

The four of them hastened out of the village and across the bridge. Natsuko was sitting on a stool outside her mill, still fuming.

'You tell that Scarface, I'll break *both* his kneecaps the next time I see him!' she crowed, waving her stick like a battleaxe.

Buoyed by her resilience, they promised to deliver her message if they had the chance.

If only all the farmers were as fearless as her, thought Jack.

Following the riverbank, Miyuki led them across the edge of the Okayama Plain and up into the forested slopes of the mountains. The bandits' trail wound along a narrow path and over a ridge. They followed it until they came to a fork in the road.

'Which way now?' asked Jack, looking at the confusion of prints in the snow.

Miyuki bent down to examine the trail.

'That way,' she said, pointing to the left.

'How can you be so sure?' asked Hayato.

'Those are the tracks of a large stag, those of a wild boar and *these* are horse's hooves,' replied Miyuki, indicating each set of prints as if she was teaching a child.

'They all look the same to me,' said Hayato, his pride ruffled by her patronizing tone.

Jack shot Miyuki a warning glance, pleading with her to be more tolerant. The last thing he needed was for the two of them to start fighting.

With a heavy sigh, Miyuki took the time to explain to Hayato, 'I'm not looking at the shape of each print. The first rule of snow-tracking is to identify the animal's track *pattern*. Even when the prints are windblown and obscured like this, their gait is often still identifiable by its distinctive arrangement in the snow.'

'Now I understand,' he replied, clearly appreciating her insight.

'And do you see that track?' she said suddenly, indicating a completely blank patch of snow.

Baffled, Hayato shook his head. Jack also strained to see what she was pointing at.

'That's a . . . ninja trail!' she exclaimed, bursting into laughter.

Getting the joke, Jack joined in too.

'I'll certainly watch out for *those*,' said Hayato, managing to crack a smile as well.

Chuckling, Sora trudged past. Despite his age, he was proving as surefooted and hardy as an old mountain goat and had kept up a steady pace since leaving Tamagashi village.

'And these are bear tracks!' he said, prodding his walking-stick at a set of huge paw prints in the snow. 'We should keep moving. Bears can be more dangerous than bandits.'

Miyuki walked over and examined them. 'They're fresh!'

At that moment, a low growling was heard coming from the undergrowth. The branches surged forward in a wave towards them and a massive bear, jet black apart from a patch of white fur on its chest, thundered out. Stopping in front of them, it sniffed the air, then snapped its jaws viciously.

'There's only one thing more lethal than a bear,' said Sora, taking several nervous steps backwards, 'and that's a *hungry* bear!'

'What should we do?' whispered Jack. 'Run?'

'No!' Miyuki hissed. 'Gather together so we look bigger, more threatening.'

But the bear wasn't intimidated. It reared up on its hind

legs, towering over them. Its razor-sharp claws were extended and ready to carve them to pieces.

Jack reached for his sword and Hayato went for an arrow, but at this range the bear would kill at least one of them before they could land their first blow.

A rock suddenly struck the animal in the chest. Another quickly followed – hitting the bear directly on his nose. Howling with rage, it turned on its attacker. Having appeared out of nowhere, Neko jumped up and down, waving her arms to distract the beast. With a great roar, the bear charged her. Neko spun on her heels and ran into the forest, leading the ferocious animal away.

'No!' cried Miyuki, sprinting after Neko, no longer concerned for her own safety.

Jack and the others followed close behind. Branches tore at their clothes and faces as they forced their way through the dense thicket. Ahead, they could hear the bear crashing through the undergrowth and see Miyuki speeding after it.

'Wait, Miyuki, WAIT!' cried Jack as they fell behind, the bear's roar growing ever more distant.

They eventually caught up with her beside a mountain stream.

'Where's Neko?' asked Jack, breathless.

Miyuki turned her tear-filled eyes upon him.

'The bear went that way,' she sniffed, pointing across the stream. 'But Neko's tracks stop *here*.'

In the distance, they heard another mighty roar.

Miyuki began to tremble. 'The bear must've got her.'

Jack suddenly felt choked with emotion too. It had all happened so fast. The bear. Neko. Her sacrifice for them. He stood beside Miyuki in grief-stricken silence, too shocked to know what to do next.

'We should go . . . before it comes back,' said Sora, nervously scanning the bushes.

'We can't just leave her –' said Jack, but stopped midsentence as he saw two cat-like eyes peer at him from a hole in a tree. 'Neko!' he exclaimed as she emerged from her hiding place, grinning victoriously.

Using the hand signs Miyuki had taught him, Jack asked, *Are you OK?*

Neko nodded, having only suffered a few scratches in her escape.

Miyuki, delighted to discover her young charge unharmed, cried, 'I told you, she'd make the perfect ninja!'

'Well, she certainly doesn't make a good samurai,' said Hayato. 'She disobeyed orders following us and almost got herself killed.'

'If it wasn't for Neko, we would be dead!' shot back Miyuki.

'And I'm thankful for that,' replied Hayato. 'But what's she doing here in the first place?'

Miyuki signed the question to her. 'She says she thought she could help.'

'Which is exactly what she *has* done!' said Jack, smiling warmly at their silent saviour.

Retracing their steps, they took up the trail once more, Neko now part of the expedition. They trekked deeper and deeper into the mountains. The land became more rugged and remote, spears of rock rising all around them. Approaching mid-afternoon, the trail led them up a hair-raising path cut into a cliff face before entering a narrow gorge.

'How much further, do you think?' Jack called to Miyuki.

She turned to reply, but Sora interrupted her.

'Quiet!' he hissed, putting a finger to his lips.

The three young warriors went for their weapons. But on looking around, the gorge was deserted.

What is it? mouthed Jack.

Sora pointed a finger upwards and whispered, 'Danger of avalanche!'

Above them, a colossal wave of snow teetered upon the edge of the gorge's upper lip. Maintaining their silence, they cautiously edged further along the ever-narrowing chasm until, at its farthest end, they saw a sheer rock face blocking the gorge.

'Are you certain they went this way?' whispered Jack.

Miyuki nodded and pointed to the two tracks that continued ahead of them.

'Maybe the bandits lost their way?' suggested Hayato.

'I don't think so,' replied Miyuki, under her breath. 'There are no fresh tracks leading back from here.'

'Then let's keep going,' said Jack.

Walking on, the walls of the gorge pressed closer until only a thin blue line of sky could be seen between the ridges of snow above. It was as if the mountain itself was trying to crush them.

'We should turn back,' said Sora, glancing up to spot dark clouds gathering. 'I don't know this area and there's a storm coming.'

But Jack was determined to follow the trail to its end. As they neared the end of the gorge, he couldn't believe his eyes. He now saw that the rock face cut hard right at the last moment. The optical illusion gave the appearance of a dead end, when in fact the track led to a narrow gap in the mountainside.

Passing through, the five of them were stunned to discover a hidden valley.

32

AKUMA

A waterfall cascaded down a cliff into a crystal-clear sliver of lake. Near the shore a patch of hardy trees clung to the steep valley sides, while further along the snow-clad bank was a knot of wooden buildings, protected in the lee of an overhanging crag. There was a storehouse, a stable and a large wooden bunkhouse, smoke rising from a hole in its thatched roof.

'This has to be it!' exclaimed Jack.

'We should wait until dusk,' said Miyuki. 'To avoid being spotted.'

Hunkering down behind a boulder, they watched the camp for signs of life. A few men wandered around tending to the horses, but it appeared that most of the bandits were within the bunkhouse itself. Snatches of raucous laughter and drunken singing could be heard drifting across the lake.

'I haven't seen any guards,' said Jack, as the sun dipped below the mountain ridge.

'Nor have I,' agreed Miyuki.

'They're overconfident,' said Hayato. 'Akuma clearly doesn't believe anyone would find them here.'

'No one ever has,' said Sora, shivering in the icy mountain air. 'Or at least, none have returned to tell the tale.'

'Don't worry, we will,' said Jack, praying he spoke the truth.

Skirting the edge of the lake, they kept to the cover of the trees for as long as they could, then used the larger boulders to creep closer. But this only took them so far.

'It's open ground from here,' said Miyuki. 'I'll go first.'

Checking the way was clear, she sprinted for the near wall of the bunkhouse. As she reached halfway, the main door opened and a bandit stepped out. In an instant, she dropped into a crouch and became still as a stone. Dressed in her white *shinobi shozoku*, she appeared no more than a mound of snow. And despite knowing exactly where she was, even Jack had difficulty spotting her in the half-light.

The bandit, shuddering against the cold, strode in her direction. He drew closer and closer. She was bound to be discovered. From behind their boulder, Hayato took an arrow from his quiver and raised his bow.

'Just in case,' he whispered, targeting the man in the throat.

But the bandit walked straight on by, completely oblivious to Miyuki at his feet. He headed over to a small outhouse. A few minutes later, he returned to the main building, closing the door behind him. Only then did Miyuki look up and dart for the shelter of the wall.

'That was *too* close,' said Hayato, lowering his weapon.

Miyuki peeked through a slat in a lower window of the bunkhouse. Satisfied no one else was coming out, she beckoned them over one at a time. After they were all safely concealed in the shadows, Jack pressed an eye to the slat for his first real look at their enemy.

Inside, a roaring fire burned in a massive hearth at the centre of the room. Bandits were sprawled everywhere, gorging themselves on bowls of rice and large jugs of *saké*. In one corner a group of men were betting on a rowdy game of dice. In another, a small crowd cheered on two bandits arm-wrestling. Their wrists were bound together and either side of the table were flaming candles. Biceps rippling, they fought furiously against one another. The wrestler on the left screamed as his hand was forced into the burning flame. His opponent just laughed at his suffering.

If this is how they treat one another, thought Jack, *what hope do we have?*

Turning his attention to the opposite end of the bunkhouse, Jack immediately spotted Nakamura and Sayomi. They knelt before a bearded man with coal-black eyes and a broad chest. He wore a breastplate as dark as the night and around his head was tied a blood-red *hachimaki*. The bandanna, reinforced with a steel plate, was as potent as any crown.

'That's Akuma!' whispered Sora, trembling at the sight of his village's tormentor.

Jack laid a calming hand on Sora's shoulder, but he too was struck by a chill of fear upon seeing the man known as Black Moon. The bandit leader's malevolent presence dominated the room and he gazed upon the proceedings with the predatory glare of a killer shark. Jack noticed the bandits never looked directly at their leader and always kept a wary distance.

Akuma snapped his fingers and a girl appeared, bearing food and a pot of *sencha*. Bowing low, her eyes averted, she poured out a measure of green tea and handed him the cup.

Without even tasting it, he said, 'The tea's cold!'

'But I just made it –'

Akuma brutally struck the girl with the back of his hand.

'I said, the tea's cold.' His tone was calm and even, as if nothing untoward had happened. But blood trickled from the girl's lower lip and a red welt bloomed across her cheek.

'Sorry, my lord,' she sobbed, scurrying off to bring him a fresh pot.

A man was dragged in by two bandits and dumped at Akuma's feet. Dressed in a tattered farming smock and trousers, the prisoner quivered in terror.

'I warned you not to resist,' said Akuma, selecting a rosy-pink slice of salmon from a plate of *sushi* and popping it into his mouth.

The ragged farmer prostrated himself on the dirt floor. 'I was only thinking of my family. I won't do it again. I promise –'

'No, you won't,' interrupted Akuma. 'I accept your pitiful apology.'

The farmer looked up in amazement. 'Thank you, O great Akuma, thank you!' he cried, bowing over and over.

Akuma rolled his eyes, quickly bored with the man's overt display of gratitude.

'Now roast him on the fire!' he ordered.

The two bandits seized the farmer and hauled him towards the blazing hearth. The room fell silent as everyone watched in grim fascination.

'B-b-but my apology!' pleaded the farmer, struggling wildly in the arms of his captors.

No longer able to stand by and watch, Jack drew his sword. But Hayato prevented him.

'No! It would be sheer suicide!'

'But we can't just do *nothing*,' protested Jack.

'We help him, we die – it's as simple as that.'

'He's right, Jack,' said Miyuki, although she was clearly as uncomfortable with the situation as they all were. 'There are too many of them. We can't sacrifice the village's safety for the fate of one man.'

A horrendous scream pierced the night.

'We *must* stop Akuma!' said Jack.

The screams went on and on, only challenged in volume by the gleeful laughter of the bandits.

'And we will,' promised Hayato, a look of fierce determination on his face. 'At the coming of the black moon, we will.'

The screaming stopped.

Sora sat back in the snow, weeping silently and trying to comfort the traumatized Neko. With great reluctance, Jack and the others forced themselves to look through the window again.

Akuma, apparently disappointed at such a short display of torture, announced, 'Feed him to the dogs!'

The two bandits pulled the unconscious farmer away from the fire and dragged his blistered body out to the back. A moment later, excited howls, yelps and growls were heard.

Akuma's the devil himself! thought Jack, sickened to the pit of his stomach.

Turning to Sayomi and Nakamura, Akuma enquired, 'I trust there'll be no such resistance from the farmers of Tamagashi village?'

Sayomi shook her head. 'Their spirit is broken after last time. Unless you count the old woman who beat Nakamura!'

Akuma let loose a booming laugh at this. Sayomi cackled too. Then, as if on cue, all the bandits joined in.

Nakamura fumed. 'Well, I'm still suspicious of that trench,' he mumbled.

'You saw the state of their paddy fields,' said Sayomi dismissively. 'It was to stop the flooding.'

'Maybe, but the old woman acted *too* bold for my liking.'

'You're just upset that a woman hit you,' smirked Sayomi.

'I'll hit you if you don't shut up!' he snapped.

'You can try,' she challenged, her eyes narrowing.

Akuma held up his hand and the two of them immediately stopped squabbling. 'So you think the farmers are planning something?'

'I doubt they're clever enough,' replied Sayomi.

'They might have sought help,' Nakamura suggested.

'But who'd listen to their pleas?' said Akuma. '*Daimyo* Ikeda doesn't care.'

'Perhaps some masterless samurai.'

Akuma considered this. 'But even *ronin* have standards. What sort of samurai would lower himself to serve a farmer?'

'A desperate one!' Out of the shadows stepped a man dressed in black and tan leather. The entire left-hand side of his face was burnt away, the skin red and rippled like candle-wax, the hair all gone. His left eye was missing, the lid melted over the empty hole.

'*Kurochi the Snake*,' whispered Sora, as Miyuki gasped in horror at the disfigured bandit.

'But we need not fear *ronin*,' sneered Kurochi. 'Not with a weapon like this.'

He raised a loaded musket, aimed it at a large *saké* barrel in the corner and pulled the trigger. It exploded with a deafening crack. Bandits scattered in panic and rice wine cascaded over the group playing dice. Kurochi gave a cackling laugh and Akuma grunted in satisfaction at the deadly display.

33

UP IN FLAMES

'We're in grave trouble,' said Hayato with dismay. 'I count forty-*five* bandits and that Kurochi has a gun!'

'It takes time to prime and reload, though,' said Jack, recalling the pistols his father had owned. 'We can hide behind our defences, then attack once he's fired his first shot.'

'But there are bound to be other bandits with muskets. And I've seen what these dishonourable weapons can do on the battlefield. They'll slaughter us without ever coming close enough to fight.'

'Muskets need gunpowder,' said Miyuki thoughtfully.

'Then we have to even up the odds,' said Jack.

Although they'd embarked on a surveillance mission, faced by such a formidable and well-armed enemy, he realized they needed to take direct action.

'What are you proposing?' asked Hayato.

'Destroy their supply.'

'Or steal it,' proposed Miyuki, a mischievous twinkle in her eyes.

'We could also let loose their horses,' said Jack.

'Why stop there?' said Hayato, warming to the idea. 'Let's fight fire with fire. Burn their camp to the ground!'

'Now you're thinking like a ninja!' said Miyuki.

Hayato grimaced at this, his samurai pride offended by the comparison, but he refrained from answering back.

'But if you attack, Akuma might suspect our village and seek revenge,' interjected Sora, an anxious look on his wrinkled face. 'He'll utterly destroy us!'

'He'll do that anyway,' said Hayato. 'Besides, Akuma has many enemies. He won't know who's responsible.'

'And without a base, horses or gunpowder, the bandits' ability to mount an attack will be severely compromised,' said Miyuki.

Jack nodded his agreement. 'We wait until they're asleep. Then strike.'

It wasn't long before the bandits fell into a drunken stupor and the sound of snoring filled the vast bunkhouse. Akuma had retired to a *futon* on an upper level, closing the screen behind him, the only one to have a room to himself.

Once they were certain everyone was asleep, Miyuki led the way to the storehouse. Keeping close to the side wall, they crept round to its entrance.

Suddenly she held up a hand for them to stop.

Jack and the others froze. Beneath the flickering light of an oil lamp, a bandit sat beside the door. Evidently meant to guard it, he was slumped on a bench, head bowed, eyes closed, an empty bottle of *saké* at his feet.

Miyuki signed for Jack and the others to wait. Using her ninja stealth walk, she approached the slumbering man. With a thumb, she pressed a nerve point in his neck. The guard barely roused before he slid to the floor in a heap.

Jack hurried over. 'Is he dead?'

Miyuki shook her head as they dragged the bandit's body into the shadows. 'No, but he'll wake up in the morning with a crippling headache and remember nothing.'

Hayato tried the door. 'It's locked!'

Miyuki searched the bandit for a key, but came up with nothing.

'We'll have to break it open,' said Jack, looking round for a heavy rock.

'That'll make too much noise,' replied Miyuki.

Jack felt a tug on his sleeve. Neko was pointing to a slatted window beneath the eaves. It was just wide enough for her to slip through. With Jack and Hayato's help, she clambered up and inside. A few moments later, the door slid open.

Good work! signed Jack.

Neko signed back, *Easy!*

Sora held up the bandit's lamp. The storehouse was packed to the rafters with goods of all kind. Bales of rice, *saké* barrels, dried fish, lamp oil, swathes of cloth, spears, swords, several muskets and gunpowder. The spoils of countless raids.

'Must you destroy *all* this?' asked Sora, his eyes hungrily taking in the mounds of rice.

'I'm afraid so,' said Hayato. 'An army marches on its stomach. This will be a serious blow to Akuma and his men.'

'But won't he just go on the rampage? Take everything we have?'

'Whatever happens, Akuma intends to raid your village

next,' reminded Jack. 'But this time, you'll be ready for him. And we'll put a stop to his attacks, once and for all.'

'Besides, we'll use the oil lamp to make it look like an accident,' said Miyuki, taking the light from Sora. She went over and examined the weaponry. 'But first we'll steal back some of this.'

She rolled out two small casks of gunpowder and a large ceramic jar of lamp oil.

'We can't carry those,' said Hayato. 'They'll slow us down.'

'You're right – we need to make a quick escape,' said Jack and turned to Sora. 'Go and free the horses, but keep five of the best for us to ride. Plus one more to carry the supplies and a bale or two of rice for the village.'

Sora seemed satisfied at this. Jack signed for Neko to help the old farmer and the two of them hurried out and across the yard to the stables. A short while later, Jack heard whinnying and hoped the noise wouldn't wake any of the bandits.

Hayato picked up a flint-and-steel firelighter and a spare jar of lamp oil. 'I'll set fire to the bunkhouse, while you two finish up here. Akuma deserves a fiery awakening!'

'We'll meet you by the trees,' said Jack. 'And don't wait around! I want us to be long gone when all this goes up in flames.'

Hayato nodded in acknowledgement.

'Be careful,' said Miyuki.

Hayato glanced back, surprised at her apparently sincere concern. 'You too.'

Then he disappeared into the night.

Miyuki selected a few more supplies and Jack hauled them outside. She then cast lamp oil over the walls and floor before running a line of gunpowder to the door. Neko reappeared with the horses and Jack hurriedly loaded them up.

'You go ahead,' said Miyuki. 'I'm nearly done.'

'I'll be waiting for you,' replied Jack, holding her gaze a moment. At times, her courage and daring reminded him so much of Akiko.

Following the edge of the lake, Jack and Neko led the horses over to the treeline, tethered them, and concealed themselves behind a boulder. They watched the camp in tense silence. Beneath the pale light of the waning moon, it was hard to make out much movement. A few horses were gathered at the water's edge drinking, but the rest had bolted. To Jack's relief, none of the bandits had stirred – or else they were too drunk to react.

Their plan was going to work.

He saw Miyuki place the lamp on the ground. She kicked it over and there was a burst of flame. For a brief moment she was silhouetted against the intense light.

Running as fast as she could, Miyuki raced across the open ground to where Jack and Neko were hiding. Behind her, an orange glow blossomed within the storehouse, smoke billowing out of the door.

Reaching the treeline, she glanced back at her handiwork.

'They'll have trouble putting that out,' she said, pleased with herself.

'Have you seen Hayato?' Jack asked.

Miyuki shook her head. 'I thought he was already with you.'

They scanned the camp for him, the fire within the storehouse illuminating the bunkhouse.

'I can't see him,' said Miyuki, concern edging her voice.

A moment later, a shadow bolted through the darkness. Hayato bounded over rocks and boulders without looking back once.

'It took a while to light,' he explained, breathless. 'The thatch is all wet, but eventually it caught. It'll take time to burn through, but we've landed our first blow against Akuma!'

They all felt a heady rush of victory.

'Let's go!' said Jack, keen to escape while they could.

'Where's Sora?' asked Hayato.

Miyuki and Jack looked at one another. In their haste, they'd completely forgotten about the old farmer.

'Surely he's freed every horse by now,' said Miyuki.

Jack looked over to the stables, but Sora wasn't anywhere in view. Miyuki signed urgently to Neko, but she didn't know where he was either.

Then in the flickering firelight, Jack spotted Sora heading towards the rear of the bunkhouse.

'What's he *doing*?' said Hayato angrily.

'Stay here!' ordered Jack. 'I'll get him.'

'Hurry!' said Miyuki. 'Those bandits won't be asleep much longer.'

Jack sprinted back to the camp, keeping his eyes peeled for the enemy. He found Sora at the back, both arms reaching through an open window.

'*What are you doing?*' hissed Jack. '*We must leave now!*'

Sora turned to him with pleading eyes. 'But we can't . . .'

He moved aside to reveal the tearful face of a young girl.

'I've found my daughter, Miya!'

34

RESCUE

Behind Miya were countless other girls, their faces forlorn and lost.

Jack turned on Sora. 'Why didn't you say something *earlier*?'

Wringing his hands, Sora sobbed, 'I'd given up hope of ever seeing her again. Then when that tea girl appeared, I just thought . . . maybe . . .'

'But Hayato's set the bunkhouse on fire!' exclaimed Jack.

Sora's eyes widened in panic and he began to yank at the barred window. The slats didn't shift at all. Jack pushed him aside. The girls were crammed into a room separate from the main area.

'Can you get out of there?' he whispered to Miya.

The girl shook her head. 'The door's locked at night and there's always a guard.'

Jack studied the bunkhouse wall. It was built of solid tree trunks. He wouldn't have any hope of breaking through. In the background, he could hear the growing crackle of the fire. He was fast running out of time to save them.

'Go back to the trees and tell Miyuki,' he ordered Sora. 'I'm going in to free your daughter and the other girls.'

Sora nodded. But he remained rooted to the spot, unable to tear himself away from his imprisoned daughter.

Jack gave him a shove. 'Hurry!'

This broke Sora's trance and, stealing a final look at Miya, he ran off into the night.

Jack spotted a back door, but it was barred shut. There was another window further along. He was about to try it, when he noticed several dark shapes outlined against the snow. A pack of dogs slept in the far corner of the yard . . . their bellies round and full.

Jack backed slowly away. He didn't want to see any more. Nor did he wish to wake the bloodthirsty hounds.

Once he was safely round the corner, he dashed to the front entrance and eased the door open. The bandits lay sprawled throughout the room, straw blankets thrown across themselves. Many looked to be comatose from the effects of too much *saké*; others were fast asleep and snoring loudly. Above, smoke poured through the thick thatch and formed a deadly cloud in the rafters, but the tang of woodsmoke from the still-burning hearth helped mask the fire in the roof. Jack prayed he could get the girls out before any of the bandits stirred.

Moving silently and swiftly, just as he'd been taught by the ninja Grandmaster, Jack weaved between the unconscious bodies to a *shoji* at the back of the room. Sliding it open a crack, he spied a large cooking area and over to his left a barred door. Beside it squatted a bandit, who gave a great yawn then began to pick at his teeth in boredom.

Although the man was completely off-guard, Jack realized that, before he had a chance to silence him, the bandit could raise the alarm. Ninja stealth wouldn't help him in this instance. But a simple disguise might work . . .

Looking around, he found a discarded *saké* bottle. Then, pulling his straw hat over his face, Jack boldly opened the door and staggered inside. In the gloom of the kitchen, he hoped to fool the guard.

'Got . . . any . . . more?' Jack slurred, holding up the empty bottle.

Barely looking at him, the guard grumbled, 'You know we're not allowed any when on guard duty.'

Stumbling closer, Jack was almost on top of the man before the bandit realized his fatal error. Reaching for his sword, the guard went to shout a warning. But Jack drove forwards and struck him with Fall Down Fist – one of the Sixteen Secret Fists of the ninja, the blow instantly knocked the man out. He dropped to the floor like a sack of cloth.

Raising the wooden bar off its mountings, Jack yanked the door open. The girls cowered in the corner, afraid he might be a bandit. Jack lifted the hat from his face and they now stared in awe. Some were even more terrified by his foreign features, clearly believing him to be a spirit.

'Follow me!' he hissed. 'And be quiet.'

Miya was the first to move and the other girls, overcoming their initial shock, quickly fell in line.

Checking the main hall, Jack discovered it had filled with smoke and the air was rapidly thickening into an impenetrable fog. Although the bandits lay below the line of the noxious grey cloud, a few were beginning to cough and splutter in their sleep.

Jack led the girls through the haze as quickly as he dared.

They tried to cover their mouths, but it was impossible not to choke on the foul air. One of the girls started having a coughing fit and Jack urged them to hurry before she woke every bandit in the room. But they were frustratingly slow, petrified of stepping on their captors. Reaching the door, he ushered Miya out.

'Run for the trees,' he whispered. 'And don't stop!'

Directing the other girls after her, Jack helped each of them out. Then the last girl, overcome by smoke, stumbled and fell on to a sleeping bandit.

The man woke angrily. 'Watch it!' he growled.

His eyes blearily focused on the girl and a momentary look of confusion passed across his face at seeing her free. Then he noticed the cloud of smoke filling the bunkhouse.

Throwing the girl off, he jumped to his feet and roared, 'FIRE! FIRE!'

35

FIRE FIGHT

Chaos reigned as the bandits awoke and scrambled for the door in panic. A few didn't rise at all, having already succumbed to the toxic fumes. The rest barged one another out of the way in a bid to escape first.

Jack dived back into the bunkhouse to rescue the girl. He forced his way against the tide of bandits, all of whom were more concerned with their own lives than the stranger in their midst. Finding the girl, he yanked her to her feet and shoved her towards the door. She had just got out when Jack was seized from behind.

'Who the hell are you?' snarled Nakamura, his scarred face appearing out of the smoke haze.

Without hesitation, Jack spun round, wrapped his arm beneath his assailant's forearm and drove it upwards in a *taijutsu* breaking technique. He wrenched hard enough to snap the elbow the opposite way.

But rather than crumple to the floor in agony, Nakamura merely laughed. 'You'll have to do better than that!' he said as he punched Jack in the gut with a hammer-like fist.

Jack dropped to his knees, gasping. Nakamura then threw

him across the room. Jack crashed into a supporting pillar. Before he could rise, Nakamura launched a stomping front kick at his chest. On instinct, Jack managed a double forearm block and rolled away. But Nakamura kept up the attack, snatching a smouldering branch from the hearth and using it to force Jack into the centre of the room.

The bunkhouse roof was now an inferno, flaming sections of thatch raining down on them. Jack knew his chances of surviving were fading by the second. Unless he regained the advantage and escaped, he'd either succumb to the smoke, be burnt alive or killed by Nakamura.

Ducking as the bandit wielded the red-hot branch like a club, Jack went to draw his swords. But he'd barely got his hands to the handles, when his head was wrenched back and a knife held to his throat.

'Are *you* the cause of all this, *gaijin*?' asked Sayomi, the female bandit's eyes red with smoke.

Jack didn't answer. His mind was focused on dealing with the cold steel at his neck.

'We don't have time to play games, boy,' said Nakamura, glancing round at the spreading blaze. 'Who sent you?'

Nakamura drove the tip of the glowing branch into Jack's right thigh. Jack cried out as the red-hot wood burnt straight through his kimono and scorched his bare skin.

'Tell us before we leave you here to burn alive!' croaked Sayomi.

Jack spluttered in pain, his throat hoarse from the smoke he'd inhaled.

Impatient for an answer, Nakamura reapplied the blazing wood. There was a sizzling sound as it seared into Jack's flesh. Gritting his teeth against the agony, Jack tried to break from Sayomi's grip, but she pressed the knife closer to his throat.

Then a ghost-like figure flew out of the smoke. A flash of steel whipped past Jack's face and Sayomi cried out as the *shuriken* embedded itself in her arm. Miyuki's simultaneous flying side-kick struck Nakamura in the chest and sent him hurtling backwards into the hearth. He landed among the glowing embers and screamed as his clothes caught alight and flames leapt up his arms and back.

Seizing the initiative, Jack grabbed Sayomi's wrist and disarmed her of the knife. Elbowing her in the stomach, he flung her over his shoulder, using *seoi nage* technique. Sayomi tumbled head first and crash-landed on the floor.

Above, a horrendous cracking alerted them to a rafter breaking free from the roof. Wasting no time, Miyuki took Jack's hand and guided him through the smoke towards the door. A sharp pain flared in his right leg with every step. Behind, they heard Sayomi cursing them.

As they burst out of the door, Nakamura dashed past wearing a cloak of fire. He didn't stop until he'd thrown himself into the lake.

The shock of their camp being set ablaze had sent the bandits into complete disarray. Some simply stared at the destruction, while others were violently sick from a combination of smoke and excess *saké*, and a desperate few were trying to douse the flames with buckets of water. The resulting mayhem covered Jack and Miyuki's escape. They ran across the open ground, every excruciating step taking them closer to safety. Up ahead, the girl he'd saved was almost to the trees.

'STOP THEM!' roared Akuma, who stood enraged before the hellfire of his burning camp.

Jack and Miyuki kept running.

There was a crack of musket fire.

The bullet missed them.

But the girl fell.

'NO!' shouted Jack.

Arrow after arrow whistled past in the opposite direction as Hayato tried to hold back the bandits that Akuma had rallied.

Jack levelled with the girl and stopped to help her up. But she was already dead, a thin stream of blood running from her lips on to the crisp white snow.

'We must keep going!' said Miyuki, dragging Jack on.

The bandits were closing fast. Hayato picked off another three before Jack and Miyuki entered the treeline. Once within the woods, Hayato led them along the edge of the lake.

'Neko and Sora have gone ahead with the girls and horses,' he explained as they fled.

Behind them, they heard the angry shouts of the bandits. Limping as fast as he could, Jack's only thoughts were of the poor girl who'd been shot so close to freedom. They entered the dogleg of the narrow gorge. As they turned the corner, Jack snatched a final glance back. The bandits' camp was consumed in fire, the crimson flames reflected in the rippling waters of the lake like lava.

At least the girl's death hadn't been in vain.

Dashing along the gorge, they'd almost caught up with Sora and the other girls when the bandits appeared behind.

'You can run, but you won't escape *me*!' Kurochi shouted, raising his loaded musket and taking aim at their backs.

He pulled the trigger. A spark ignited the explosion of gunpowder and a bullet shot towards the fleeing young warriors.

Miyuki dived at Hayato, knocking him to the ground. The bullet ricocheted off the rock face where Hayato had been just moments before.

'You saved my life!' he exclaimed as Miyuki rolled off him.

'Not yet,' she replied, looking over her shoulder at the advancing bandits.

They scrambled to their feet.

'We'll have to make a stand here,' said Jack, unsheathing his *katana*. 'Give Sora and the others a chance to escape.'

The three of them understood the futility of trying to outrun the bandits in their own mountains. This narrow section of the gorge was their best chance of holding them off. Drawing their weapons, they prepared to fight when an ominous rumbling was heard from above.

Everyone looked up.

The gunfire had triggered an avalanche and a colossal wave of snow now thundered into the ravine.

'RUN!' shouted Sora, as he urged the girls to safety.

As if the sky had fallen, snow surged down the rock face, threatening to consume all in its path.

Jack, Miyuki and Hayato sprinted for the entrance to the gorge. The bandits fled in the opposite direction.

Miyuki and Hayato pulled ahead of Jack, whose right leg protested against his every stride.

'Come on, Jack!' cried Miyuki.

Fighting the pain, Jack lurched forwards just as the avalanche struck the bottom of the gorge.

36

AN ICY GRAVE

Jack felt as if he was cocooned in a white coffin. He could barely breathe beneath the crushing weight of the snow. All sound had been drowned out. Only the rush of his blood and the beat of his heart were still audible.

Had the others made it out alive? He could only pray they had.

He began using his fingers to dig at the snow, but he had no idea which way was up. Completely disorientated, he could be burying himself *deeper* into the avalanche. He tried to move, but was pinned on all sides. The only good thing about his predicament was that the cold snow numbed the burning sensation in his leg.

After much scraping away, Jack managed to create a small hollow for himself. But no sooner had he done this than the roof collapsed. As the snow engulfed his tiny haven, he started panicking. Gasping for breath, he struggled wildly to free himself from his icy grave. But the snow merely embraced him like an old friend.

Jack tried to calm himself. He had to think straight if he was going to survive. He had no intention of dying here. That wasn't his fate. He hadn't got this far on his journey simply to end up a victim of the mountain. He was determined to return home to his sister, Jess, in England.

Jack kept burrowing.

He lost all sense of time, his strength ebbing away as the cold gnawed at his bones. Then his fingers came across something hard. A red handle. His *katana*! Digging furiously around it, he managed to get a good grip. Hoping to find the surface, he levered his sword upwards with all his might. The razor-sharp blade sliced through the snow. He pushed for freedom . . .

But met resistance every inch of the way.

He was buried deep. Too deep.

He *would* die . . . never to be found.

Despair gripped him. After all his struggles against Dragon Eye, Kazuki and the Shogun, it was to be Mother Nature herself who proved his executioner.

Jack tried to turn his mind to happier thoughts. He pictured Akiko, the time they'd sat together on the slopes of Mount Hiei to wait for *hatsuhinode*, the first sunrise of the new year, her head resting on his shoulder, her smile as radiant and warming as a new dawn . . .

He began to drift into unconsciousness, when the snow over his head parted.

'I've found him!' cried Miyuki, furiously clearing a hole to pull him out.

Hayato and Neko joined her, hands digging on all sides.

Dragged clear, Jack breathed in a lungful of fresh mountain air. Above him, the stars seemed to shine brighter than ever. He looked around. The gorge was completely blocked, a wall of snow and ice rising upwards. He was lucky to have been so near to the gorge entrance when the avalanche had struck.

'I can't believe you found me!' Jack exclaimed, scanning the vast mounds of snow that surrounded him.

Hayato helped him to his feet and Miyuki handed him his *katana*.

'If it wasn't for the tip of your sword poking out, we never would,' explained Miyuki. 'Neko's got good eyesight!'

Turning to Neko, Jack signed *thank you*, but this seemed so inadequate for saving his life. On an impulse, he embraced her as a friend. Neko smiled shyly at the unexpected affection and gave a humble bow in response.

The four of them carefully headed over to where the rescued girls and horses waited.

'At least the avalanche has stopped Akuma,' said Jack.

'I'm afraid not,' replied Sora. 'My daughter says there's another way out of the valley. It'll take him an extra day or so. But Black Moon *will* come.'

'Then we'd best get moving,' said Hayato, mounting his horse.

Jack clambered on to his, relieved to take the strain off his injured leg.

'Akuma may well come,' said Jack to Sora, before glancing at Miya and the rest of the girls. 'But we're returning with good news too.'

The villagers wept with joy upon seeing their daughters alive – a miracle beyond their wildest dreams. Even Sora's usual hangdog expression vanished, replaced by one of pure rapture at the sight of Miya running into her mother's arms. That alone was enough to convince Jack all their efforts so far had been worthwhile.

Junichi greeted them with the deepest of bows. 'If only all

samurai and ninja were as courageous as you, then there wouldn't be devils like Akuma!'

Yoshi tottered out of the farmhouse, his old eyes brimming with tears.

'I never thought I'd see the day,' he croaked. 'You've given life back to our village!'

While the families were reunited and the daughters from neighbouring villages welcomed with equal affection, Jack hobbled over to Sora's farmhouse with Miyuki, Hayato and Neko. They were all exhausted from the night's escape and Jack was now in serious pain from his wound.

Yori, Saburo and Yuudai were waiting to greet them.

'What happened to you?' asked Yori, his face etched with concern at Jack's woeful state.

'Apart from being beaten, burnt and buried alive?' Jack joked. 'We dealt our first blow against Akuma.'

'That's something worth celebrating!' said Yuudai, clearly relieved to see them back safe and sound, if a little battle-worn. 'Let's get you inside and fed and rested.'

He opened the door for them to enter, when they heard a great wailing.

'*Where's Suki?*' cried a despondent mother, searching the faces of the girls. 'Where's my Suki?'

The woman was becoming more and more frantic. Sora hurried over and spoke softly to her. For a moment, she just stared at him in disbelief. Then burst into floods of tears. Sora tried to comfort the woman, but she shrugged him off and strode over to Jack and the others.

'M-m-my Suki was shot . . . by Akuma?' she asked, her voice trembling with grief.

Jack now had a name for the poor girl. 'Yes. One of his men, Kurochi, did it.'

'I know you tried to save her,' she said, her sorrow turning to anger. 'But promise me, you'll set my daughter's soul at peace! Promise me, you'll put an end to Akuma!'

Jack held the mother's gaze and felt the torment in her broken heart. He could see in her features her own daughter's face and remembered the girl, not much older than himself, sprawled in the bloodstained snow. Nodding, Jack gave his sworn promise as the memory of the girl's senseless slaughter hardened his resolve to stop Akuma's reign of terror . . . *whatever* it took.

37

HEALING

While the village emotionally healed itself, Miyuki set to work healing Jack's wound. Crushing up herbs she'd taken from a winter garden and mixing them with a fine powder she carried in a small container on her *obi*, Miyuki cooked up a thick green paste. She applied this to Jack's blistered skin as he lay on his bed in Sora's farmhouse.

Jack cried out, 'Ow, that stings!'

'Still the big samurai baby, I see,' she teased, covering the rest of the wound.

Biting his lower lip against the pain, Jack asked, 'How bad is it?'

Miyuki examined the injury, then replied gravely, 'You could lose the leg.'

Jack swallowed in shock, his face going pale at the thought.

'But don't worry,' added Miyuki, 'Yuudai's offered to cut it off cleanly with his *nodachi*.'

Jack glanced fearfully at the formidable sword on Yuudai's back, before catching the smirk on Miyuki's face.

'Another ninja joke!' he said, forcing a laugh as a wave of relief flooded him.

'It should be fine in a day or so,' Miyuki revealed, smiling warmly at him as she put aside the medicine. 'The cold snow from the avalanche reduced the swelling. And with these herbs, there won't even be a scar.'

Kneeling by his side, she clasped her hands together, her fingers interlaced, the index finger and thumb both extended. Closing her eyes, she began to chant softly.

'*On haya baishiraman taya sowaka . . .*'

Her hands hovered over his wound, moving in a figure-of-eight pattern, and Jack felt a familiar warm tingle beneath his skin as the *Sha* healing ritual did its work.

'What's she doing?' muttered Saburo, eyeing Miyuki suspiciously.

'*Kuji-in* . . . Ninja magic!' whispered Yori reverentially. 'Sensei Yamada told me about it, but I've never seen it in action.'

Yori watched rapt as Miyuki went deeper into her trance, channelling her healing energies into the wound. Jack noticed his friend copying her hand position and silently mouthing the mantra as he tried to commit the words to memory. Always the most diligent student among them, Yori loved to learn such mystical techniques and Jack made a mental note to ask Miyuki to teach his friend some more.

After an hour, Miyuki opened her eyes. She looked exhausted from the intense healing session.

'You still have healing hands,' said Jack, sitting up. 'I can feel my leg getting better already.'

'It's never any trouble . . . for you,' she replied, wearily getting up and heading for her bed. Within moments, she was fast asleep.

Saburo and Hayato came over.

'Does it *really* work?' Saburo asked dubiously.

Jack nodded his head. 'Have a look.'

The wound had lost much of its red rawness and the blisters beneath the green paste were starting to disappear.

'The ninja possess some unique talents,' said Yori admiringly as he continued to practise the hand sign, moving it in a figure-of-eight through the air.

'I can see why you're so impressed with her,' conceded Hayato, now heading to bed himself. 'Even if she is a ninja.'

'Ninja or not, Miyuki's proved to be a good friend,' said Jack, a little defensive at Hayato's inherent prejudice towards her.

'Well, it's obvious she thinks the world of you,' said Yori, too wrapped up in his *kuji-in* to realize what he'd just said.

Jack glanced guiltily over at the sleeping Miyuki. He hadn't been aware that her feelings ran that deep or were so apparent to everyone else.

Saburo raised an eyebrow archly at him. 'Does Akiko know about her?'

'Y-yes,' said Jack, awkward at the implication. 'They met once in the Iga mountains.'

'I bet some sparks flew when they were introduced!' Saburo laughed.

'You're not far from the truth,' Jack admitted, recalling the girls' first tense encounter within a blazing farmhouse, set alight during *daimyo* Akechi's invasion of the ninja village.

Wanting to shift the focus from Miyuki and Akiko, he asked, 'How's Kiku? Have you seen her since the Shogun closed the school?'

It was now Saburo's turn to look flustered. 'She's well,' he replied, suddenly finding the hilt of his new *katana* of great interest. 'In fact . . . she was the other reason I went on my *musha shugyō* . . . to impress her father!'

Jack grinned at discovering Saburo's romance blossoming. He'd suspected as much when Kiku had stayed behind following Saburo's injury in the attack on the *Niten Ichi Ryū*.

'Well, if we survive beyond the black moon, you'll have enough tales of courage to win her father over.'

'*If* we survive?' queried Saburo, shifting uncomfortably in his seat. 'I thought you'd burnt the bandit's camp to the ground. Surely Akuma's no longer such a threat?'

'Jack entered the cave and roused the bear,' said Yori, now anxiously rubbing a set of prayer beads at the thought of the impending raid.

'But the bandits will be weakened from hunger and without supplies or weaponry,' Saburo argued.

'Perhaps,' said Jack. 'But I wouldn't be surprised if Akuma doesn't have some hidden reserves.'

Alone with his two close friends, Jack felt he could admit his true concerns.

'Having seen Akuma for myself, I'm even more worried than before. The man isn't called Black Moon for nothing. His heart is black. He didn't show an ounce of pity or remorse when torturing that farmer. Akuma's not just cruel, he's pure evil. We either win this battle outright . . . or we must prepare ourselves for the worst.'

38

STRAW SOLDIERS

The celebratory mood among the villagers quickly disappeared in the cold light of morning. Fear and worry returned with a vengeance when they realized that the black moon was little more than a day away. Noticing the growing panic, Jack immediately put the village to work and the furious last-minute preparations helped to distract the farmers from the coming attack.

Most were involved in the final push to finish the dry moat. When they showed signs of flagging, Saburo shrewdly split the workforce between the two ends and challenged his unit to race Yuudai's to the completion point. A samurai's sense of pride soon took over. Saburo and Yuudai's competitiveness was heard throughout the village in their increasingly vocal shouts of encouragement.

While this digging race went on, Jack took the opportunity to inspect the state of the other defences with Yori. Thanks to Miyuki's ninja healing, he no longer walked with a limp and she promised a full recovery in time for the battle.

Heading first to the barricade, Jack was stunned to discover it guarded by a line of samurai.

'Where did all these *ronin* come from?'

Yori simply grinned at this reaction.

'How did you persuade –'

It took Jack a second look to realize their new recruits were straw dummies wearing the spare samurai helmets and armour. Crossing the wooden gangway and drawing closer, it was now obvious. But from a distance, the impression had been entirely convincing.

'This was *your* idea?' said Jack, rapping his knuckles upon the helmet of the nearest straw soldier.

Yori nodded. 'They're no good at fighting, of course. But hopefully Akuma will be fooled into thinking we've got a whole battalion of samurai! We can also use them to draw musket fire.'

'Yori, you're a genius!'

'I merely remembered one of Sensei Kano's lessons,' Yori replied humbly. '*The eye sees only what the mind believes it sees.*'

'Well, my mind fooled me,' said Jack. 'And the bandits will definitely be deceived.'

The two of them made their way over to the forest. As before, the defences appeared to be non-existent – apart from Miyuki's basic wooden barrier and Saburo's thorn-filled ditch that now cut across the main path.

Yori glanced nervously at Jack. 'Akuma could march straight in here.'

'*To see with eyes alone is not to see at all*,' said Jack with a wry smile, as he recited another of Sensei Kano's teachings. 'When you're dealing with a ninja, it's what you *don't* see that you should be afraid of!'

As they crossed the southern paddy fields to the bridge,

Jack's heart dropped like a stone. In all directions, the water had become encrusted with ice.

'We've flooded these too early!' he exclaimed.

'It can't be very thick yet,' said Yori, picking up a rock from the pathway and tossing it high into the air.

The rock bounced and skittered across the hardened surface.

'Well . . . I doubt it'll take the weight of a man,' said Yori.

He placed a tentative foot on the ice. It crackled around the edges, but held firm. He stepped on with his other foot.

'Oh dear,' said Yori, fully supported by the ice. 'It seems that –'

All of a sudden he fell through, ending up thigh deep in ice, water and mud. Yori looked down as he began to sink.

'I suppose that's good news,' he said, trying to pull his feet out.

'Let's pray it stays that way,' replied Jack, quickly hauling his friend back on to the path. 'But if not, we'll just have to station the majority of the farmers along this front line – and hope.'

They headed over to the bridge, Yori squelching at his side. As they approached the river, they heard sounds of bickering further back up the road. Miyuki and Hayato were positioned beside the hay bales at the village's eastern entrance.

'I thought you were a skilled archer!' cried Miyuki.

'I am,' Hayato snapped, drawing another arrow from his quiver.

'Then how come you missed?'

'Because I've got you breathing down my neck.'

Jack and Yori hurried over.

'What's the problem?' asked Jack.

'Miyuki wants me to hit that charge with a flaming arrow

from *here*!' Hayato explained, indicating the gunpowder cask half hidden beneath the bridge.

A small wooden target had been set up in front for practice. From where they stood, the distance and awkward angle made the shot difficult for any archer. However, bushes near the bridge obstructed the view and made the task even more challenging. An arrow from Hayato's previous attempt was embedded in the bridge's supporting strut, a good hand's breadth off-target.

'It would be simpler and less risky to dismantle the bridge,' Hayato urged Jack.

'But we'd lose an opportunity to reduce Akuma's force,' Miyuki argued.

'Can't you move the gunpowder?' suggested Yori.

Miyuki shook her head. 'We have to put the main charge there,' she explained. 'Otherwise the bridge won't collapse. And we can't get any closer, since Hayato would become a target for musket fire.'

'Why not use a line of gunpowder and light it from here?' said Jack.

'Over this distance? It'd be impossible to get the timing right. Akuma's men could be across before it blew.'

'I don't understand why we can't place *two* charges,' demanded Hayato, indicating a second cask of gunpowder next to Miyuki. 'Put that one where I *can* hit it and have the explosion set off the other.'

'Sorry, but I need that cask,' she replied.

'More invisible ninja defences?' said Hayato sarcastically.

Jack turned to Hayato. 'Try again. I'm sure it's just a matter of practice.'

Nocking the arrow, Hayato raised his bow, took aim and fired. They all watched with bated breath as the arrow sped through the air, its feathered flights whipping past the bushes. A moment later it clipped the target, but flew beyond and disappeared into the river. It was a good shot, but not good enough.

'Missed again,' Miyuki tutted.

Hayato glared at her. 'I'd like to see you do any better!'

Jack stepped forward and handed Hayato another arrow. 'Remember how you hit a moving target in that boat on the river. Just use the same technique now.'

Reluctantly, Hayato accepted the arrow and took aim a third time. But in mid-flow he paused and looked hard at Miyuki. A sly grin spread across his lips. Narrowing his eyes, he refocused on the target and fired.

The arrow shot towards the bridge and struck the target dead centre.

'I *knew* you could do it!' said Jack.

'Yes,' said Hayato, shooting Miyuki a sideways glance. 'I just had to imagine the target was a ninja!'

Miyuki took the insult in her stride.

'Whatever it takes,' she replied coolly. 'But you'd best hit it *first* time when Akuma comes, because you won't get a second chance . . . just as you wouldn't with a ninja.'

39

BATTLE CRY

A massive shout erupted from the moat.

Jack and the others turned to see Saburo astride the built-up wall of earth, punching the air.

'We won!' he cried in jubilation.

Exhausted and covered in mud, his unit crawled out of the trench and admired their work. The thorn-filled ditch now encircled the entire village, forming a daunting barrier to any invader.

'The village wins,' corrected Jack, his and everyone else's spirits lifted by the accomplishment of such a monumental feat. At the start no one would have believed the task was possible.

Yuudai's team laid the last of the thorn bushes.

'Let Akuma come if he dares!' he said to Jack, giving the barbed defence a final inspection. 'That bandit's about to get one very nasty shock.'

Flopped in the snow, Kunio was picking thorns out of the palms of his hands. With a pained expression, the boy begged, 'Can we rest now?'

'Tonight,' said Jack, clapping him encouragingly on the back. 'But first you must practise your spear drills.'

Groaning at the thought, Kunio marched off with the other farmers to fetch their weapons. After their last training experience, none of the villagers showed much enthusiasm. But the imminent threat of Akuma compelled them to make an effort and the return of their daughters had given them hope that the impossible could happen.

They obediently gathered in the square in their assigned units. Toge was the last to arrive and found his position at the front.

'Let's hope Akuma is late too!' Hayato remarked, the farmers laughing at his jest.

Toge bowed his head in apology. This was the first time Jack had seen him since their return from Akuma's camp and he hoped the farmer was coping with his grief. It must be hard to see all the other families reunited when his own never would be.

Under Hayato's command, the units went through their drill formations. Jack was as relieved as Hayato when the farmers managed to keep in line and maintain at least a semblance of coordinated defence. But in spite of their efforts, their skills were still greatly lacking. Practising their attack manoeuvres, the units were hesitant and would run all ways rather than make a concerted charge.

After several false starts, Hayato called for a break and the young commanders gathered together on the farmhouse veranda.

'They wouldn't scare off a flock of birds!' he muttered.

Jack nodded reluctantly in agreement. 'Akuma's going to plough straight through them. They've got no confidence in their abilities.'

'These farmers lack courage,' stated Hayato. 'And we need a *fighting* force if we're to have any hope of defeating the bandits.'

Yori raised a hand. 'Even a sparrow has courage when it flies with others. Individually the farmers know they're weak. We need to convince them there's strength in numbers.'

'What do you suggest?' said Jack.

Yori thought for a moment. 'A battle cry. One that will unite them.'

'Good idea,' said Hayato, nodding approvingly. 'By all means, give it a try.'

'I meant for you to teach them . . .' said Yori, but Hayato had already stepped aside for him.

Jack offered him an encouraging smile as his friend nervously took centre stage on the veranda. The villagers stared back, wondering what the little monk was about to do.

'A lion's roar . . . can frighten the greatest foe . . . even if the lion has no claws,' Yori began in a timid voice. 'A strong battle –'

'Speak up!' cried a farmer near the back.

Yori cleared his throat and tried again. 'A strong battle cry will scare your enemy; help focus and strengthen your attack; even overcome your own fear. So I want you all to shout.'

The farmers looked doubtfully at him.

'Scream as loud as you can,' urged Yori.

Feeling self-conscious, only half the farmers made an attempt.

'You can do better than that!' said Yori. 'Roar like a lion.'

The second shout was louder, more farmers taking part, but they still lacked any conviction. Their third effort was no better. Yori began to despair.

'You need to shout from your *hara*, your centre,' he explained, pointing to his stomach. 'Put your *ki*, all your energy into it. Like this!'

Taking a deep breath, Yori opened his mouth and roared.

'YAAAAAH!'

The ear-splitting yell was so unexpected from a boy of his size that everyone was temporarily stunned. Kunio, who was directly in line, staggered backwards and landed on his rear. He lay there, clasping his chest, his face screwed up in agony.

'What did you do?' he wheezed. 'It feels like you've hit me!'

'Sorry,' said Yori, smiling apologetically. 'I . . . I got carried away.'

The farmers now all stared at Yori, dumbfounded.

Hayato and Miyuki glanced at Jack for an explanation.

'*Kiaijutsu*,' said Jack, referring to the secret fighting art of the Sohei monks, whereby warriors channelled their inner energy, *ki*, into their battle cry and used it as a weapon. Sensei Yamada had attempted to teach his students the skill at the *Niten Ichi Ryū*, but Yori was the only one to master it.

Yori's convincing demonstration reinvigorated the farmers and he soon had them shouting in units at one another. Although there was no chance of them mastering *kiaijutsu*, their spirited battle cries gave them courage and gradually they bonded into a single united force . . . a *fighting* force.

40

DOUBTS

Jack stood on the rise overlooking the village. The square was deserted, all the farmers having retreated into their homes. After the tumultuous noise of so many battle cries, a deathly silence now took hold. Alone with their families, each farmer's courage turned small and their confidence faded into fear once more.

Jack too felt an overwhelming sense of foreboding as he watched the sun sink below the horizon and the shadow of the mountains creep back over the plain. Compared to their towering peaks, the village's improvised defences appeared weak and insubstantial. He began to question their ability to repel the almighty Akuma.

Ever since laying eyes upon the bandit leader, a seed of doubt had been growing within him. When he'd first agreed to the job, he'd foolishly presumed the bandits would be disorganized – little more than bullies made brave by their swords.

How wrong he had been.

While this might apply to some of the bandits, Nakamura, Sayomi and Kurochi were an entirely different matter. They'd proved to be deadly adversaries – skilled in fighting, devious in tactics and merciless in attitude. None would prove easy targets and all three would be highly dangerous in the forth-coming battle. Jack still felt a twinge of pain when he recalled Nakamura driving the burning branch into his leg.

Akuma himself was even more cause for concern.

The bandit leader's heartless disposition chilled Jack to the bone. The man reminded him of the ninja Dragon Eye. Both shared the same ruthless and inhuman nature, and they matched one another in their sickening appetite for torture. Yet what worried Jack the most was Akuma's reaction to the destruction of his camp. The bandit leader had paid no attention to the fire. His only focus had been the capture and punishment of those responsible. Akuma was clearly a man who would go to the ends of the earth to exact his revenge.

This worried Jack greatly and he wasn't alone in his concerns.

Over by the eastern entrance Hayato was firing arrow after arrow at the target beneath the bridge. He'd been practising non-stop. Although Jack couldn't judge the accuracy of his shots, Hayato's furious determination suggested he still wasn't satisfied with his performance. Like Jack, this young samurai understood none of them could afford to make a single mistake against a foe as formidable as Akuma.

Booming laughter suddenly burst forth from Sora's farm-house. It sounded strange and out of place against the tense atmosphere gripping the rest of the village. Neko came flying out of the door, Yuudai in close pursuit. They were re-enacting her episode with the bear again. Neko scampered away in delight and hid behind a wall as Yuudai stalked her. Then she jumped out, arms raised. Yuudai feigned shock and ran away, before they both charged back inside the farmhouse.

Smiling to himself, Jack thought, *At least they're managing to keep their spirits up*.

The jingle of metal rings alerted Jack to Yori climbing the rise with his *shakujō*.

'Dinner will be ready soon,' he said. 'Not that I feel much like eating.'

The thought of the impending battle was evidently tying his stomach in knots. Jack didn't blame him. He knew the ordeal his friend had gone through during the Battle of Osaka Castle. Yori still suffered nightmares from thinking about the corpses he'd hidden beneath in order to escape certain death. That was one of the reasons he'd become a monk rather than remain a samurai warrior.

Jack placed an arm round his friend's shoulder. 'When the time comes, your role will be as lookout in the watchtower. Stay there. But if our defences are breached, stick with me. I promise not to let any harm come to you.'

Yori put on a brave face. 'I'll be fine,' he insisted. 'Everyone's worried about what tomorrow will bring. It's just that as a monk I need to show strength of spirit to the villagers. They want to be reassured by my faith.'

'I have total faith in you,' said Jack. 'I couldn't have done any of this without your wisdom.'

Yori bowed his head in humble acknowledgement.

They gazed over the freezing paddy fields as the last rays of the sun disappeared and the sky began to fill with stars. Glancing down at the moat, Yori spotted Miyuki crouching at its edge.

'What's she doing?' he asked.

'Looking for weaknesses and gaps, I presume,' Jack replied, admiring her commitment to the cause. 'She's walked the whole stretch this evening.'

'It's good to have a ninja on our side,' said Yori unexpectedly.

'I wish everyone saw it that way.'

'I believe they do,' replied Yori, looking over towards the bridge. 'But samurai pride won't allow them to admit it.'

Snow began to fall around them and settle on the ground.

'A storm's brewing,' Yori observed, hugging himself against the icy wind that blew across the plain.

Jack looked up. Dark clouds gradually extinguished each of the stars, a thin sliver of moon barely visible in the sky.

Tomorrow, even that would be gone.

41

FEAR

The next day the snow lay crisp and even over the plain, a chill blanket muffling all sound and stripping the world of features. The village, tiny against the mountains, was the sole island in this sea of white. Keeping watch over the deserted landscape, both farmers and young samurai found it hard to believe that, in a few hours with the coming of the black moon, Tamagashi would turn into a bloody battleground.

On Hayato's suggestion, a guard rota had been organized so that everyone's strength would be preserved for the fight itself. A small contingent of farmers was assigned to each defence, while a young samurai patrolled the village, ready to raise the alarm at a moment's notice.

So far it had all been quiet.

Jack was finishing his rounds when he heard a clink of armour. Coming to relieve him of his duty, Saburo was dressed in full battle garb — he wore a skirted breastplate of red lacquered leather, decorative gold and brown shin guards and a pair of heavy black gauntlets. From his shoulders hung blue rectangular pads for protecting his upper torso and on his head was a bronzed helmet with curving red horns. The final touch was a *menpō* across his face, a gruesome half-mask with razor-teeth and a hook nose, designed to protect the wearer and at the same time instil fear in the enemy.

Cocooned within his layers of armour, Saburo waded stiffly through the snow over to Jack.

'You'll collapse with exhaustion wearing all that!' exclaimed Jack, staring in astonishment at his friend.

'I'm not taking any chances!' Saburo replied, only his eyes and black bushy brows visible, his voice slightly muffled behind the mask. 'Not after what happened last time.'

'Better safe than sorry,' agreed Jack. Having experienced the pain of an arrow wound himself, he understood Saburo's precautions. But with the Two Heavens sword technique at his disposal, Jack favoured freedom of movement over protection of armour.

'Neko's cooked up a feast, by the way. I got her to understand that a samurai can't fight on an empty stomach,' said Saburo, patting his armoured belly. 'But you'd best hurry – Yuudai has an even bigger appetite than *me*!'

'I'll be left starving then,' said Jack, heading over to the farmhouse for a much-needed meal and, if he could, some sleep too.

Jack was woken by Yori shaking his shoulder. Before he'd even opened his eyes, he'd grabbed his swords and was rising from his bed.

'Akuma?' he asked, blinking away the remnants of sleep.

'Not yet,' replied Yori, relief evident in his voice. 'But dusk isn't far off.'

Yori had apparently followed Saburo's lead and kitted himself out in some armour too. But his diminutive size meant the breastplate and helmet he'd chosen swamped him. He looked more like one of his straw soldiers than a monk.

Everyone apart from Miyuki, who was on guard duty, had gathered around the hearth, warming themselves in preparation for the long night ahead. Neko had her *katana* in hand and Yuudai was offering last-minute tips on wielding it. Saburo was tucking into another bowl of rice, clearly worried it might be his last. On the other side of the fire, Hayato sat cross-legged, eyes half-closed in meditation, as he prepared his mind for the coming conflict.

With night soon to fall, everyone would join the watch and take their posts. This was the time of Black Moon. The attack could occur at any moment. The unpredictability, combined with Akuma's fearsome reputation, put them on edge and Jack could see the strain in his friends' faces. When he joined them by the fire, they all looked expectantly his way.

But words of reassurance failed Jack. He was as uneasy as they were. They were about to wage their first war. Although each of them had been in battle before, they'd had the support and experience of adult warriors leading them. This time they were to face their enemy alone. If things went wrong, they had no one to turn to but themselves.

'Gather your units in the square,' said Jack, attempting to keep his voice steady and at least give an outward appearance of confidence.

Bowing their obedience, the young samurai got to their feet, collected their weapons and marched out the door.

'I couldn't think of anything else to say,' said Jack to Yori, his tone apologetic, as he secured his swords and put his five *shuriken* within the folds of his *obi*.

'Don't worry. Leadership is often more about attitude and actions than words,' replied Yori, picking up his ringed staff and heading slowly for the door. 'A call to action is reassurance enough for us. It shows you're in command and know what you're doing.'

But do I? thought Jack.

Outside the light was fading fast as the farmers took up position and Jack stepped on to the veranda. Junichi emerged from the farmhouse to greet him. His face was grizzled with stubble and his eyes were hollowed black rings from many sleepless nights.

'The time of judgement has come,' said Junichi gravely, glancing up at the darkening sky. 'Do not fail us. Otherwise Akuma will burn this village to the ground and everyone with it. Our fate is in your hands, Jack Fletcher.'

Jack felt the weight of responsibility fall heavily upon his shoulders.

Yoshi tottered out. 'Ignore Junichi's doomsaying. He's afraid, like all of us,' wheezed the old man, waving his walking-stick at the gathered villagers. 'Whatever happens, young samurai, know that your answer to our cry of help is *all* that matters. Win or lose this battle, as long as there is good like that shown by you in this world, evil can never conquer.'

Jack bowed his head. 'I appreciate your faith in me. I will not fail you.'

But turning to the row upon row of terrified farmers'

faces, Jack seriously questioned whether he'd made a promise that he couldn't keep. The farmers shuffled nervously on the spot, their fear intensifying as the sun dropped below the horizon. Barely a handful of stars lit the night. The moon was nowhere to be seen and the invasive darkness fuelled their fright.

'Words are needed to reassure them, however,' Yori whispered urgently.

'Any suggestions?' said Jack, out of the corner of his mouth.

'I'm not Sensei Yamada!' replied Yori with uncharacteristic sharpness. 'I don't have all the answers on the tip of my tongue.'

Jack was taken by surprise with his curt reply and realized he'd put too much pressure on his friend. 'Sorry, I was only asking for *your* wisdom, not his.'

Yori bit his lip, thinking hard, determined to help Jack. He made to speak, then stopped himself. Eventually he said, 'The farmers' fear is greater than ours . . . That makes us brave and courageous in their eyes, so you must appear strong in whatever you say and they'll gain strength from you.'

'That's all I needed,' said Jack, his friend's advice triggering a memory from the *Niten Ichi Ryū*.

Jack took a breath and addressed the petrified farmers.

'When I first trained as a samurai,' he began, 'I was told: *Courage isn't the absence of fear but rather the judgement that something else is more important than fear*.'

Jack let the lesson sink in.

'I know you're afraid, but this village, your families, your rice and your fields are all more important than your fear of

Akuma. So tonight . . . fight like *samurai* . . . so that tomorrow you can be *farmers* once again!'

Roused by his heartfelt speech, they raised their weapons as one and gave an almighty battle cry that echoed across the plain.

42

NIGHT WATCH

'Any sign of him?' whispered Jack, crouching down beside Miyuki.

She lay well hidden within a clump of bushes at the edge of the forest. The rest of her unit were stationed behind the wooden barrier, staying close to the sentry fire to stave off the cold and keep their fears at bay.

'Nothing,' she replied, her eyes constantly scanning the inky forest for the slightest sign of movement.

'Do you want me to take over?' offered Jack, aware she hadn't rested for several hours.

'No, I'm fine. The Grandmaster trained us for night operations. You quickly learnt not to fall asleep on your watch. Otherwise you'd wake up with all your hair cut off and bound to a tree until the following day.'

She shuffled over in the snow to make space for him. 'Some company would be nice, though. The farmers are too wary of ninja to talk much to me.'

Jack lay down next to her. The ground was cold, but he could sense the warmth of Miyuki's body close by his side.

As she resumed her watch, she asked, 'What will your plans be if we survive all this?'

'I'll head south again,' Jack replied. 'Get to Nagasaki, somehow.'

'My offer was genuine,' she said, her gaze softening as she turned to him. 'I'll go with you . . . if you want.'

Jack truly valued Miyuki's loyalty and friendship. Yet after Yori's observation about her feelings towards him, he felt compelled to say something.

'I –' Then he hesitated. What if Yori had been wrong? He might insult her and things could become awkward between them. Then again if Yori was right, he had to be clear that, much as he admired and liked her, he couldn't feel the same way. 'I'd like you to join me, but –'

Miyuki placed a finger to his lips. 'Shh!'

All of a sudden her senses were on full alert, her eyes and ears tuned in to the forest.

Jack's breath caught in his throat as he too heard the rustle of bushes and the crunch of snow. He couldn't see anything moving, but he could hear the noise getting closer.

Is Akuma finally here?

Jack reached for his *katana* and prepared to run back to the defensive line to raise the alarm. But Miyuki stopped him.

A deer nosed its way out of the undergrowth in search of food.

Jack relaxed his grip on his sword. As the creature foraged towards the path, Miyuki picked up a small stone and threw it. The deer bolted away in shock.

'That was one lucky deer,' she whispered. 'Any closer and it would have been tomorrow's lunch.'

Aware Akuma could come from any direction, Jack's mind now turned to the northern, eastern and southern approaches. 'I must check on the other defences,' he said, getting to his feet.

Miyuki nodded in response and waited for Jack to say more. But the moment had passed and Jack left their previous conversation unfinished.

'It's been as quiet as a mouse,' Yuudai informed Jack.

His unit were taking turns to patrol the barricade, their presence reinforced by the line of straw soldiers. Two farmers paced nervously up and down, building up their courage to peer every so often through the gaps. Beyond the spiked defence and the light of their fire, the road rapidly disappeared into sinister blackness.

If Akuma approached from the north, as Jack knew he was likely to, they wouldn't have much of a warning.

'The men are becoming tired and edgy,' said Yuudai, under his breath. 'They're not used to guard duty.'

'They shouldn't have to wait much longer,' replied Jack. 'Junichi told me that Akuma always raids before midnight.'

'Yes, he'll come at the darkest hour to gain the best advantage,' said Yuudai, grimly contemplating the unseen road. 'How are the other units holding up?'

'I'm visiting Saburo, then Hayato next. Miyuki's had one false scare. Otherwise it's just as quiet and her unit is just as scared.'

'And Neko?'

Jack smiled at him. 'Neko's the bravest – the only one who dares venture beyond the firelight.'

Yuudai laughed, making some of the farmers jump in fright. 'She's fearless, that one. How I wish I'd seen her confront that bear.'

'But if you'd been with us,' said Jack, laughing too, 'the bear would've run away *before* Neko got there!'

Confident that Yuudai had everything under control, Jack made his way down to the square. Yori was perched in the watchtower, keeping his eye out for the warning beacon.

'Are you all right up there?' called Jack.

'Yes,' replied Yori. 'It's so peaceful it's easy to forget we'll be fighting soon.'

'Who knows? If Akuma's repelled by our defences, we may not even have to,' said Jack, although deep down he knew Akuma would never give up, especially when the bandit realized this was the village that had attacked his camp and freed the girls. 'Ring the alarm if you see anything.'

Yori waved to him and resumed watching the skyline.

Jack joined Saburo on the village's southern border. The whole stretch felt terribly exposed, with just the frozen paddy fields and the thorn-filled moat for defence.

'It's freezing,' complained Saburo, stamping his feet for warmth. 'No sane bandit would want to raid in these conditions.'

'That's because Akuma's mad!' said Kunio, shuddering despite sitting so close to their sentry fire he was almost in the flames.

'Don't make the mistake of thinking Akuma's mad,' Jack corrected the boy. 'He knows exactly what he's doing. This is the best time to attack, when you're at your weakest and most vulnerable.'

'So where is he?'

Jack looked into the night. 'Out there. Somewhere. Waiting to strike.'

The long night stretched on. The biting cold made the farmers shiver and fatigue made them yawn. The task of the young samurai commanders was as much to keep the farmers awake and focused as to watch out for Akuma.

Jack stood beside Hayato at the eastern entrance. They both listened hard for the sound of horses' hooves and the crunch of footfalls in the snow. But apart from the crackling of the sentry fires, the night was as deaf as it was blind.

'He's not coming,' said Toge, crouched behind the hay bales out of the wind.

'This night's not over,' Hayato reminded him.

'Akuma has always raided us by now.'

'Maybe our attack on his camp scared him off,' Sora suggested, a hopeful expression lighting up his face as he tried to warm his hands by the fire.

'I wouldn't count on it,' said Jack. 'He didn't look the sort of man to be frightened.'

'Then he could be trapped, his back route out of the valley blocked by snow too.'

'Wishful thinking,' said Hayato. 'Akuma would find a way – or make one. He's probably just been delayed by last night's storm.'

But the farmers preferred the idea that Akuma had failed to show up.

'I think Toge's right,' said another man. 'It'll soon be dawn. Black Moon never attacks in the day.'

'All this training, ditch digging and barricade building has been a complete waste of time,' complained Toge bitterly.

'You don't know Akuma won't come,' said Hayato. 'There's still time.'

'But he isn't here now,' argued a farmer, beginning to rejoice. 'And he won't be. Akuma's *not* coming!'

Jack and Hayato glanced anxiously at one another as the false victory spread like wildfire among the gathered farmers.

'Look!' cried Sora, pointing to a faint glow in the mountains. 'The sun's about to rise.'

But it wasn't the sun.

The furious clang of the alarm broke the peace of the night as a warning beacon lit up the sky.

43

THE RAID

'He's attacking from the north!' cried Yori as Jack sprinted into the village square.

'You stay there,' shouted Jack. 'Keep an eye out in case Akuma has split his forces.'

He dashed up the road to the barricade. Yuudai had already rallied his men. They crouched in two rows behind the secondary wall of hay bales, their spears at the ready. The beacon on the hill burnt brightly, but down in the valley it remained pitch black. The thunder of horses' hooves grew louder and disembodied howls and shouts sent shudders of fear through the farmers. Some began to back away, their overwhelming instinct to flee their posts.

'Stay in line!' ordered Yuudai fiercely.

Out of the veil of darkness rode Akuma and his bandits. Like black ghosts, they charged down the road. Caught in the flickering light of the sentry fire, their faces appeared savage and bloodthirsty. They descended upon the village, swords and weapons drawn to massacre any who stood in their way.

Jack now comprehended the utter terror the farmers

harboured for Black Moon. Even in his worst nightmares, he couldn't imagine a more fearsome and bone-chilling sight.

Only at the last moment did Akuma register the barricade in the darkness. He furiously brought his horse to a halt. The bandits around him did the same. But a number, too intent upon the attack to notice, continued the charge. As the barricade loomed into view, their horses broke from their gallop, straining every sinew to stop. The bandits were thrown head first off their mounts to crash into the wooden barricade. Some were knocked unconscious on impact. One victim landed upon a spike, its tip driving straight through his chest.

Confounded by the fortification, the bandits were bottlenecked in the valley and chaos reigned. With their normal strategy foiled, most were at a loss as to what to do next. Akuma, quickest to adapt to the unexpected resistance, barked out orders and marshalled his forces at a safe distance. Then he mobilized a contingent of men to launch a fresh attack. Dismounting, these bandits stormed the barricade on foot.

'First row, get ready,' hissed Yuudai to the farmers.

Although they were terrified out of their wits, their confidence had been boosted at seeing the bandits in such disarray. Yuudai picked up one of the samurai spears in preparation for their defence. Jack squatted beside him, his *katana* drawn.

'We only need to go hand to hand if the barricade is breached,' explained Yuudai, indicating for Jack to stay where he was. 'I'll need you to lead the second division, if required.'

Jack nodded his understanding.

The bandits had started to scale the outer defences. It was hard going and their weapons hampered them as they climbed.

This gave the farmers a vital advantage. When the bandits were halfway, Yuudai gave the signal.

'*KIAI!*' he cried, leading the charge across the wooden gangway.

The farmers rose from their hiding place and rushed the barricade, their spear tips aiming between the gaps for the invaders. The attack was so sudden and swift that the bandits could do little about it. Cries of pain pierced the night as they dropped to the ground, one by one. Most met their fate where they fell, but one survived. Clutching his bleeding stomach, he crawled desperately back towards Akuma.

'SAMURAI!' he warned, pointing to the row of armoured figures behind the barricade.

On Yuudai's instruction, the farmers quickly retreated back across the moat so as to maintain the illusion of an all-samurai force. Hidden behind the hay bales, breathless from the rush of combat, they grinned at one another, exhilarated by their first flush of success.

Paying no attention to his wounded men, Akuma glared in disbelief at such bold opposition.

'Hear me, *ronin*!' he roared. 'This isn't your battle. There's no glory in fighting for farmers. If it's rice you need, there's more than enough to go round. I'll even double what these farmers are paying. Stand aside now.'

Jack and Yuudai glanced at one another.

'It's a good offer,' said Yuudai, with a playful grin. 'Shall we take it?'

The nearby farmers looked shocked at his suggestion, but Jack was impressed that Yuudai could still make jokes under the circumstances.

'Tempting as it is, I think we should refuse,' he replied.

Nodding in agreement, Yuudai grabbed a spare spear. 'Allow me to answer on your behalf.'

He launched the spear, his immense throw sending it soaring into the night. A moment later, they heard a crunch and a startled whinny as it embedded itself in the ground right next to Akuma and his horse.

'You'll regret that, samurai!' snarled Akuma.

Yuudai turned to Jack. 'I'm afraid the spear didn't quite strike home.'

'Don't worry. There'll be plenty more chances to deliver the message.'

Mustering his men, Akuma sent another bandit force to storm the eastern end of the barricade. Yuudai once again led his first division to engage with the attackers. Having lost the element of surprise, though, they found it harder to fend off the bandits. Akuma's men were more cautious this time, keeping their weapons to hand, so they could deflect the lethal spear thrusts as they climbed.

While the farmers battled to bring them down, Akuma ordered a second wave to strike at the western end of the barricade. With Yuudai and his farmers distracted, these bandits climbed unopposed.

Spotting Akuma's tactic, Jack took command of Yuudai's second division and rushed to defend the unguarded end. He and the farmers fought furiously to stop the bandits breaching their defences. But one was already nearing the top. Without hesitation, Jack pulled a *shuriken* from his *obi* and threw it at the man. The ninja star flashed through the air and struck the bandit in the neck. Crying out in shock and pain as blood spurted out, the man lost his grip on the barricade. He crashed into the other bandits, dislodging them as he tumbled to the ground.

Fear and adrenalin driving them on, the farmers kept stabbing with their spears. Confronted with such a relentless defence, the bandits quickly lost the momentum of their assault.

Then a gunshot went off.

The farmers froze like startled deer.

One of Yuudai's unit fell to the ground.

'Got one!' cried a delighted Kurochi, who stood beside Akuma reloading his musket.

Jack raced over to the lifeless man. An arm had been blasted off, but it still made a convincing samurai in the dark. Pushing the straw dummy back into position, Jack taunted, 'You missed, snake head!'

Kurochi swore in disbelief. Furiously packing the gunpowder into the barrel, he reloaded his musket with a lead ball, aimed and fired.

This time the gunshot took off the dummy's head . . . and Jack's almost with it.

'I *never* miss!' shouted Kurochi.

But even though the musket had made an impact, the bandits were failing to make any dent in the farmers' defences.

Realizing he was losing men and gaining nothing, Akuma bellowed, '*FALL BACK!*'

The surviving bandits hurriedly withdrew to their horses.

Pulling hard on his reins, Akuma turned and rode off into the mountains, his men following close behind.

'They're retreating!' cried a farmer in amazement.

'We've WON!' exclaimed another.

Exhilarated by their combat experience, the villagers started to shout in delight.

But Jack and Yuudai knew different. The battle had only just begun.

44

THE MILL

The sun bled above the horizon, bringing with it a crimson dawn. As Jack stood with Junichi in the village square, he was reminded of the mariner's weather lore:

Red sky at night, shepherd's delight
Red sky in the morning, sailor's warning

The prediction couldn't be more accurate. Although Akuma had yet to return, the young samurai kept up a vigilant watch while the exhausted farmers grabbed snatches of fitful sleep.

'Are you certain he'll come back?' Junichi asked, scratching his stubbled chin.

Jack nodded and glanced towards the village's rice store. 'Akuma has few, if any, supplies. He needs your rice to survive the winter.'

'Now he knows how *we* feel,' said Junichi, his expression hardening. 'But we dealt him a severe blow. I was told eight bandits were killed!'

'That means nothing to him,' said Jack, recalling the

wounded bandit that Akuma had left to die. 'He'd sacrifice *all* his men to win.'

'Maybe he's decided to raid another village instead?'

'I doubt it. We've just made Akuma very angry,' argued Jack. 'And now we don't have the element of surprise, our next encounter will be even more dangerous.'

Hearing footsteps, Jack turned to see Miyuki approaching from the direction of the forest.

'Is everything all right?' said Jack, surprised to see her deserting her post.

'Neko's taken over the watch while I rest,' she explained, rubbing her eyes, bloodshot with tiredness.

'Do you need me to go and help her?' he asked.

'No, she's got eagle eyes. Nothing will get past her without us knowing about it.' Wiping the snow from the veranda, she sat down and pulled off her hood. 'I hear Yuudai didn't lose a single man during the attack.'

'Not entirely true,' said Jack, his expression grief-stricken.

Miyuki looked up at him in shock. 'Oh no! Who was killed?'

Jack dabbed a dry tear from his cheek and replied in his gravest tone, 'One of Yori's straw soldiers.'

Miyuki blinked, then registered what he'd said. 'A *hilarious* samurai joke!' she laughed. 'I suppose that makes us even.'

Getting up, she headed wearily for the farmhouse. 'Wake me in an hour or so, will you?'

'Don't worry,' said Jack. 'I won't let you miss any of the action.'

Miyuki was almost to the door, when the alarm clanged a second time.

'No chance of that!' she called, running back.

Up in the watchtower, Yori pointed and yelled, 'Horses to the east!'

Now on full alert, Jack dashed down to Hayato's defensive line, Miyuki and Junichi close on his heels. Hayato stood behind the protective wall of hay bales at the eastern entrance, his hand shading his eyes as he looked to the horizon. Silhouetted against the rising sun, the bandits could be seen in the distance, galloping across the plain.

'It won't be long before they're here,' said Hayato, picking up his bow.

'Good luck with your shot,' encouraged Miyuki.

'I don't need luck,' replied Hayato irritably. 'I've practised.'

He selected an arrow from his quiver. A cloth dipped in lamp oil had been bound to the shaft near the tip.

'I just need to compensate for the arrow's extra weight and drag, that's all.'

Jack looked over to the bridge. The wooden target had been removed and the cask of gunpowder was just visible beside the main supporting strut. Although he had every faith in Hayato's skills, it was still an extremely difficult shot – one made harder by the fact he was firing into the sun.

'I'll send for reinforcements,' said Jack. 'Just in case.'

He turned to one of the younger farmers. 'Tell Yuudai we need his second division here *now*.'

Nodding obediently, the farmer dashed away as if his life depended upon it.

Hayato stood by the sentry fire in preparation to ignite the arrow. The bandits were still a good distance off and his timing would have to be perfect. He couldn't fire too early or else they wouldn't catch Akuma's forces in the blast. But if he shot too late, the village would be in serious danger of invasion. And if he missed . . .

The farmers fell silent as the tension grew.

Jack tried to count the enemy as they approached. Although too far away to be accurate, he judged there were more than thirty left.

Then Jack noticed something odd. A thin stream of smoke was rising from the roof of the mill.

'Where's your mother?' Jack asked Junichi.

'My mother is stubborn,' he replied, with a sad but resigned look on his face.

'Natsuko's still *there*!'

'I tried to persuade her so many times, but –'

Jack leapt the line of hay bales. Having seen what Akuma and his henchmen were capable of, he couldn't leave the old woman to such a fate. He ordered two of the farmers to help him carry the wooden board used to cross the moat during construction.

'NO, Jack!' Miyuki cried. 'You'll never make it back in time.'

Jack bounded over the wooden board, crossing the thorn-filled ditch in a few strides.

'Wait!' called Junichi, running after him. 'My mother will never listen to you.'

'She doesn't listen to you either!'

'Then you'll need my help to carry her out. She won't go any other way.'

Jack didn't have time to argue and they both sprinted down the road towards the bridge.

45

THE BRIDGE

On the plain, Akuma and his bandits rode ever nearer.

The snow crunched under Jack's feet as he urged himself to go faster. He flew on to the bridge and almost slipped upon its icy surface. Panting heavily, Junichi struggled to keep up. By the time he reached the river, Jack was already across.

The bandits were now close enough that Jack could make out Akuma by the distinctive red *hachimaki* on his head.

Hammering on the door, Jack cried, 'Natsuko! Open up!'

'Coming,' croaked a voice from within.

The old woman seemed to take an age, while with every second the thunder of horses' hooves grew louder. Jack was about to kick in the door, when there was a wooden clunk and it slid open. Natsuko's wrinkled face appeared.

'It's about time you paid me a visit,' she said, turning back inside before Jack could grab her. 'Come in, breakfast's almost ready.'

Jack chased after her. 'We've got to go *now*,' he urged, grabbing hold of her arm.

'But we've not even had *sencha*,' she said, appalled at Jack's apparent rudeness.

Junichi ran up to the doorway, breathless. 'Mother, Akuma is coming!'

She sighed heavily. 'I told you before, son, I'm too old to be scared any more.'

'We don't have time for this,' despaired Junichi, glancing over his shoulder. 'He's almost at your door!'

'Let him in then,' she said, brandishing her walking-stick. 'I'll give him a black moon he won't forget!'

'*Please*, Mother, don't argue –'

A distant crack of a musket preceded the gruesome thud of a lead shot. Junichi was thrown against the door frame, blood spewing from his mouth. He weakly clutched at his chest as he slid helpless to the floor. Jack ran to him, but Junichi was fading fast, his tattered kimono soaked red with blood. Natsuko tottered over and fell to her knees.

'I told you to leave me be!' she sobbed, cradling her dying son in her arms.

Junichi's face had gone deathly pale and his breathing was laboured. Focusing on Jack, he spluttered, 'Young samurai . . . don't let Akuma win . . . save Mother . . . save the village . . .'

Then his eyes lost the spark of life and he fell silent.

Consumed with grief, Natsuko stroked her son's hair, no longer aware of the world around her.

Jack could hear the baleful shouts of the bandits nearby. Sticking his head out to check the bridge was still clear, he hurriedly withdrew it as an arrow thudded into the wooden framework. Akuma's bandits were almost on top of them. Grabbing Natsuko, he threw the old woman over his shoulder and ran for the bridge.

Natsuko protested at being torn from her son. Then she saw Akuma bearing down on them.

'You devil!' she cried, raising her stick in defiance. 'I'll see you dead before I die!'

Jack's heart pounded in his chest. Natsuko wasn't heavy, but she was enough to slow him down. He risked a glance back. High in her saddle, her black hair streaming out behind, Sayomi was drawing her bow and taking aim. The ghostly woman's lips parted into a hideous smile as she released the arrow.

In sheer desperation Jack threw himself to the ground, Natsuko protesting at the sudden jolt. She shut up when the arrow missed them by a whisker and drove into the icy deck of the bridge.

Sayomi shrieked in frustration and reached for another arrow.

'GET UP!' screamed Miyuki from the village's eastern defence.

Jack and the old woman were now directly in the path of the bandits' stampeding horses. Using all his strength, Jack rose to his feet with Natsuko and broke into a staggering run. They were completely exposed as he crossed the bridge. Although Kurochi couldn't reload while riding, Sayomi would have no problems rearming her bow.

At the boundary to the village, Jack could see Hayato and Miyuki arguing over when to shoot the gunpowder cask. He wasn't yet across, but behind he heard the leading horses clatter on to the bridge.

'SHOOT!' he bawled, running with all his might.

Hayato seemed reluctant to fire. But if he waited any longer, the bandits would breach their primary line of defence.

'SHOOT!' ordered Jack.

The flaming arrow hurtled towards him.

Jack made a last-ditch effort as it shot past.

Behind he heard a *whoosh*, then a huge explosion. He was knocked off his feet by the blast and landed face first in a ditch by the side of the road. Natsuko dropped next to him, stunned by the detonation.

Dragging her away from the blazing heat, he looked back to see the bridge engulfed in a ball of flame. Its structure had collapsed entirely, preventing any chance of crossing the river. The lead riders and their horses had plummeted into the icy waters and were being washed downstream by the current. While the men struggled to stay afloat, the stronger-swimming horses were able to reach the safety of the bank.

To Jack's dismay, though, Sayomi had survived. Blown by the blast from her horse, she'd landed upon the mill-side bank. Her hair wild and her pale face blackened with smoke, she swayed unsteadily as her eyes hunted for her missing prey. Kurochi and Nakamura had also escaped the trap and gazed in disbelief at the destroyed bridge.

Through the haze of heat and hell-fire, Akuma roared in fury at being foiled a second time.

46

ICE

'Be warned!' Akuma bellowed, seizing a burning fragment of bridge. 'Farmers who fight fire with fire end up with ashes!'

He threw the flaming chunk of wood into the mill and watched it catch light. Leaving the building to burn, Akuma rallied his bandits and rode south for the ford. Sayomi hung back a while to scan the opposite bank one last time. Infuriated, she spurred her steed on with a kick and galloped after her leader.

Jack stayed hidden in the ditch until certain she was gone, then helped the distraught Natsuko to her feet. Behind him, the farmers were wailing at the loss of both their mill and the head of their village.

'Junichi was a good man . . . and brave,' said Jack, trying to comfort the old woman.

'I do not weep for my son. In death, there is no suffering,' she said, staring at the blaze that was her home and now Junichi's grave. 'I weep for all those he left behind. With a tyrant like Akuma, it's those who survive that suffer most.'

Jack helped Natsuko over the wooden board spanning the moat, before leaving her in Sora's care. Miyuki raced up and immediately began checking Jack for injuries.

'I'm fine,' Jack insisted.

'Hayato almost killed you!' she exclaimed in outrage, as she brushed charred splinters from his hair.

'I was following orders,' said Hayato, striding up behind. 'Besides, it's your fault. I always said the plan was *highly* risky.'

'But it worked,' reminded Jack, hoping to prevent a full-blown argument. 'Thanks to Miyuki's cunning *and* your skill.'

Nodding reluctantly, Hayato conceded, 'There's no doubt it was effective. Four bandits were caught in the explosion. That leaves Akuma with a force of less than thirty men.'

'The odds are improving,' said Miyuki with a grin.

Jack's expression remained serious. 'True, but we don't have long before Akuma attacks again. We need to remain vigilant. Miyuki, you'd best return to the forest. Hayato, we need every spare man on the southern defence. We must convince Akuma there's an army waiting to greet him.'

The farmers assembled along the edge of the moat, their forest of spears pointed to the sky. Every eye was turned towards the horizon, nervously awaiting the arrival of Akuma. Beyond the thorn-filled ditch, the patchwork of snow and ice that covered the paddy fields seemed scant defence against such a ruthless enemy. However, having successfully repelled Akuma twice, the farmers now had faith in Jack's strategy.

Jack too was more confident in his role as samurai leader. Tactical planning seemed more instinctive and he positioned the Sword unit to engage any bandits who broke through the line of farmers. He then walked the length of the southern defences with Hayato and Saburo, offering words of encouragement and advice to the most anxious villagers. They listened attentively, assured by the proven capability of their young protectors.

One boy, not much older than Jack, was quivering with fear at the prospect of the coming battle.

'A wise man once told me, *In order to be walked on, you have to be lying down*,' said Jack, recalling Sensei Yamada's very first life lesson to him. 'Are you lying down?'

The young farmer shook his head, somewhat confused at the question.

'Then Akuma can't walk over you, can he?'

'No!' replied the boy, standing a little taller and grasping his spear tighter as he understood the lesson.

Then for the third time that day, the alarm rang out.

'Bandits to the south!' cried Yori.

Like an approaching storm, Akuma and his men came into view, galloping up the southern track. When they reached the first of the paddy fields, he raised a fist and the bandits came to a halt. Akuma wasn't taking any chances this time. Noticing the land had been flooded, he ordered one of his men to dismount and test the way ahead. The bandit hesitantly stepped on to the frozen paddy field.

Jack watched with bated breath as the man made his way across the ice. The surface held his weight and continued to do so. When he reached the middle, Akuma ordered the man to jump up and down.

The ice held.

'I was afraid of that,' said Jack, sharing an uneasy look with Hayato and Saburo.

'Akuma's got a clear run at us,' Hayato replied gravely. 'That means we've only the farmers' fighting spirit to rely upon to win this battle.'

Then the bandit slipped and landed hard on his rear. The spectacular fall caused riotous amusement among the farmers, as well as Akuma's bandits who laughed at their floundering comrade.

'Well, that's raised everyone's spirits!' grinned Saburo.

'It'll certainly dissuade Akuma from charging at speed,' said Jack, glad that despite the freezing their defence had some effect.

As the humiliated man scrambled to find his feet, Hayato took the opportunity to carefully aim his bow. He released an arrow just as the bandit got to his hands and knees. It soared through the air and struck the man directly in his behind. He howled in pain and hobbled in retreat back to the edge of the paddy field.

'Just helping him off the ice,' said Hayato with a smirk.

47

A DEAL

The bandits spread themselves out in preparation to attack. They glared at the army of ragtag farmers with derision, unfazed by their display of resistance. On Akuma's command, they rattled their weapons and bellowed a bloodthirsty battle cry, whooping and hollering abuse.

The farmers instinctively backed away from this ferocious display.

'Hold your lines!' ordered Jack. 'Akuma's just trying to frighten you.'

'He's doing a good job of it!' exclaimed Kunio, trembling so much he was barely able to stand.

'You wanted to play at being samurai,' said Hayato sternly. 'This is your chance. Show some backbone.'

Suddenly Yori appeared at Jack's side.

'I ordered you to stay in the watchtower,' said Jack.

'You need *every* samurai to fight this battle,' replied Yori, striding determinedly forward to stand upon the ridge of the moat. Planting his *shakujō* in the earth, he drew in a deep breath and yelled back at the bandits, 'KIAAAI!'

Realizing the guts it would have taken his friend to perform such a bold act, Jack raised his *katana* and bellowed at the top of his lungs too, urging the farmers to do likewise. Taking courage from Yori's spirited cry, the farmers clattered their spears and roared their defiance.

'KIAAAI!'

As the farmers' battle cry faded, a scornful laugh was heard echoing across the fields.

'Farmers pretending to be samurai!' shouted Akuma. 'I've never seen anything so pathetic.'

He rode forward with Sayomi and Nakamura to the border of the next paddy field. Decked out in jet-black armour, the steel plate of his red *hachimaki* glinting in the morning sun, Akuma was a fearsome sight. He held a barbed trident in one hand and upon his hip were two black-handled swords. Beside him in her blood-red armour, Sayomi had stowed her bow in favour of her lethal double-edged *naginata*. On his other side, Nakamura brandished his terrifying battleaxe, its blade chipped and worn from use. He was still recognizable by his red scar, but now half his beard was missing, his skin scorched red with burns.

'If you resist further, you'll *all* be slaughtered!' declared Akuma. 'Surrender now or face the consequences.'

When the villagers didn't respond, Akuma continued, 'Everyone knows that farmers don't possess the courage or skills to fight. You'd be better off putting a sword in the hand of a child! This is your last –'

'They *have*!' interrupted Nakamura, suddenly spotting Jack among the ranks and pointing furiously. 'That's the *gaijin* boy who attacked our camp.'

Akuma fixed his gaze upon the blond-haired blue-eyed

warrior, who stood sword in hand beside a small warrior monk, a samurai in full-body armour and another *ronin* with a bow. His expression grew dark and murderous.

'I demand to speak to your leader *now*,' snarled Akuma, addressing the farmers.

With Junichi dead, the villagers glanced at one another in confusion. There had been no time to consider who would be his replacement. Then slowly, like a change in the direction of the wind, all eyes turned to Jack.

Saburo patted him on the shoulder. 'It appears *you* have the honour.'

Jack stepped forward, doing his best to appear as poised and confident as his opponent.

'*You're* their leader?' spat Akuma, incredulous. 'What mad man put the infamous *gaijin* samurai in charge – and a mere boy at that?'

'You did,' shouted Jack. 'When you killed Junichi, the head of their village.'

Akuma now reassessed Hayato, Saburo and Yori. 'You're *all* children!'

He turned to his brigade of bandits and said mockingly, 'They've hired *young* samurai.'

Astounded, the bandits howled with laughter. The farmers shifted uncomfortably, their confidence wavering in the face of such ridicule.

'You farmers must be desperate,' said Akuma, letting out a cruel laugh.

'They've beaten you twice!' shouted Sora, stepping forward from the ranks. 'And they'll defeat you again!'

Akuma stopped laughing. 'Not *this* time,' he replied, furious. He eyed the extensive moat surrounding the village, noting the spiky thorn bushes. 'A ditch won't save you. But . . . I'm not a merciless man. Hand over your rice now and we'll spare you and your families.'

Jack almost laughed at the suggestion. He'd witnessed the sort of mercy Akuma gave out – it involved torture and death.

'Leave this village alone and we'll spare *you*!'

Akuma looked outraged. 'Beware, *gaijin*, you're delivering this village a death sentence.'

Sayomi leant over from her horse and spoke softly to her leader. Akuma's expression transformed from thunderous to triumphant. He addressed the farmers again. 'I have a better deal for you. Hand over the *gaijin* samurai and I promise – *on my honour* – to leave you and the rice untouched.'

Pulling on his reins, Akuma retreated to his line of bandits and rammed his trident into the snow. Holding up his hands, he cried, 'As you can see, my intentions are honest.'

Jack heard an argument break out among the ranks of farmers.

'We should do it,' urged the elderly farmer who'd led the vote against Jack before. 'He just wants the reward.'

'You believe that devil?' said Yuto, standing up to the old man yet again. 'Once he has Jack, he'll destroy us all. Jack's our saviour!'

'But if we fight Akuma, who knows how many of us will die? This could be our last chance to save the village.'

'NO!' Yoshi the elder overruled, leaning heavily on his walking-stick as he tottered to the front line. 'We must reap what we have sown. We agreed when Junichi was alive and we must respect his memory. There's no going back now.'

Yoshi stepped on to the moat beside Jack and bowed to him. Then turning to Akuma, he called, 'We know your game, Akuma. We no longer bow to you. No deal!'

Akuma glared in disbelief at the outrageous defiance of the villagers.

'Know this,' he thundered. 'YOU'VE JUST DECLARED WAR!'

48

SCARED

Seeing Akuma snatch up his trident, Saburo pulled out his *katana* in preparation for battle. The polished blade shone like quicksilver in the sun.

'Time to make use of my father's gift,' he said, offering Jack a grim smile.

'You'll make him proud,' Jack replied. 'And Kiku's father.'

Saburo forced a laugh. 'I only wish I was able to write *haiku*. Poetry is a far less dangerous way of impressing a girl.'

'But no easier,' said Jack, remembering the *haiku* he'd written for Akiko. It had taken him months to compose, even with Yori's help.

Determined to keep the farmers focused on fighting rather than fear — as well as demonstrate to Akuma their military capability — Jack gave the signal to begin defensive formations. On Hayato's command, the farmers lowered their spears and advanced to the front line, ready to fend off the invading bandits. A fearful tension hung in the air as they waited for Akuma to make his move.

But Akuma didn't give the order to attack. In fact, the

bandits appeared in little rush to go anywhere, satisfied merely to intimidate their victims.

'Why's he not attacking?' asked Saburo.

Jack looked along the line. Only now did he notice Kurochi the Snake wasn't among them. He did a quick count. The bandits numbered just twenty-three.

'Hayato, take command,' said Jack urgently.

'Where are you going?'

'Akuma's tricked us,' cried Jack, beckoning three men from the Sword unit to follow him. 'I must warn Miyuki.' And he ran off towards the forest.

As Jack flew along the path, he heard the distinctive blast of a musket shot. Turning the corner of the last house, he found the small group of defending farmers cowering behind their wooden barrier. On the ground lay a body.

Neko knelt beside the dying victim, trying to stem the bleeding. No match for the power of a lead bullet, the barrier hadn't provided much protection and the musket shot had gone straight through. Fearing the worst, Jack rushed over just as the unfortunate farmer gave a guttural groan and fell still.

Neko continued to hold the wound closed, silently imploring the man to come back round. But there was little hope of that. Jack respectfully closed the dead farmer's eyes and pulled Neko away.

Where's Miyuki? Jack signed.

With a bloodstained hand, Neko pointed to the forest. Jack peered round the barrier. Kurochi and seven bandits were cautiously edging along the main track in single file. But there was no sign of Miyuki.

He tried not to worry about her, realizing she was probably well hidden. Yet seeing the bandits approach unopposed, he couldn't help question the effectiveness of her defences. With his *katana* at the ready, he urged the other three farmers to unsheathe theirs and prepare to engage.

The bandits' confidence grew, the further along the snowy track they came. Clearly believing Akuma's diversion had drawn all the *ronin* to the southern boundary, the leading bandit began to stride towards the village.

Then he was gone.

In the blink of an eye, the man had completely vanished from the path. Kurochi and the other bandits came to an abrupt halt, all of them sharing the same shocked expression. Even the farmers were surprised by his sudden disappearance.

Then a pained moan rose from the hidden pit. 'My legs . . . my legs . . . they're broken!'

'Spread out!' ordered Kurochi, making a sweep of the forest with his musket.

His remaining six men fanned out. They kept their eyes on the ground, worried they too might fall into another snow-covered trap.

Rebuking himself for even doubting Miyuki, Jack now watched their advance with eager expectation. As the bandits worked their way through the undergrowth, he wondered who the next victim would be. He didn't have to wait long. One man was concentrating so hard on where he was placing his feet that he never saw what hit him. Pushing his way between two bushes, he triggered the release of a pre-sprung branch. It snapped back into place, striking the bandit in the forehead with such force that it sent him flying backwards. He rebounded off a tree trunk and dropped unconscious into the snow.

The other bandits were now petrified of making *any* movement.

'Keep going!' urged Kurochi, although he remained where he stood.

A grunt of pain alerted Kurochi to the loss of a third man. He lay slumped on the ground, having apparently been attacked by a mound of snow.

The four bandits left were frozen with fear as they imagined death awaiting them in every bush, tree and snowdrift. But Kurochi wasn't so easily put off. He raised his loaded musket and took careful aim.

Jack's heart leapt into his mouth when he realized his intended target. As Kurochi pulled the trigger, Miyuki burst from her hiding place.

The snowdrift exploded behind her.

'Kill that ninja!' roared Kurochi, reloading, furious to have missed his quarry.

Miyuki sprinted for the shelter of the barrier. A bandit followed in hot pursuit, wielding a vicious spiked club. Jack and Neko urged Miyuki on as she bounded headlong through the undergrowth. But the bandit, even faster, gained on her and swung his club. Jack shouted a warning. Miyuki ducked and switched direction.

The bandit cursed and raced after her. Too far from the barrier, Jack realized Miyuki would never reach them alive. The bandit swung his deadly club at her head again. But it never made contact. Like a startled bird, the man flailed as his feet were whipped from under him. Screaming in terror, he flew high into the forest canopy. Caught by the hidden snare, the bandit was left swinging back and forth with little hope of escape.

Weaving her way along the path, Miyuki avoided all her other traps then jumped high over the thorn ditch, somersaulting to land safely on the other side. Before Kurochi had another chance to aim at her, she dived behind the barrier and rolled to a stop beside Jack.

'That was a little *too* close,' she panted.

'Where are *you* going?' shouted Kurochi as his three surviving bandits beat a hasty retreat.

'No one said anything about ninja!' cried one of the men.

'This area's a death trap!' said another, terrified.

The third bandit, running as fast as he could, didn't even bother replying.

For a brief moment, Kurochi considered his chances of surviving a forest full of hidden traps. Then his better judgement prevailed and he hurriedly followed his fleeing men.

As the first bandit found his way to the path, he cried out in pain and began to hop around.

'*Tetsu-bishi?*' asked Jack, with a knowing smile.

Miyuki nodded and Jack almost felt pity for the men trying to escape the minefield of *tetsu-bishi* – iron spikes – hidden beneath the snow.

'They won't come this way again,' said Miyuki confidently. 'As the Grandmaster taught me – *a scared enemy is as good as a dead enemy*.'

49

SHOT DOWN

'Why doesn't he just give up?' Sora asked in desperation.

He stood with his spear unit beside the moat, red-faced and breathless from fending off another of the bandits' advances. It was now late afternoon and Akuma's dogged determination was wearing the farmers down. While used to long hours labouring in the fields, they didn't have the mental and physical stamina to fight for prolonged periods.

'Akuma won't stop until he's won . . . or dead,' replied Jack, flicking blood from his blade. 'But as long as we keep fighting, he *won't* win!'

Having failed to outflank them by the forest entry, Akuma had focused all his forces on the southern moat. His first assault had been quickly repelled. Despite the bandits' savage charge, the farmers had kept them at bay, the combination of spears, thorns and ditch proving effective. But Jack soon realized that Akuma had been merely testing the farmers' nerve – the bandit leader withdrew his forces before losing a single man. Then with calculated precision, Akuma selected different sections of the moat and sent groups of bandits to attack in turn, probing for weaknesses in the farmers' defence.

Shouting broke out from Jack's far right. The farmers under Saburo's command rushed to defend their quarter. The detachment of bandits on the other side of the moat clashed violently against the spears. Some deflected the thrusts, while others attempted to cut their way through the thorn bushes.

A farmer stepped forward to drive his spear into the nearest bandit when an arrow lanced his neck. Choking as blood gushed forth, he toppled into the moat.

'Father!' cried a farmboy, dropping his spear and rushing to pull him out.

The ominous *crack* of a musket echoed across the fields. The farmboy was blown backwards as the deadly shot ripped through him.

Saburo's unit began to break up, their courage crumbling in the face of such destructive force.

'Keep your lines!' ordered Saburo, having to battle a bandit who'd breached the moat. Blocking the man's sword thrust with his *katana*, he kicked the bandit squarely in the chest and sent him flying back into the thorn bushes. Flailing like a fish caught in a net, the bandit struggled to escape. A woman, howling with rage, ran from behind the ranks and grabbed a spear.

'This is for my husband!' she cried, harpooning the man. She pulled out the spear and thrust again. 'And that's for my son!'

Then she fell to her knees, sobbing beside her murdered family.

Saburo dragged the woman away before she too suffered the same fate.

The farmers fought on, but their resolve was weakening as an arrow brought down another farmer.

Hayato ran up to Jack and Yori. 'Akuma's waging a war of attrition,' he said gravely. 'He's got Kurochi and Sayomi picking us off one by one.'

'We *must* keep up morale,' insisted Jack. 'Our only chance is to keep fighting.'

'But if we continue to lose men like this, they'll soon be too scared to even approach the moat.'

'I don't see that we have any other choice.'

Hayato bit his lip in frustration, lost for an alternative too.

'To kill a snake, you have to cut off its head,' observed Yori.

Jack and Hayato exchanged glances, both appreciating the danger such a tactic entailed and both a little surprised that Yori had been the one to come up with it.

Looking across the fields to Akuma, Jack asked, 'Hayato, can you get him with your bow from here?'

Hayato shook his head. 'He's out of range. Always is.'

'Then you need to get closer.'

'Even if I got past the bandits, Kurochi or Sayomi would kill me first –'

A musket shot rang out.

'NO!' cried Yori, his eyes widening in horror.

Jack spun round to see Saburo falling to the ground. At the same time, Akuma launched a second group of bandits to attack the left end of the moat.

'Hayato, take your unit to stop them,' Jack ordered, as he and Yori ran the other way to Saburo's aid.

Dropping down beside their friend, they found him lifeless.

'Saburo!' cried Jack, removing the mask from his face.

His friend didn't respond. Yori began to pray as they frantically tried to revive him. Jack was in shock himself. He couldn't imagine losing Saburo like this. He should never have asked his friend to join this suicidal mission in the first place.

With their commander down, Saburo's unit started to flounder and gaps appeared in their defence. Taking advantage of the loss of leadership, the bandits stormed the moat. At the opposite end, Hayato fought to keep the second wave from breaking through.

With the farmers split between two battles, Akuma's strategy had succeeded and he now sent a third and final division of men to attack the undefended centre. They immediately went to work on the thorn bushes, hacking at them with their axes and swords.

The bandits fighting Saburo's unit were the first to breach the defences. The lead invader carved his way through the farmers, causing bloody chaos as he slaughtered all in his path.

Yori, enraged with grief, leapt up and faced the oncoming bandit.

'YAAAH!' he screamed.

The bandit crumpled as if he'd run straight into a brick wall.

Drawing his breath, Yori prepared to unleash another devastating *kiaijutsu* attack. Meanwhile, Jack searched for Saburo's wound to stem any bleeding.

'YAAAH!'

'Tell Yori . . . to stop shouting,' groaned Saburo, groggily opening his eyes. 'My head's ringing . . . like a temple bell.'

Jack stared in disbelief at his fallen friend. 'You're alive!' Then he spotted the lead shot – embedded in Saburo's helmet.

'Help me up, Jack,' said Saburo, stunned but otherwise unharmed. 'This armour weighs a ton!'

The farmers cheered in amazement at seeing their commander rise to his feet.

'Better safe than sorry,' said Saburo, tapping his helmet. After swaying unsteadily for a moment, he regained his balance and focus. Holding his sword aloft, he rallied his men together, then with a loud *kiai* charged the invading bandits.

Jack called to his Sword unit and mustered them to defend the centre. Everyone's spirits had been lifted by Saburo's miraculous survival and all the farmers fought with renewed vigour. But a hole had been cut in the moat's central defences and the bandits now clambered through.

Jack with his Sword unit intercepted them. The fighting was brutal and the farmers' sword skill no match for the bandits' battle-hardened experience. A farmer on Jack's left crumpled under the tremendous blows from one attacker. Jack ran to his aid but was too late to save him. The bandit, as big and ferocious as a bear, went to skewer another poor farmer on the blade of his *nodachi*.

'No!' cried Jack, jumping between them, both his *katana* and *wakizashi* drawn.

'Your head's mine, *gaijin*,' growled the bandit as he swung his massive sword at Jack's neck.

Jack blocked the attack with his own short sword, his arm jarring under the force. At the same time, he thrust his *katana* at the man's stomach. But the bandit's armour proved too thick and the tip of his blade deflected harmlessly to one side.

Laughing at Jack's failure to cause little more than a scratch, the bandit kicked him in the chest. Jack went sprawling in the snow. The bandit then lumbered forward to slice him head to foot. Without a second to lose, Jack flipped to his feet and cross-blocked the attack with both his swords.

Realizing any thrust to the bandit's protected torso was pointless, Jack cut to the head with his *katana* instead. The bandit instinctively raised his sword arm to block it and that's when he exposed the weak point in his armour. With devastating accuracy, Jack drove the tip of his *wakizashi* between the joint in its metal plates. The bandit grunted in pain as the blade plunged deep into his flesh.

With his sword arm now out of action, the bandit knew he stood little chance against Jack's Two Heavens technique and rapidly retreated to the safety of the plain. To Jack's surprise, the other bandits followed close on his tail. The women of the village – having seen the Sword unit in trouble – had rushed forward and were hurling rock after rock at the invaders. The ferocious bombardment drove them backwards, allowing for replacement thorn bushes to be dragged quickly over to plug the gap in their defences.

Glancing along the moat, Jack was relieved to see that Hayato was also repelling his attackers and Saburo's unit had succeeded in sending the remainder of Akuma's forces back across the moat.

The tide of battle had turned. They'd survived, but only by the skin of their teeth.

50

ASSASSINATION

'How many did we lose?' asked Jack, having summoned the young samurai and Miyuki together in the village square.

Akuma's men, bloodied and taken aback by the farmers' spirited resistance, had retreated to the far boundary of the paddy fields. There they remained, licking their wounds, kept under surveillance by Neko, stationed in the watchtower.

'Seven farmers . . . and the boy,' replied Hayato.

'His name was Riku,' said Yori mournfully. 'He was the same age as us.'

Jack sat upon the edge of the veranda, his head in his hands. 'Two of them were from *my* Sword unit.'

'You can't blame yourself, Jack,' said Yuudai. 'This is war.'

'But I trained them. I led them –'

'And that's why four of them are still alive.'

Jack appreciated Yuudai's sentiment, but it still didn't make him feel any better. And despite repelling the bandits, he could see that the farmers' morale had taken a severe blow.

'We'll be lucky to survive another attack like that,' he said.

'I did!' said Saburo, proudly inspecting his dented helmet. 'Even my father will be impressed with this.'

'Don't forget five of the bandits didn't make it back,' said Hayato. 'That leaves Akuma with around twenty men – and four of those are injured. We may have suffered losses, but he's in no rush to attack again.'

'But neither has he gone,' Miyuki observed. 'Akuma's merely waiting until nightfall.'

'Then it's time we cut the head off the snake,' said Jack, his anguish at the farmers' deaths hardening into action.

'You mean assassinate him?' said Miyuki, her eyes twinkling mischievously. 'Who came up with *that* plan?'

Jack and Hayato glanced in Yori's direction.

'For a monk, you're full of surprises,' said Miyuki. 'Tell me, how do you intend to do it?'

Yori looked startled at the suggestion that *he* would be the assassin.

'He's not. I am,' said Hayato. 'With my bow.'

'It won't work,' stated Miyuki flatly.

'I *know* Akuma's out of range,' Hayato sighed, irritated by her swift dismissal of the plan. 'That's why I need to get closer – without getting shot by Kurochi or Sayomi in the process.'

'That's not your problem,' said Miyuki.

'Then what *is*?' demanded Hayato, his patience run dry.

'Akuma's armour is too thick. Your arrow will simply bounce off. To assassinate Akuma, you need to get in close. Real close.'

'What do *you* suggest then?'

'This is a job for a *ninja* . . . not a samurai.'

★

The moon remained unseen in the sky, only starlight reflecting off the snow-covered plain. With nightfall came the return of the farmers' fears. Aware Akuma was out there biding his time to strike, they were scared to venture beyond the safe glow of the sentry fires. To them, Akuma was a devil who lived off the night and all believed he drew strength from the darkness.

But so did the ninja.

'I'll attack at midnight,' said Miyuki, checking her *ninjatō* was secure upon her back.

'You don't have to do this,' said Jack, fearing she'd never return from such a dangerous mission.

'This is what I'm trained for.'

'I know. But men like Akuma are prepared for assassination attempts.'

'You're not worried about *me*, are you, Jack?' she said, a teasing smile upon her lips.

'Of course I am,' he replied and pulled a *shuriken* from his *obi*. 'Take this, just in case.'

Passing her the ninja star, their hands closed around each other's and their eyes met.

'I'll be careful,' she promised, holding his gaze as she accepted the *shuriken*.

Then she pulled on her hood and ran off through the forest.

Jack watched her leap the moat, skirting the hidden traps until she disappeared into the night. Her plan was to work her way through the forest, down on to the plain and sneak up behind Akuma. Her fearless courage and daring astonished Jack. He wondered if he would ever see her again.

Appearing at his side, Neko signed, *You will*.

Jack smiled at her, grateful for her reassurance. Silent as Neko's world was, she wasn't deaf to the many things that went unsaid.

Leaving Neko to keep watch over the forest approach, Jack returned to the square and made his way to the southern moat boundary. Hayato was patrolling the central section of the moat with Saburo at the western end and Yori at the eastern end. Yuudai remained at his post on the northern barricade with a small division of farmers. There was always the chance Akuma had left some men behind to mount a secondary attack and Jack couldn't risk leaving such a gap in their defences.

'She's gone,' Jack informed Hayato.

'That's one brave ninja.'

'Miyuki *will* be back,' said Jack, rather sharper than he intended.

Hayato glanced at him. Understanding his anxiety, he added, 'With Akuma's head, I hope.'

His eyes returned to scanning the dark expanse of the Okayama Plain. 'It's been strangely quiet. I've got a bad feeling Akuma's up to something.'

Jack felt it too. 'Whatever it is, his time is running out.'

As Jack went to check on Saburo, shouts punctured the night air. Originating from Yori's unit, it appeared Akuma had made his move. Snatching a flaming torch from the sentry fire, Jack and Hayato ran along the moat.

A startled face appeared out of the gloom.

'They came at us . . . from nowhere,' gasped Sora.

'Where are they?' said Jack, his *katana* at the ready.

'Gone . . . but not before . . . snatching him.'

'Who?' demanded Hayato.

But Jack didn't need to hear the answer. He already knew.

In the snow, beside a patch of blood, lay Yori's abandoned *shakujō*.

51

EXECUTION

The two bandits held up flaming torches so everyone in the village could see the wooden pyre in the centre of the paddy field. Logs scavenged from the forest had been heaped at the foot of a stake rammed into the ground. Bound to this post was a small figure dressed in the robes of a monk and the armour of a samurai – Yori.

Jack stood powerless at the edge of the moat, staring in horror at the planned execution. Hayato, Saburo and the farmers gathered beside him, their faces mirroring his anguish.

Hidden deep within the darkness, Akuma gave a callous laugh at their reaction.

'You have until midnight to surrender,' he declared. 'Otherwise the monk burns.'

'*Don't surrender!*' shouted Yori, his voice trembling in spite of his courageous cry.

Nakamura stepped into the light of the torches and slammed the butt of his axe against Yori's helmet. 'Hold your tongue, or I'll cut it out.'

Yori went limp, knocked unconscious by the blow.

Jack surged forwards in rage, determined to break his way through the thorn bushes and rescue his friend.

But Hayato seized him. 'No! You'll be killed.'

'I *must* save him.'

'That's exactly what Akuma wants you to do.'

Jack fought against his grip.

'He's using Yori as bait to draw you out,' insisted Hayato. 'You'd be dead before you got even halfway.'

Realizing the truth in Hayato's words, Jack stopped struggling.

'I hope you like roasted monk!' Nakamura taunted, before retreating into the darkness.

The two bandits followed, leaving a single torch to flicker in the wind.

'We have to do *something*,' insisted Saburo, who was as desperate as Jack at seeing their friend about to be sacrificed.

'We could charge the bandits – all of us at once,' Jack proposed.

'Good idea! Akuma would never expect us to attack him,' agreed Saburo, his sword already half-drawn at the suggestion.

Hayato pulled Jack and Saburo aside. 'Our army consists of farmers, *not* samurai,' he reminded them. 'Without the advantage of our defences, the bandits would cut them down as if they were harvesting a field of rice.'

'Then why not a small force of samurai – just us?' said Jack.

'You were at the Battle of Osaka Castle. Don't you remember what happened when Satoshi's forces were drawn out of the castle? Our side lost! This village is our fortress. It would be suicidal to leave.'

Stepping away from the sentry fire, Toge strode up to the conferring young samurai.

'You're not thinking of surrender, are you?' he accused, paranoid with their whispering. 'If you do, Akuma will burn you, your friend and *everyone* in this village. The earth will be scorched black by the time that devil's finished.'

'A samurai isn't fickle like a farmer,' said Hayato, insulted by the allegation. 'Our code of *bushido* means *our* loyalties stay constant.'

'We're figuring out how to save Yori,' Jack explained to the abashed Toge.

Toge observed the distance across paddy fields to the pyre. 'You're willing to sacrifice *all* your lives for one person?'

'That's what it means to be samurai,' Jack replied, recalling his guardian Masamoto's core belief – and the one Yamato had followed to his tragic end to save him and Akiko. 'Besides, Yori's my friend. I'd willingly give my life for his.'

'It may not come to that,' said Hayato, a smile coming to his lips. 'We still have one hope . . . Miyuki.'

Jack kept a vigil, watching over Yori from afar. He now realized Akuma's tactic to take a hostage hadn't been to force a surrender. The execution was being staged to terrorize and intimidate the young samurai – a show of cruelty designed to break their fighting spirit and poison their morale.

Hayato's arguments against an immediate rescue attempt had been difficult to accept. But even Jack could see that it would be foolish to run blindly into a trap – particularly one they had no chance of coming out from alive. Still, he felt as if he was betraying his dear friend yet again, breaking his promise to protect him – just as he'd failed to do during the Battle of Osaka Castle. Now all Jack could do was pray Miyuki succeeded in her mission before midnight. Yori's life depended upon it.

But looking up at the stars, Jack judged she didn't have long left.

The torch in the paddy field had finally burnt out and Yori was enveloped in darkness. Jack could still picture his friend tied to the stake, the logs at his feet waiting to be ignited. He listened hard for any indication Akuma might have been killed . . . Nothing.

In the distance, a new flaming torch was lit. The ominous light floated through the dark like the disembodied head of a fiery demon. Then it stopped level with the pyre.

Yori still hung limp from his bindings, his head bowed upon his chest.

Nakamura's face, both burnt and scarred, appeared fiendish in the red glow of the flames.

'*GAIJIN!*' he called, looking for Jack among the farmers who huddled by their sentry fires. When he spied Jack's blond hair, a malicious grin spread across his blistered lips. 'Do you surrender?'

Jack stared into the surrounding darkness. *Where are you, Miyuki?*

'I asked you a question, *gaijin*!' shouted Nakamura, holding the torch aloft.

Against all his natural instincts, Jack gave his defiant reply. 'WE DO . . . *NOT* SURRENDER!'

52

THE BURNING PYRE

Nakamura threw the burning torch on to the pyre. The logs quickly caught alight and the fire began to spread. Yori's head remained bowed in prayer as the flames encircled him and smoke billowed into the night sky.

'We *can't* wait for Miyuki,' said Jack, drawing his sword to charge.

Saburo with a handful of farmers, who'd volunteered for the task, prepared to race across the paddy fields and rescue Yori.

Hayato barred their way. 'STOP! This wasn't the plan.'

'But Yori will die if we don't go *now*.'

'We agreed *only* if Miyuki killed Akuma.'

'STAND ASIDE!' ordered Jack.

Hayato refused to budge. 'Miyuki's clearly failed in her mission. Unless the bandits are leaderless, any rescue attempt is a death sentence to those who go.'

Upon hearing this, the volunteer farmers shuffled back from the moat, their nerve gone.

'Then I'll go alone,' Jack insisted.

'Not without me,' said Saburo.

'I'll go too,' insisted Yuto, terrified but determined to pay back his life debt to Jack.

From the paddy fields, the crackle and spit of burning wood could be heard.

'Listen, both of you,' said Hayato, confronting Jack and Saburo. 'Being a samurai may mean sacrifice. But in this case it is Yori who must pay that price. Don't throw your lives away. If you do, Akuma wins. The village will fall. And *everyone's* sacrifice will have been in vain.'

In his head, Jack knew Hayato was talking sense. But in his heart, the torment of such a decision was insufferable. He'd prefer to die trying, than do nothing and watch his friend burn alive.

Countless sparks flew up into the night sky and the flickering flames of the fiercely burning pyre lit the paddy field. At its boundary where the darkness still prevailed, blades glinted and shadowy figures moved.

'See! Akuma's men are waiting for you,' said Hayato.

'He's right. It's a trap,' said Saburo, hanging his head in defeat.

'Yori wouldn't want you to die for nothing,' insisted Hayato. 'But I'll no longer stand in your way . . .'

All of a sudden the pyre became a bonfire and Yori was engulfed in flames. His helmet and breastplate offered scant protection against the raging heat. Yet Yori didn't struggle or cry out. He remained courageous until the end.

'*YORI!*' cried Jack, dropping to his knees, weak with grief.

Saburo sobbed beside him, tears streaming down his face.

Hayato forced himself to watch, feeling wretched for having prevented the rescue. 'He's truly a brave samurai, not even screaming –'

'It's not in a monk's nature to,' said a voice.

Miyuki emerged from the darkness. Jack's relief at seeing her safe was mixed with his despair at Yori's fate.

'Is Akuma *dead* then?' he demanded.

Miyuki shook her head with regret.

'Why ever not?' Jack snapped, his sorrow boiling over into anger.

'I had to make a choice,' she explained. 'Kill Akuma or . . .'

Stepping aside, Yori miraculously appeared behind her.

Jack and Saburo did a double take.

'YORI!' cried Jack, hardly able to believe his eyes. Running over, he pulled his friend into an all-enveloping embrace. Then, falling to his knees, he bowed his head in shame. 'How can you ever forgive me for abandoning you like that?'

'Don't listen to him,' interrupted Hayato. 'Jack *was* coming for you. I'm the one who stopped him.'

'I'm glad you did,' said Yori, smiling warmly. 'It would have been a needless sacrifice for my dear friend.'

'But if you are here, who's that?' asked Saburo, pointing to the figure tied to the burning stake.

'A straw soldier, of course.'

Jack laughed in astonishment. Only now did he notice Yori was no longer wearing his armour.

'But we were watching you all the time. How's that possible?' said Hayato.

Miyuki shot him a playful grin and replied, 'Ninja magic.'

A howl of fury was heard from the paddy fields as Nakamura also discovered the truth. With the straw gone up in flames, the armour collapsed and an empty helmet bounced off the pyre. Nakamura glared in crazed disbelief when he spotted Yori safely behind the village defences. Yori gave him a little bow. This incensed the bandit even more and, kicking the helmet in a fit of rage, he stormed back to Akuma.

'In order for us to escape without being detected, I needed to leave a decoy,' explained Miyuki. 'There wasn't time to tell anyone of my plan. As it was, I barely reached Yori before midnight.'

'So it was *you* who put out the torch?' said Jack, his admiration for her growing even stronger.

'With a snowball,' Miyuki nodded.

'Akuma's going to be *really* furious now,' said Saburo with a roguish grin.

Out in the paddy fields, the sound of cracking ice drew everyone's attention. The heat from the fire had melted its frozen surface and the burning pyre dropped through to the waters beneath. The flames were extinguished and the plain once more fell into darkness.

53

GONE

The battle was to stay awake.

A second sleepless night meant exhaustion threatened to defeat the farmers before Akuma did. They sat beside the sentry fires, heads bobbing drowsily as they fought their fatigue. Barely able to keep their own eyes open, the young samurai took turns to patrol the boundary with their units. The moonless night forced them to rely solely upon their ears to warn of an attack. So every noise became the prelude to a bandit advance, every sound the beginning of an assault. Hayato reported hearing footsteps in the snow, but no bandits materialized to storm the moat. On Jack's round, he heard the splintering of wood – soon realizing the remains of the bridge were being washed away by the river, piece by piece. The sound of horses' hooves sent everyone on high alert, but again nothing came of it.

After that, the night settled into an uneasy quiet.

'What do you think Akuma's planning?' asked Miyuki, finding the silence more disturbing than any noise.

'Maybe he's decided to lay siege,' said Saburo, stifling a yawn.

'But without supplies, the bandits must be starving by now,' said Yori.

'That makes them more dangerous,' said Jack, stamping his feet for warmth. 'Like a pack of wild dogs.'

Jack glanced round at the farmers, who shivered with both cold and dread. None ventured far from the firelight, terrified they too might be taken hostage by the bandits. Worn out and grieving for the loss of their friends, the strain in their haggard faces was evident – the farmers had reached their limit.

'Whatever happens,' said Jack, 'the next battle will be decisive.'

'I should have gone back to assassinate Akuma,' said Miyuki. 'This could've been all over by now.'

Jack shook his head. 'After Yori's rescue, Akuma will have doubled his guard. It's too much of a risk . . . even for a ninja.'

Sora's daughter Miya appeared with some rice.

'From my mother, to keep your strength up,' she said, bowing and handing out the steaming straw containers. She glanced across the moat to the paddy fields. 'Do you think Akuma's finally given up?'

Sitting by the fire to eat, Jack shook his head.

'I'm afraid that would be too much to hope for.'

'Wake up, Jack!' urged Sora, roughly shaking him.

Blinking against the early light of dawn, Jack cursed for allowing himself to fall asleep. In an instant, he was back on his feet, sword in hand.

'Where's Akuma?' he demanded.

'He's gone!' Sora exclaimed, excitedly pointing to the abandoned paddy fields.

Jack rubbed his eyes, but it was true. Akuma was nowhere in sight. The glistening snow-covered plain was deserted as far as the eye could see. A blackened hole in the middle of one paddy field was the sole reminder that the bandits had been there at all.

Hayato strode over. 'I've walked the length of the moat. There's no sign of him.'

'He's moved on to another village,' said Toge, shielding his face from the rising sun as he too scanned the horizon.

Jack couldn't believe it. But the farmers clearly did. They were already rejoicing.

'We've beaten Black Moon!' cried Kunio, grinning ear to ear.

The farmers raised their spears and cheered their victory.

'Akuma can't be gone. He *must* be hiding somewhere,' insisted Jack, unwilling to celebrate so quickly.

Running into the square, he clambered up to the top of the watchtower. Miyuki was already on the platform with Yori, looking in all directions.

'I can't see him or any bandits,' said Miyuki.

Jack's view from the watchtower only confirmed the paddy fields to be empty. To the east, the mill was a burnt-out shell, smoke curling into the sky like a black snake. What little remained of the bridge was impassable, just a few charred stubs poking out of the water. Otherwise, there wasn't a single soul in sight. The mountain approach to the north was equally bereft of life.

Spotting Neko enter the square, Jack asked Miyuki, 'What about the forest?'

Miyuki caught Neko's attention and signed to her. 'Neko says the forest is clear too.'

In the village below, the farmers began downing weapons and disbanding their units. Even Yuudai's men abandoned their post to join the others in the square to celebrate Akuma's departure.

Toge stood upon the farmhouse veranda with Yoshi. He called up to Jack, 'Can you see Akuma anywhere?'

'No, but –'

The farmers' shouts of delight drowned him out before he could voice his doubts.

Toge now addressed the villagers. 'Thanks to the young samurai and *your* bravery, we're free of Black Moon!'

More cheers and cries filled the square. Up in the watchtower, Jack shook his head, unconvinced. 'Akuma wouldn't up and leave like this.'

'Perhaps the shame of defeat was too bitter a pill for him to swallow,' Yori suggested.

'Or else, as Toge said, he's decided to attack an easier target,' said Miyuki.

'Akuma's cunning. He knows the farmers are tired – they're desperate to believe him gone,' Jack insisted. 'He's simply waiting for us to lower our guard like this.'

'But the bandits can't appear from *nowhere*,' argued Yori.

Jack hunted the landscape for their enemy and saw only snow. He kept searching . . .

With each passing moment, Jack's conviction wavered. Perhaps Akuma had *really* gone.

The sun rose fully above the horizon, its golden light heralding a new day and banishing all the fears of the previous night. With the battle seemingly over, Jack was suddenly overwhelmed with exhaustion.

'Since Akuma's not here – for now – we should rest,' said Jack. 'But we must remain vigilant.'

'I'll take the first watch,' Miyuki offered, just as reluctant as Jack to believe Akuma had gone for good.

Too tired to protest, Jack nodded his agreement and ushered Yori down the ladder. He was just about to follow when his eye caught a flicker of movement. He stopped and stared at the nearest paddy field. There was nothing but snowdrifts. Convincing himself he was just burnt out and seeing things, Jack stepped on to the ladder.

Then he heard an ominous rumbling in the distance.

At the same time, Miyuki yelled, 'Bandits to the north!'

Jack spun to see a massive boulder thundering down the valley. It had been dislodged from the rocky ridge and now careered towards the barricade. Chasing behind it, five bandits charged along on horseback, Sayomi riding upon the ridge above.

In the square, there were cries of disbelief and alarm from the farmers.

Yuudai shouted above the panic, 'BARRICADE UNIT!'

To Jack's horror, he discovered his instincts had been right all along. When he glanced back at the paddy fields, snowdrifts started to rise up and fall apart before his eyes. Two bandits hidden beneath ran at the moat. Between them, they carried a wide wooden plank scavenged from the destroyed bridge. As they went to throw it across the thorn-filled ditch, more snowdrifts burst apart. Nakamura and three other fully armed bandits rushed for the makeshift crossing.

'Bandits to the south!' warned Jack.

Saburo rallied his men to head for the moat.

'Bandits to the east!' cried Miyuki and Jack saw another pair explode from the snow to lay a wooden board across the eastern side of the moat. Having used the cover of the river-bank to reach the bridge undetected, Akuma now led a charge on horseback up the road and towards the gangway.

Hayato called for his unit. As the farmers rushed in all directions to retrieve their weapons and follow their young commanders, mayhem reigned in the village square.

Stunned by Akuma's all-out assault, Jack turned to Miyuki in horrified disbelief. 'They're going to overrun us!'

54

THE RING OF FIRE

Yuudai was the first to reach his post. But he was already too late.

The boulder hurtling along the last stretch of path smashed into the centre of the barricade. It tore a massive hole in the spiked wall of beams and branches, before rolling to a stop in the moat. As the bandits galloped for the gap unopposed, Yuudai frantically heaved back the wooden gangway to prevent them crossing. But Sayomi, from her position on the ridge, launched an arrow at him. The barbed point struck Yuudai in the chest, knocking him to the ground.

Now nothing stood between the bandits and the terrified farmers.

Meanwhile, Hayato desperately attempted to muster his unit along the eastern entrance. Akuma was halfway up the track and his bandits would soon cross the thorn ditch. Pulling an arrow from his quiver, Hayato rose up from behind the protection of the haybales and took aim with his bow. The bandit leader rode boldly towards him, as if daring him to shoot. Hayato had Akuma in his sights when another snowdrift burst apart. Kurochi the Snake appeared, musket in hand, and fired before Hayato did.

Taken completely by surprise, Hayato had no chance of avoiding the deadly bullet. He was blown backwards by the blast to land in a bloody heap in the snow.

Jack witnessed all of this in the first few chaotic moments of Akuma's attack.

'Yori!' he cried to his friend in the square below. 'Hayato needs your help.'

As Yori ran off, Jack turned to Miyuki who was crouched behind the protective screen.

'Come on!' Jack urged. 'Yuudai's also hit.'

'You go,' replied Miyuki, urgently striking a flint and steel over a small black tube. She cursed and struck again. 'I hoped we wouldn't have to use this.'

'What are you talking about?'

More sparks flew until a bright light flared in Miyuki's hands.

'The Ring of Fire!' cried Miyuki, standing up with the tube's fuse burning fiercely. 'Our *last* line of defence.'

With a snap of her arm, she hurled the container of gunpowder into the air. It flew over the rice store and towards the southern moat. Jack and Miyuki watched it tumble towards its target . . . and land short.

'I'll get it,' said Jack, scrambling for the ladder.

But Miyuki grabbed him. 'There isn't time,' she explained, furious with her failed throw. 'It'll detonate before you get there.'

Jack's eyes flicked to the still-burning charge and knew she was right.

'NO!' he cried, suddenly spotting Neko dart from the square towards it.

But Neko couldn't hear him. She ran like the wind, snatched up the tube and flung it into the ditch. By now the bandits were storming the moat from all directions. A second later, the detonator exploded and a wall of fire rocketed into the sky.

Neko was blown off her feet and engulfed in flames. Explosions shook the ground as each gunpowder charge Miyuki had laid was triggered. The fire raced along the moat, following the trails of lamp oil she'd carefully poured over the thorn bushes the night before the black moon.

Farmers and bandits alike stared in abject terror as a blazing ring of fire encircled the village. The unfortunate bandits caught up in the inferno screamed as they were incinerated in a matter of seconds.

Jack gazed upon the scene in shock and awe. 'I never imagined the Five Rings could be *so* powerful,' he breathed.

'Too powerful . . . sometimes,' replied Miyuki, a tear running down her cheek. 'Neko's gone.'

Jack looked down at the spot where Neko had stood. There wasn't a trace of her left. He felt his heart crack with grief. They may have dealt a devastating blow to Akuma, but the price had been high. Neko had been the reason Jack had agreed to save the village in the first place . . . and now she was dead.

Miyuki started to sob. 'It's . . . my . . . fault.'

'No, the blame lies with Akuma – and always will,' said Jack firmly. 'Neko may have been silent as a mouse, but she had the courage of a lion. Without her sacrifice, Akuma's men would be slaughtering everyone in the village by now.'

Jack's thoughts turned to Hayato and Yuudai, praying they'd somehow survived. He couldn't see Hayato from the watchtower, but Yuudai was propped up against a hay bale, a small group of farmers gathered by his side.

Then a man next to Yuudai suddenly collapsed, an arrow protruding from his back. Jack's eyes darted to a figure standing on the massive boulder dislodged from the ridge. Through the gap in the flames, Sayomi began to pick off Yuudai's men one by one with her bow. The farmers dived behind the hay bales as she shot another villager through the neck.

From the eastern entrance, Jack heard cries of panic and the noise of battle. Clearly, not every bandit had been killed by the Ring of Fire.

55

OVERRUN

Jack and Miyuki dropped down the ladder as fast as they could.

'You stop Sayomi; I'll help Hayato and Yori,' said Jack, drawing his swords.

But no sooner had Miyuki disappeared up the track to the barricade than Hayato's unit, along with many women and children, came screaming into the square. They ran in all directions, desperate to escape the horror that pursued them. A musket shot rang out, creating even more panic.

Not far behind the villagers, Yori struggled to help a bleeding Hayato, the farmboy Kunio carrying his bow and quiver. Using Yori's *shakujō* as a crutch, the three of them staggered into the square.

'*Akuma!*' was all that Yori could gasp.

Rushing over, Jack helped them to the cover of Kunio's parents' house beside the pond.

'Akuma's armour . . . protected him . . . from the flames . . .' Hayato wheezed, clasping his stomach as he collapsed against the wall.

A second later, the thunder of horses' hooves signalled the entrance of Black Moon. He charged through the square upon his armoured steed, his face a savage mask of murder. Chasing down a villager, he drove his trident into her back, the barbs bursting through her ribcage. He wrenched the lethal weapon out and the poor woman dropped lifeless to the ground.

Another four bandits on horseback charged into the square, unleashing more death and destruction. Akuma seemed intent on killing any and everyone in the village.

Without Hayato to command them, his unit of farmers fell into disarray and forgot all their training. They tried to fend off the attackers in small vulnerable groups, but the bandits simply cut a swathe through their feeble defences.

Jack ran into the midst of the chaos.

'TO ME!' he cried, attempting to rally the farmers.

But they were lost in their panic.

'Kill the *gaijin*!' roared Akuma, as he hunted down a group of screaming villagers.

A horse galloped towards Jack. Upon it a fearsome bandit wielded a bloodstained *katana*. Crossing his swords above his head, Jack barely managed to deflect the attack and the force of the blow almost took his right arm off.

The bandit wheeled round to charge again. Jack realized he had little chance against a mounted opponent. The speed and power of the horse, along with the advantage of height, meant Jack would be beheaded before he could land a counterblow.

Sheathing his swords, Jack ran for his life as the bandit rode him down. The horse's hot breath was almost on his neck, when he snatched up the bamboo spear he'd been heading for and spun on his attacker. The bandit, unable to halt his charge, was struck in the chest by its pointed tip. The bamboo shaft split on impact against his armour, but the blow was enough to knock him out of his saddle.

Jack dived aside as the horse continued on its charge. Winded but otherwise unhurt, the bandit scrambled after his *katana*, determined to fulfil Akuma's wishes and kill Jack. Finally gathering their wits, a group of farmers led by Yuto rushed to Jack's defence. Stabbing furiously with their spears, they brought the bandit's life to a swift end.

Jack, amazed to have survived the encounter, hurried over to Yuto.

'Stay together. Remember what Hayato said: *in a storm a single tree falls, but a forest still stands.*'

Yuto nodded mutely, traumatized by having killed a man, even a sworn enemy.

'Set up a defensive wall of spears to protect those women and children,' ordered Jack, pointing to a group of villagers cowering next to the rice store.

Glad to have instruction, Yuto and the other farmers immediately fell into line and surrounded the defenceless group.

On the other side of the square, Jack spotted Sora being knocked to the ground by the charging riderless horse. The old farmer lay at the mercy of the bandits. One outlaw wielding a heavy club bore down on Sora as he struggled to find his feet.

Running with all his might, Jack fought to reach his friend before the bandit did. Dodging and weaving between the panicked villagers and mounted bandits, Jack dived in front of the horse's flying hooves, grabbed Sora by the arm and bundled him out of its path.

Thwarted from killing his intended victim, the bandit

lashed out at Jack with his club as he shot by. The studded end caught Jack on the back of the head. It was a glancing blow, but enough to send him reeling to the ground.

With his head ringing, and the taste of blood in his mouth, Jack felt sick and disorientated as if caught in the worst of sea storms. Dimly aware he was an easy target for the enemy, he forced himself to his knees. But the pain in his head intensified. On the verge of blacking out, the village spun around him, glimpses of the battle flashing before his eyes . . .

The farmers scattering as Akuma rampaged through the village . . .

Yori in mortal danger, confronted by a bandit seemingly immune to his *kiaijutsu* . . .

Nakamura Scarface in the square, swinging his deadly axe with wild abandon . . .

In the distance, Miyuki using her *manriki* chain to disarm Sayomi of her bow. Then Sayomi wielding her double-edged *naginata*. Miyuki fighting a losing battle, only her swift reactions and acrobatic skills keeping her from being sliced in half . . .

Jack rubbed his temples, trying to relieve the throbbing in his head and recover enough to fight.

At that moment, Akuma spotted him alive yet helpless in the middle of the square and turned his horse to charge at him. With a triumphant expression, he raised his trident, aiming its cruel barbs at Jack's chest.

Unable to stand, let alone run, Jack could only watch as Akuma closed in for the kill.

56

SHAKUJŌ

All was lost. He had failed. The village was to be conquered by the devil, Akuma.

Jack had been foolish to think that he and his friends could make a stand against such bandits and win. After all, he was just a *young* samurai . . . and soon to be a dead samurai.

As Jack knelt powerless to avoid his fate, he stared into the unforgiving eyes of his enemy. Black as a moonless night, they harboured only hate for him along with a cold callous pleasure at exacting revenge.

'I'll rip your heart out!' Akuma roared as he thundered ever closer, trident thrust forward.

Jack made a final attempt to rise, but his legs gave beneath him.

And then he was encircled by a protective ring of spears. They formed an impenetrable barrier, forcing Akuma's horse to rear up and break from its charge. The unit of farmers held their ground as Akuma, along with two other bandits, attempted to penetrate the ranks. But with their charges blocked by the steel-tipped samurai spears, Akuma snarled, 'I'll leave you till last, *gaijin*!'

Angrily whipping his horse, he then rode off with his bandits to find easier prey.

'I said you'd need me to save your miserable life yet again!' jested Saburo, pulling Jack to his feet. 'For the time being, at least.'

Jack clamped his hand on Saburo's shoulder as much to thank him as to steady his own legs. The sickness eased and although his head still hurt, his world was no longer spinning like a top.

'What took you so long?' said Jack, smiling despite the pain.

'Not all the bandits from the paddy field were fried by Miyuki's bonfire,' replied Saburo.

A blast of gunfire scattered a bunch of villagers hiding behind a woodpile; one fell dead before he'd taken two steps.

Jack hunted for the deadly Kurochi among the bandits, but the square was too chaotic to pinpoint where he was firing from. To Jack's relief, though, Yori was still holding off his attacker. The bandit, on foot and armed with a battle-chipped *katana*, fought to bring the little monk down. But Yori used his ringed staff to deflect the strikes.

Jack was amazed at the skill with which Yori wielded his *shakujō*. Apparently Sensei Yamada had been teaching his friend a great deal more than Zen philosophy and meditation. As the bandit thrust for Yori's gut, Yori drove his staff directly at the sword's tip. He hooked the blade through one of his *shakujō*'s iron rings, then wrenched it upwards. The steel blade snapped in two.

Stunned at the loss of his weapon, the bandit was taken by surprise when the end of the *shakujō* whipped round and struck him in the jaw. The blow dropped him in a heap. A group of farmers, emboldened by Yori's spirited defence, charged forward and the bandit disappeared beneath a forest of spears. Offering the dead man a quick blessing, Yori hurried back to tend to Hayato.

His mind now clear, Jack recalled Miyuki's plight. Looking to the barricade, he saw Sayomi with her *naginata* poised to cut straight through the exhausted ninja.

'*Miyuki!*' Jack cried in despair, too far away to prevent her death.

Then he spotted a familiar glint of steel flash through the air. Sayomi flinched as the *shuriken* Jack had given Miyuki embedded itself in her upper chest. But Sayomi's armour prevented the throwing star from penetrating deeply. She recovered quickly from the attack and swung the *naginata*'s blade down on to Miyuki.

Jack was unable to tear his eyes away, however much it tortured him to witness Miyuki's murder.

At the last second, Yuudai rose from the hay bales and caught the *naginata*'s wooden shaft, halting the blade in mid-swing a fraction from Miyuki's head. He yanked the weapon from Sayomi's grasp and snapped it in half. Seizing her with his great hands, Yuudai then lifted the bandit off her feet and over his head.

Sayomi flailed helplessly in his grip. With a tremendous shout, Yuudai tossed the woman into the air. She flew through the flames of the moat to crash into the top of the barricade. As she tumbled over the other side, her long black hair became entangled in the spikes. Sayomi ended up swinging high above the sharpened bamboo stakes that were planted at the foot of the barricade. Her screams echoed up the valley as her hair ripped from her head and she dropped to the ground.

Yuudai, the arrow still embedded in his chest, turned to Miyuki. Grimacing against the pain of his wound, he offered his hand to help her to her feet. Seeing Miyuki rise, Jack realized the young samurai were far from defeated by Akuma's men.

'Rally the other units,' said Jack to Saburo. 'Order them to corner the remaining bandits using their spear drills. It's time we brought Akuma's reign of terror to an end, once and for all.'

As Saburo began barking out commands, Jack spotted Nakamura, his leather armour scorched black, leaping on to the veranda of Junichi's farmhouse. The bandit began kicking at the door. From inside came the screams of women and children. Unable to break it down, Nakamura took his axe and in a single swipe shattered the door open.

Leaving Saburo to lead the units, Jack dashed over to the farmhouse. He burst through the entrance just as Nakamura prepared to chop Yoshi's head from his shoulders. The bandit kicked Yoshi to his hands and knees and raised the axe.

'Say *sayonara* to Grandpa!' laughed Nakamura.

57

THE POND

Jack dived head first at Nakamura as the axe blade came hurtling down. There was no time for any other strategy. Yoshi was seconds from death.

Charging forward, Jack kept his back straight and neck in line just as he'd been taught during his Sixteen Secret Fists *ninjutsu* training. His head collided with Nakamura's ribcage and the bandit experienced the full crushing force of Demon Horn Fist. There was a crunch of fracturing bones and Nakamura was sent flying into the back wall. His axe fell from his hands, missing Yoshi by a whisker.

Gasping but not defeated, Nakamura seized Jack before he could roll away. Caught in a massive bear grip, Jack struggled to break free as he felt the life being squeezed from him.

'You won't get away this time,' Nakamura growled, his scarred face a knot of fury.

Drawing a forearm across Jack's throat, he began to crush his windpipe. Jack choked, the veins in his neck bulging under the crippling pressure. Clawing at Nakamura's arms, he kicked and writhed. But the bandit's iron-like grip didn't give at all. Black spots blurred his vision and his head once more throbbed as if about to explode. With his strength ebbing away, Jack knew he didn't have long to live.

Across the room, the women and children looked on, paralysed with fear.

As he spluttered his last breaths, one of the girls finally plucked up the courage and ran over. Clasping her hand into a ninja fist, she drove her thumb into Nakamura's injured ribs. The bandit howled in agony as Finger Sword Fist dug deep.

In his pain, he batted the girl away. But Jack managed to wrench himself free and roll to his feet. Turning on the bandit, he launched a stomping front kick at his chest. Nakamura caught his foot and twisted it, intending to snap the ankle. Jack whirled in the air, spinning with the attack. At the same time, he thrust out his other leg. His free foot caught Nakamura in the jaw and the bandit went sprawling to the floor.

Jack hoped this would be the end of it, but Nakamura was even tougher than he imagined. Despite being dazed, the bandit snatched up his battleaxe and swung it at Jack's legs. Jack jumped in the air, the steel blade whistling beneath his feet. As he landed, Nakamura rose up and chopped madly with his axe.

The women and children scattered, desperate to avoid the deadly swipes.

Jack leapt away from the attack, but failed to notice the hearth behind him. He stumbled into the hot ashes of the dying fire, lost his footing and fell.

Nakamura rushed forward, his axe raised to cleave him in half.

Yoshi, still on his hands and knees, found his walking-stick and thrust it between Nakamura's legs. Nakamura tripped and the axe head buried itself in the wall just above Jack's head, splinters flying everywhere.

Cursing, Nakamura brutally kicked the old man to the ground. Jack jumped up but before he could draw his swords, Nakamura barrelled into him like a raging bull. The two of them careered into the rear wall which, already split by the axe, now disintegrated. They tumbled out of the farmhouse and down the slope, throwing kicks and punches as they fell.

In the square, Akuma and his bandits had returned, but Saburo was marshalling the farmers to corral them. One bandit had been knocked from his horse and was making a frenzied attempt at an escape. The villagers soon caught the doomed man. But Akuma rode defiantly straight at the farmers, driving them back again and again with his trident.

Jack and Nakamura rolled to a stop. Nakamura stunned Jack with a head butt, then scrambled through the snow to retrieve his battleaxe.

'I'm going to take your head, *gaijin*,' said Nakamura, spitting blood. 'And your arms and your legs and your . . .'

Grunting with the effort, Nakamura brought his axe hurtling down.

Jack rolled aside as the blade thudded into the frozen ground. Scrambling to his feet, he unsheathed his swords and went on the attack. His *katana* flashed through the air, slicing for the bandit's neck.

Nakamura blocked the blade with his axe head, sparks flying on contact. Jack spun and thrust with his *wakizashi*. Almost skewered on its tip, Nakamura twisted away at the last second and brought the axe handle down on to Jack's left arm. Pain rocketed through Jack and he was forced to drop the short sword.

'Your fancy sword techniques won't beat an axe blow!' laughed Nakamura.

Swinging the massive weapon in a lethal series of arcs, he forced Jack on the retreat. Realizing the axe could shatter his *katana*'s blade, Jack had to hope for a gap in Nakamura's attack before retaliating. But his foot slipped from under him. As he tried to regain his balance, Nakamura chopped down with all his might. The axe head skimmed past Jack's face and chest to hit the ground with an ear-splitting *crack*. Fissures in the snow snaked their way out from where they stood. Water spurted up and the ground shifted beneath their feet.

Jack dived away. But Nakamura, too slow to realize what was happening, dropped through the ice and disappeared with his axe into the freezing depths of the pond.

Jack lay as still as he could, spreading his weight to prevent the pond's surface breaking up any more. But all around he heard ominous cracking. He saw Yori leave Hayato and come running over, quickly followed by Yuudai and Miyuki who'd witnessed the brutal fight.

'Stop!' cried Jack. 'No closer.'

Throwing his *katana* clear, he began to ease himself away from the hole and towards the bank.

'I'll get a spear!' cried Miyuki.

A moment later she was back, lying on the ground, the spear outstretched towards him. Jack grabbed the shaft and she began to haul him in.

All of a sudden, a hand seized Jack's ankle, dragging him the other way into the ice hole.

'Not s-s-so f-f-fast,' spluttered Nakamura, his scarred face turned blue.

Jack slid into the freezing waters, pulling Miyuki off the bank. Half on the ice, half in the pond, he lashed out at Nakamura. But the bandit refused to let go.

Fighting the cold and Nakamura, Jack felt his fingers slipping off the spear.

58

END OF A NIGHTMARE

'I can't hold on much longer!' yelled Jack.

Yuudai reached for Miyuki to pull them *all* in. But Naka-mura yanked on Jack's leg, seemingly determined to drown them both.

'Let Jack go!' Yori shouted, throwing a snowball at the bandit.

But Nakamura kept tugging Jack into the hole. Jack's grasp slid to the very end of the spear. Gritting his teeth, he clung on for dear life. Nakamura began to crawl up his back, trying to prise him away from his lifeline. At the same time, the frigid waters of the pond lapped at Jack's waist, chilling him to the bone and sapping his strength.

He was about to give up all hope when an arrow shot past his shoulder and struck Nakamura. Jack heard a pained groan followed by the slosh of water as Nakamura lost his grip and slipped beneath the surface. Looking up, Jack saw Hayato propped up against the little farmhouse, bow in hand, Kunio holding his quiver. The effort of firing the arrow, however, had proved too much. Clutching his wounded stomach, he collapsed to the ground.

Hauling Jack out of the pond, the four of them rushed to Hayato's side. He was still breathing, but a thin stream of blood trickled from his mouth. Yori gently eased him into a sitting position.

'Is . . . the battle . . . over?' Hayato gasped, his face deathly pale, the snow around him a pool of red.

Jack looked to the square. Only Akuma and a single bandit remained. Having lost their mounts, they were trapped within an ever-tightening circle of armed farmers. The fearsome Black Moon had no chance of victory . . . or escape.

'We've won.'

Hayato smiled at their triumph. He turned his eyes on Miyuki.

'Was the Ring of Fire . . . your idea?'

Miyuki nodded.

'I wish . . . I'd thought of it,' said Hayato. With his last breath, he proffered a final truce. 'Ninja have all the best ideas . . .'

Reaching out, Miyuki tenderly touched his cheek and shed a tear. For a moment, no one spoke. Jack was choked at their tragic loss so close to victory. Hayato had just saved his life – and he hadn't even had the chance to thank him.

A shout from the square broke their grieving silence.

'This nightmare needs to end *now*,' said Jack with determination born out of sorrow. Standing up, he retrieved his swords.

In the square, Saburo was commanding the farmers to hold back.

'What's the problem?' Jack asked, looking over the crowd of agitated villagers.

'Akuma won't admit defeat,' Saburo explained. 'And he's demanded to talk with you.'

The farmers parted to allow Jack through.

'Be careful,' said Saburo, sticking close to his side, his sword at the ready.

Nodding, Jack stepped into the circle.

'Face to face with the infamous *gaijin* samurai, at last!' snarled Akuma, looking him up and down with contempt. He stood defiantly in the centre, seemingly indifferent to the ring of steel-tipped spears that surrounded him. 'I'd heard the rumours but never believed them to be true. It appears I've paid the price for not heeding the myth. It just sounded so improbable – a foreign boy trained as a samurai who'd mastered the Two Heavens. And, to my eyes, one who appears to be a ninja as well! What other powers do you possess, *gaijin*?'

'I don't have any *powers*,' replied Jack, keeping a wary distance.

Akuma snorted. '*My* power is fear.'

He faked an attack with his trident and the farmers jumped nervously away. 'See how they still tremble! Yet *you* don't show fear.'

Jack stared into Akuma's demonic eyes and felt a cold chill run through him.

'I have loyal friends by my side, so I've no need to be scared of you,' Jack explained. '*That's* the reason we defeated you. Now lay down your arms and surrender.'

Akuma laughed. 'And you'll let us live?'

'Unlike you, I am merciful,' replied Jack, his leniency shocking the villagers. 'I'm a samurai and follow the code of *bushido.* And these villagers are farmers, not bandits. We didn't train them to become cold-blooded killers – only to defend their lives against the likes of you.'

The bandit with Akuma immediately threw down his sword and bowed his submission to Jack and the farmers. The next moment he was dead.

'We do *not* surrender,' said Akuma coldly, leaving the trident sticking in the bandit's back.

Jack was sickened by Akuma's cruel nature. The man's heart was made of stone.

'I no longer care if I die,' roared Akuma, 'as long as *you* die too!'

Drawing his black-handled blades, he charged at Jack.

But Akuma hadn't taken two paces when he suddenly gasped and dropped to his knees. Behind him, Natsuko stood with her bony hands clasped round the shaft of a spear.

'A devil like you deserves to be stabbed in the back,' stated the old woman. 'That's for my son.'

As Akuma rose to his feet, Toge stepped from the ranks and planted another spear in the bandit's back. 'That's for my wife and child,' he cried.

But Akuma kept coming for Jack, determined to have his revenge.

Another farmer pierced the bandit in the stomach. 'That's for my daughter, Naoko.'

Still Akuma refused to surrender.

One by one, then in a rush, the villagers surged forward to defend Jack and vent their fury and grief. The naming of Akuma's victims went on. And so did the spear thrusts.

'Shouldn't we stop them?' said Saburo.

'I think they must end their nightmare their own way,' Jack replied, as Black Moon fell beneath the torrent of spears.

Jack and Saburo made their way back to the pond, where Yori was chanting prayers over Hayato's body. Yuudai and Miyuki stood nearby, their heads bowed in respect.

As they approached, Yuudai looked up. 'Where's Neko?' he asked.

Jack glanced at Miyuki, who was distraught at the reminder.

'She's . . . dead,' said Jack, much to Yuudai's alarm. 'But if it wasn't for Neko, the Ring of Fire wouldn't have worked . . .'

Yuudai swallowed hard and, for the first time since Jack had met him, he appeared vulnerable. Heaving a great sigh of sorrow, he said, 'Neko may have been born a farmer, but to me she had the heart of a samurai.' A great tear rolled down his cheek.

'And the makings of a . . . ninja,' added Miyuki, her voice choking with sorrow.

Their grieving was interrupted by Kunio. 'Jack, do you think I can keep Hayato's bow and arrow?'

'Show some respect!' Saburo snapped, shooting him a scolding look. 'Hayato's spirit is not even departed and Yuudai's just found out Neko's dead.'

Kunio blanched. Then pointed behind them. 'If she is dead, then that must be her ghost!'

A blackened figure emerged from the rice store. Her eyebrows were burnt off and her clothes singed, but otherwise she appeared alive and unhurt. Everyone gasped in astonishment at her miraculous survival. Despite the pain in his chest, Yuudai ran to meet her. But before he could get halfway, a musket shot blasted out.

Yuudai stumbled and fell to the ground. Neko gave a strangled cry. Jack and the others searched for the source of the shot as the villagers scattered for cover.

'Up there!' cried Miyuki, pointing to the top of the watch-tower.

Behind the protective screen, Kurochi was loading another round.

Neko took one look at Yuudai writhing helpless on the ground and ran away.

Jack and Saburo sprinted across the square to drag Yuudai to safety, but he was heavy. They were still pulling him towards the cover of a building, when Kurochi took aim once more.

But suddenly the watchtower swayed.

Neko was furiously hacking at one of the supporting pillars with the axe she'd taken from the woodpile. Kurochi screamed as the structure keeled over into the still-burning moat. Fuelled by the bandit's gunpowder, the watchtower exploded in a ball of flame . . . taking Kurochi the Snake with it.

59

TEARS AND CELEBRATION

Snow fell across the Okayama Plain like the tears of a thousand angels. The patches of blood, so stark and red, gradually disappeared beneath a fresh blanket of white. Even the moat scorched black by the fire lost its colour and faded from view. All around, the land was healing itself from the previous days and nights of battle.

And so too were the farmers and young warriors.

The villagers gathered quietly in the square to honour and bury their dead, while upon the rise overlooking the village Yori made the final preparations for a funeral pyre.

As Jack crossed the square with Miyuki and Saburo, he spotted a glint of steel in the snow. A red cloth fluttered in the breeze. Bending down, he picked up Akuma's abandoned *hachimaki*. The blood-red bandanna was all that was left of the mountain bandit. But even this seemed to harbour evil – a grim reminder of all the pain, suffering and death that Black Moon had once caused.

Asking his friends to wait, Jack made his way over to the pond. Standing upon the bank, he threw the *hachimaki* into the ice hole and watched it sink without trace.

The three of them then climbed the rise and joined Yori beside the funeral pyre. Yori was wafting incense over Hayato's body and quietly chanting a sutra. Hayato had been laid carefully upon the stacked wood, his arms crossed over his chest, his bow and quiver by his side, a white *hachimaki* tied round his head. He looked like a true warrior at peace with himself.

'Is there anything more we can do?' asked Jack, when Yori had ceased chanting.

Yori solemnly shook his head. 'I've not performed funeral rites before, but I think everything is in place. We're just waiting on Yuudai now.'

Jack and the others turned to watch Yuudai limp up the rise, Neko helping him along.

'You're a powerful healer,' Yori remarked to Miyuki.

Humbly acknowledging the compliment, Miyuki replied, 'He's strong, as well as lucky that the bullet only hit him in the leg.'

Yuudai stiffly bowed his respects to his fallen comrade. In a quiet voice, he said, 'A courageous warrior, an honourable samurai and a loyal friend. We'll never forget your sacrifice.'

Offering more incense to the pyre, Yori now began the ritual and they all fell silent. Then the fire was lit and Hayato's body was given to the flames.

Below in the square, the villagers knelt in honour of the young samurai. The sound of their weeping drifted up as tears of grief flowed for Hayato and all who'd lost their lives.

'Like the snow covering this earth, there will be new

beginnings,' Yori proclaimed. 'Winter will pass, spring will bring new life and this village will blossom once more.'

Later that morning, Junichi's remains were cremated in the same manner as Hayato and his ashes buried in the fields. Once these rites had been observed, Toge was duly appointed as the new village leader. Over the course of the next few days, he organized the farmers to bring down the barricade and start the building of a new bridge. All the weapons, including the bandits', were collected together and offered to the young samurai and Miyuki out of respect. But it was agreed that the farmers should keep them – they had earned the right.

While Miyuki and Neko cleared the forest of traps, Jack and Saburo helped in salvaging what they could from the burnt-out mill. Yori visited each family in turn, offering spiritual comfort and guidance where needed. And Yuudai, despite his injuries, refused to rest and spent his time chopping the watchtower into firewood.

On the fourth day, a celebration was deemed in order. That afternoon, everyone gathered in the square to eat, drink and rejoice in their victory over Akuma and his bandits. Breaking into their most precious of stores, a feast was laid on by the women of the village. Along with mounds of rice, they'd prepared miso soup, tofu, pickled vegetables, grilled fish, and even a barrel or two of *saké* had been opened.

'Yuudai seems quite settled here,' remarked Miyuki, nodding in the boy's direction.

Jack looked over to where Yuudai was sitting. Their friend was trying not to laugh as Neko stuffed another pickled vegetable in his already-brimming mouth.

Jack smiled. 'Neko looks happy too.'

Miyuki considered the couple. 'Perhaps a ninja's life isn't for her, after all.'

She turned to Jack. 'So have you thought about when we're leaving for Nagasaki?'

With Akuma dead, the village now safe and his health restored after four nights of rest, Jack realized he had no further reason to stay – other than to be in the company of good friends. Thick snow still covered the roads in and out of the village, but with the weather improving every day it wouldn't be long before the Funasaka Pass opened up and the Shogun's samurai resumed their hunt for him. It was time to move on.

'In a couple of days,' he replied. 'Let's gather our strength and supplies first.'

Miyuki nodded her agreement. Then she looked Jack directly in the eye. 'You do *want* me to come with you, don't you?'

Jack returned her gaze. She'd already done so much for him and asked for nothing in return. Over the past month, he'd come to rely upon her bravery, her bold spirit and, most of all, her friendship.

'Of course I do,' said Jack, smiling warmly at her.

Yori and Saburo wandered over.

'I could get used to this,' said Saburo, through a mouthful of rice and fish. On his head, he wore the dented helmet as a badge of honour. 'I can't wait to tell my father about the battle. We're heroes, thanks to you, Jack!'

'I wouldn't have survived one day without all of you by my side,' replied Jack. 'I'd agreed to an impossible task. But having your belief, Saburo, along with Yuudai's strength, Hayato's skill, Miyuki's cunning and Yori's wisdom, *together* we achieved the impossible and saved this village. As Hayato said, *in a storm a single tree falls, but a forest still stands*.'

'But it takes a captain to sail a ship safely through a storm,' said Yori, raising his eyebrows meaningfully at him.

Jack laughed. *Trust Yori to have the last word*, he thought.

Toge took to the veranda and clapped for everyone's attention. He beckoned for Jack and the others to join him. Since the death of Akuma and his ascendancy to village leader, he'd become less sullen and more friendly. Addressing the villagers, he said, 'The black moon is no longer a cause for fear . . . but one for celebration!'

The farmers applauded and shouted their delight.

'We may have lost much in our past, but with Akuma gone we've gained a future – one made possible by these young warriors. For that, we shall be forever grateful.'

Toge bowed low to Jack and his friends.

The villagers chanted 'YOUNG . . . SAMURAI!' then bowed as one to their saviours.

Yoshi tottered over to Jack, smiling a toothless grin.

'I've always believed, a child is not a vase to be filled but a fire to be lit,' he said. 'And your fire burns the brightest of anyone I know.'

Jack felt humbled by his praise. 'I only wanted to help.'

Stepping down from the veranda, Jack was greeted by Sora, his wife, and his daughter, Miya.

'Thank you for your faith in us, Jack,' said Sora, bowing deeply. 'If it hadn't been for you, we would never have seen our daughter again.'

Miya stepped forward and presented Jack with a new straw hat.

'For your journey home,' she said.

As Jack accepted their gift and bowed his gratitude, Kunio ran into the square shouting, 'SAMURAI! SAMURAI ARE COMING!'

60

KOBAN

The celebrations came to a swift end. The villagers looked anxiously to Toge, whose expression was especially grave at the news. He issued urgent instructions to hide all the food and prepare for their arrival.

'*Daimyo* Ikeda's samurai only ever visit us to collect his rice tax,' Sora explained to Jack. 'But they already have this season's. I can only think they're looking for you!'

As the villagers hurriedly cleared away all signs of a celebration, Sora bundled Jack, Miyuki and the other young samurai into the rice store, closing the door behind him. They peered, unseen, through gaps in the wooden wall.

Toge and Yoshi were waiting on the veranda to greet the samurai, while the rest of the farmers gathered round the edges of the square, heads bowed. The sound of horses' hooves drew nearer. Then ten fully armed samurai rode in. Dismounting, the lead samurai strode on to the veranda. Toge and Yoshi bowed deeply, keeping their eyes lowered to the ground as he approached.

'What happened to your bridge?' demanded the samurai.

'It was destroyed by Akuma,' Toge replied.

'Where's that troublesome bandit now?'

'Dead.'

The samurai looked surprised. 'Dead! Who killed him?'

'Some *ronin*,' explained Toge.

'*You* hired masterless samurai,' he said, incredulous. 'What with?'

'Rice. It's all we have.'

Laughing, the samurai glanced at the submissive villagers. 'No wonder you all look so hungry!' He turned back to Toge, his hand upon the hilt of his sword. 'Now, where's the *gaijin* samurai?' he demanded.

Toge swallowed nervously, keeping his eyes fixed on the ground.

'Come on, I don't have all day. *You* told us he was here.'

'I don't believe it!' cried Sora. 'Toge, of all people, betrayed you.'

Jack was equally shocked. He'd known the farmer was bitter, but hadn't thought him a traitor.

'*That* explains why Toge wasn't around when you went to look for Akuma's camp,' whispered Yori, shaking his head in dismay.

'Don't worry, you'll be paid,' said the samurai, pulling four *koban* from a purse.

Toge's eyes alighted on the glittering gold coins. Then he glanced towards the rice store.

'He's about to tell!' exclaimed Sora.

Saburo drew his sword. 'We won't let them take you, Jack.'

'I'll distract them, while you three run for the forest,' said Miyuki, her *ninjatō* at the ready.

'No, I won't let you sacrifice yourselves,' said Jack. 'This isn't your battle.'

Toge looked back down at the ground. 'The *gaijin* samurai is . . . dead.'

Jack and his friends held their ground, stunned by Toge's reversal.

The samurai studied the farmer with suspicion. 'Where's the body then?'

Toge struggled for an answer.

The samurai jingled the coins in his hand. 'Alive or dead, he's still worth four *koban*.'

Yoshi shuffled forward. 'As much as we want to serve our Shogun, the *gaijin* was killed by Akuma during the battle. Unfortunately, both their bodies were burnt in the fire.'

The samurai grabbed Toge by the hair and wrenched his head back to face him.

'I should cut out your tongue for wasting our time.' He threw the farmer to the floor with disgust. '*If* the *gaijin* samurai is dead, our job is done. But no body, no reward.'

Turning on his heel, he pocketed the four *koban* and mounted his horse. The samurai gave one last look around the square. For a moment, he stared directly at the rice store. Then he urged his horse on and the ten samurai warriors rode out of the village.

'That was close,' said Saburo, sheathing his sword. 'At least now the samurai won't be looking for you, Jack.'

'I'm afraid you're wrong,' said Sora, shaking his head with regret. 'Samurai *never* believe us farmers. They'll be back.'

61

FUGITIVES

Early next morning, Sora helped Jack gather the supplies he needed for the long journey south to Nagasaki. With every chance that *daimyo* Ikeda's samurai would return, Jack decided he had to leave as soon as possible.

While the old farmer filled four straw containers with rice, Jack retrieved his pack from beneath the floorboards. Safe inside were Akiko's black pearl, his four remaining *shuriken* and, most important of all, his father's *rutter*. His thoughts once more turned to home and his sister, Jess.

Neko came over with some water and *mochi*. Kneeling before Jack, she gazed silently at him with doleful eyes.

I made these for you, she signed, and handed him the rice cakes.

Smiling gratefully, Jack took a bite of one. Filled with red bean paste, it was deliciously sweet.

Very tasty, signed Jack. *You're a good cook.*

Neko bowed at the compliment, then signed, *Are you coming back?*

Jack shook his head.

Neko's eyes welled with tears. *Friends forever?*

Jack signed, *Yes, friends forever*, and she beamed at him.

Getting to her feet, Neko joined Miyuki for another tearful goodbye.

Jack stowed the *mochi*, water and rice containers Sora had prepared in his pack. Picking up his red-handled samurai swords, he secured them in his *obi* and felt reassured by their presence on his hip. He was ready to go.

Yori and Saburo entered the farmhouse, their packs already on their backs.

'You don't have to come with me,' said Jack, fearing for his friends. 'This journey is going to be very dangerous.'

Saburo looked at him and laughed. 'And fighting a bloodthirsty group of bandits *wasn't* dangerous?'

'But you'll be fugitives,' argued Jack.

'Some roads aren't meant to be travelled alone,' said Yori, picking up his *shakujō*.

Thinking of all the challenges ahead, the treacherous journey seemed impossible. And for that reason Jack would welcome having his friends by his side. Together, they might stand a chance. Shouldering his pack, Jack walked out of the door.

The entire village was waiting to wish them farewell. Familiar faces bowed and offered their thanks for all they had done.

Yuudai stepped up. 'I trust you understand my reasons for staying. We can't leave this village completely defenceless.'

'Of course we understand,' replied Jack, exchanging a knowing glance with Miyuki as Neko stood proudly at Yuudai's side. 'But we'll miss you, my friend. I've come to rely upon your strength and good humour.'

Yuudai smiled broadly. 'It was an honour to fight alongside you. I hope our paths cross again one day.'

They bowed to one another. Then, as Saburo, Yori and Miyuki were saying their goodbyes, Toge burst through the crowd and threw himself at Jack's feet.

'I made a terrible mistake in judgement,' he confessed. 'I truly believed that turning you in for the reward was our only chance . . . How wrong I was . . . I beg your forgiveness.'

Toge's forehead touched the ground in abject apology, expecting at any moment to feel the edge of Jack's sword. Jack realized Toge had brought great shame upon himself and lost all respect among the farmers. But Toge had also redeemed himself at the crucial moment and Jack recognized that the village needed a strong leader at this time, one who could rebuild their community.

'There's no such thing as a mistake,' said Jack, remembering what Sensei Yamada had once said when he himself had needed a second chance. 'As long as you learn from it, then it's a lesson.'

Toge humbly bowed his understanding. Forgiven and absolved in the eyes of the villagers, he returned to the veranda to stand beside Yoshi.

His mission to save the village accomplished, Jack put on his new straw hat and waved a final goodbye.

With the rising sun at their backs, Jack and his friends hiked south-west across the glistening snow-clad plain, leaving four sets of footprints where before there had been only one.

Notes on the Sources

The following quotes are referenced within *Young Samurai: The Ring of Fire* (with the page numbers in square brackets below) and their sources are acknowledged here:

1. [Page 154] 'Know yourself, know your enemy. A thousand battles, a thousand victories.' By Sun Tsu (Chinese military commander).
2. [Page 212] 'Courage is not the absence of fear but rather the judgement that something else is more important than fear.' Excerpt from 'No Peaceful Warriors!', *Gnosis: A Journal of the Western Inner Traditions*, © 1991 by Ambrose Hollingworth Redmoon (pseudonym of James Neil Hollingworth, 1933–96).
3. [Page 234] 'People who fight fire with fire usually end up with ashes.' By Abigail Van Buren (pen-name of American journalist Pauline Phillips, b.1918).
4. [Page 236] 'In order to be walked on, you have to be lying down.' From Brian Weir (original source unknown; no evidence of publication).

5. [Page 300] 'A child is not a vase to be filled but a fire to be lit.' By François Rabelais (French writer and doctor, 1494–1553).

CHARACTER NAMES

A Young Samurai website competition was held to suggest the name for the fearsome bandit leader who would be Jack's enemy in this book.

The winner was:

Rozina Bashir

For her suggestion of **Akuma**, which means 'devil' or 'demon' in Japanese, and perfectly complemented the evil nature of my villain.

With so many excellent names entered by Young Samurai fans, the following were also chosen for the book:

Black Moon (*Kuro Tsuki*) submitted by Miranda Chong – I loved the concept of the black or new moon as a nickname for the bandit leader and the time for him to strike.

Hayato submitted by Rachel Andrews and by Sharuk Rahman – meaning 'falcon person', which reflected this character's skill with the bow.

Yuudai submitted by Andrew Dent – meaning 'great or large hero'. For obvious reasons, this name was ideal for this towering character.

Neko submitted by Maria Hoffman – meaning 'cat'. Although the actual suggestion was Bakeneko, meaning 'black cat', I was enchanted by the idea of comparing this character to a cat.

Toge submitted by Shray Bhandary – meaning 'thorn'. As Shray wrote in his entry, he's got to be a thorn in people's side.

Nakamura submitted by Carl Petzer – this is the name of a real bandit peasant from the sixteenth century who is rumoured to have killed the famous general Akechi Mitsuhide.

Sayomi submitted by Sharuk Rahman – meaning 'born in the night' – was a fantastic suggestion for an evil female bandit and created a character I hadn't thought of.

Arigatō gozaimasu for your suggestions!

Look out for more competitions and prizes on the Young Samurai Facebook page and *www.youngsamurai.com*

JAPANESE GLOSSARY

Bushido

Bushido, meaning the 'Way of the Warrior', is a Japanese code of conduct similar to the concept of chivalry. Samurai warriors were meant to adhere to the seven moral principles in their martial arts training and in their day-to-day lives.

Virtue 1: *Gi* – Rectitude
Gi is the ability to make the right decision with moral confidence and to be fair and equal towards all people no matter what colour, race, gender or age.

Virtue 2: *Yu* – Courage
Yu is the ability to handle any situation with valour and confidence.

Virtue 3: *Jin* – Benevolence

Jin is a combination of compassion and generosity. This virtue works together with *Gi* and discourages samurai from using their skills arrogantly or for domination.

Virtue 4: *Rei* – Respect

Rei is a matter of courtesy and proper behaviour towards others. This virtue means to have respect for all.

Virtue 5: *Makoto* – Honesty

Makoto is about being honest to oneself as much as to others. It means acting in ways that are morally right and always doing things to the best of your ability.

Virtue 6: *Meiyo* – Honour

Meiyo is sought with a positive attitude in mind, but will only follow with correct behaviour. Success is an honourable goal to strive for.

Virtue 7: *Chungi* – Loyalty

Chungi is the foundation of all the virtues; without dedication and loyalty to the task at hand and to one another, one cannot hope to achieve the desired outcome.

A Short Guide to Pronouncing Japanese Words

Vowels are pronounced in the following way:
'a' as the 'a' in 'at'
'e' as the 'e' in 'bet'
'i' as the 'i' in 'police'
'o' as the 'o' in 'dot'
'u' as the 'u' in 'put'
'ai' as in 'eye'
'ii' as in 'week'
'ō' as in 'go'
'ū' as in 'blue'

Consonants are pronounced in the same way as English:
'g' is hard as in 'get'
'j' is soft as in 'jelly'
'ch' as in 'church'
'z' as in 'zoo'
'ts' as in 'itself'

Each syllable is pronounced separately:
A-ki-ko
Ya-ma-to
Ma-sa-mo-to
Ka-zu-ki

arigatō gozaimasu	thank you very much
bōjutsu	the Art of the Bō (a wooden fighting staff)
bokken	wooden sword
Boshi-ken	Finger Sword Fist

bushido	the Way of the Warrior – the samurai code
daimyo	feudal lord
daishō	pair of swords, *wakizashi* and *katana*, that are the traditional weapons of the samurai
dojo	training hall
futon	Japanese bed: flat mattress placed directly on *tatami* flooring, and folded away during the day
gaijin	foreigner, outsider (derogatory term)
geisha	a Japanese girl trained to entertain men with conversation, dance and song
gi	training uniform
gotonpo	the Art of Concealment
hachimaki	headbands, sometimes reinforced with metal strips
haiku	Japanese short poem
hakama	traditional Japanese trousers
hara	Japanese martial arts term referring to the stomach, 'the centre of being'
hatsuhinode	the first sunrise of the new year
inro	a little case for holding small objects
kajutsu	the Art of Fire
katana	long sword
kenjutsu	the Art of the Sword
kesagiri	diagonal cut, or 'Monk's Robe' cut
ki	energy flow or life force (Chinese: *chi* or *qi*)
kiai	a shout; but also used in Go to describe a player's fighting spirit in the face of adversity

kiaijutsu	the Art of the Kiai
kimono	traditional Japanese clothing
koban	Japanese oval gold coin
kuji-in	nine syllable seals – a specialized form of Buddhist and ninja meditation
kyujutsu	the Art of the Bow
manriki	a short chain weapon with two steel weights on the ends
menpō	protective metal mask covering part or all of the face
mochi	rice cake
mon	family crest
musha shugyō	warrior pilgrimage
naginata	a long pole weapon with a curved blade on the end
ninja	Japanese assassin
ninjatō	straight-bladed sword used by ninja
ninjutsu	the Art of Stealth
Niten Ichi Ryū	the 'One School of Two Heavens'
nodachi	a very large two-handed sword
obi	belt
ronin	masterless samurai
saké	rice wine
samurai	Japanese warrior
saya	scabbard
sayonara	goodbye
sencha	green tea
sensei	teacher
seoi nage	shoulder throw

Sha	ninja hand sign, interpreted as healing for *ninjutsu* purposes
shakujō	Buddhist ringed staff used primarily in prayer, and as a weapon
shinobi	shadow warrior, another term for ninja
shinobi shozoku	the clothing of a ninja
Shogun	the military dictator of Japan
shoji	Japanese sliding door
shuriken	metal throwing stars
sumimasen	excuse me; my apologies
taijutsu	the Art of the Body (hand-to-hand combat)
tamashiwari	Trial by Wood
Taryu-Jiai	interschool martial arts competition
tetsu–bishi	small sharp iron spike
Tōshiya	literally 'passing arrow'; archery exhibition contest
wakizashi	side-arm short sword

Japanese names usually consist of a family name (surname) followed by a given name, unlike in the Western world where the given name comes before the surname. In feudal Japan, names reflected a person's social status and spiritual beliefs. Also, when addressing someone, *san* is added to that person's surname (or given names in less formal situations) as a sign of courtesy, in the same way that we use Mr or Mrs in English, and for higher-status people *sama* is used. In Japan, *sensei* is usually added after a person's name if they are a teacher, although in the Young Samurai books a traditional English order has been retained. Boys and girls are usually addressed using *kun* and *chan*, respectively.

ACKNOWLEDGEMENTS

This story is written as a homage to the film *Seven Samurai* by Akira Kurosawa, one of the greatest directors of Japanese samurai movies. If you have the opportunity, I recommend that you watch all his films. *The Hidden Fortress* inspired George Lucas's *Star Wars*. *Yojimbo* (*The Bodyguard*) was the basis for Clint Eastwood's classic western *A Fistful of Dollars*. *Seven Samurai* was remade as a western too – *The Magnificent Seven*. Likewise, Kurosawa's films have greatly influenced my passion for all things samurai and have been a source of inspiration for my *Young Samurai* novels. For that I sincerely thank him. *Arigatō gozaimashita.*

With the sixth title in this series, my list of people to thank grows ever longer. My gratitude goes out to all my fans, teachers and librarians. Without your support, these books could never happen.

I wish to express my continued appreciation of Shannon Park, my editor, and all at Puffin for their hard work and endless enthusiasm for the Young Samurai series – Wendy Tse, Helen Gray, Vanessa Godden, Julie Teece, Jayde Lynch, Sara Flavell and Paul Young (for his fantastic covers!).

I also must thank Charlie Viney, a great agent and an even greater friend, as well as Franca Bernatavicius and Nicki Kennedy, my overseas agents at ILA, for their passion and enthusiasm.

And, most importantly, my family – thank you for all your support and encouragement, especially my mum and dad, my godparents Ann and Andrew Smeeton, Sue and Simon Mole, Steve and Sam, my wife Sarah and my son, Zach, to whom this book is dedicated.

If I have one lesson for you in life, my son, it is 'No man is a failure who has friends'.

And so I want to thank my friends for their support of me . . .

Karen and Rob Rose, Geoff and Lucy Roy, Matt Bould, Charlie Wallace, Hayley Drewery, Russell and Jackie Holdaway, Andy and Sarah Hitt (and Martha and Ellen!), Nick and Zelia O'Donnell, Emma and Simon Gibbins, the evergrowing Dyson family, Lisa and Simon Martin, Rob and Robbie Cooper, Barbara and Scott Horsfield, Heather and Steve Miller, Nick and Jane Coward, Mike and Sonia Evans, Rob and Michelle Dunkerley, Steve Backshall, Oli Bishop, Stephan Bedelian, Anthony Varney, Danny and Kate Fitzpatrick . . . to name only a few.

Oh, and Gazebo Man for protecting my 'swords'!

Any fans can keep in touch with me and the progress of the Young Samurai series on my Facebook page, or via the website at *www.youngsamurai.com*

Arigatō gozaimasu!

CAN'T WAIT
FOR THE NEXT
JACK FLETCHER
BLOCKBUSTER?

THE RING OF WIND

Here's a **sneak preview** . . .

I

AMBUSH

Japan, spring 1615

Miyuki held a finger to her lips in warning. Jack, Saburo and Yori fell silent, glancing with unease round the forest clearing. It was barely dawn and, although the four friends hadn't encountered anyone in days, they remained on their guard.

The Shogun's samurai were proving relentless in their hunt for Jack. As a foreigner, a *gaijin*, Jack had been banished from Japan. But he was *also* a samurai warrior. Having fought against the Shogun in the Battle of Osaka Castle, he'd been accused of treason. It didn't matter he was merely a boy of fifteen. There was a price on his head and the *gaijin* samurai was wanted dead or alive.

The dirt track ahead looked deserted. There was no movement among the bushes. Nor any sounds to betray a hidden enemy. But Jack trusted Miyuki's instincts. Being a ninja, her senses were highly attuned to danger.

'Ten or so men passed through here,' Miyuki whispered,

studying a patch of downtrodden grass. 'Less than an hour ago.'

'Which way were they headed?' asked Jack, not wishing to cross their path.

'That's the problem,' she replied, her dark eyes narrowing. 'They went in *all* directions.'

At once, Jack understood what she was implying. An ominous feeling like the tightening of a noose seized him. His awareness heightened by the potential threat, he scanned the undergrowth a second time. Having trained as a ninja himself, he knew what signs to look for. Almost at once, he spotted several broken stems among the bushes and debris disturbed underfoot. He then realized the forest was too quiet; not even the birds were singing.

'We must get out of here!' said Jack.

But it was already too late.

A flutter, like the wings of a startled sparrow, heralded the ambush. Ducking at the last second, Jack dodged the steel-tipped arrow targeted for his head. It clipped his straw hat before embedding itself in a nearby tree trunk. A moment later, a troop of fully armed samurai burst from the bushes on all sides and charged towards them.

Instinctively Miyuki, Saburo and Yori formed a protective circle round Jack.

'We won't let them take you,' Yori promised, holding his *shakujō* in both hands. The wooden staff with its pointed iron tip and six metal rings was the symbol of a Buddhist monk. But it was also a formidable weapon. The rings jingled as the terrified yet valiant Yori braced himself for a fight.

'And I won't let them harm you,' said Jack, drawing both

his *katana* and *wakizashi*. A parting gift from his best friend, Akiko, their perfectly balanced razor-sharp blades glinted in the early morning light as he raised them into a Two Heavens guard.

Saburo boldly unsheathed his *katana* in preparation to do battle. Although he'd trained at the *Niten Ichi Ryū* with Jack, neither he nor Yori had been taught this legendary double-sword technique.

'At least the odds are better than last time,' Saburo quipped, referring to the forty bandits they'd confronted in Tamagashi village.

Sounding a battle cry and brandishing their weapons, the samurai soldiers closed in for the kill. Miyuki turned to face the first of their attackers. Before he was within striking distance, she flicked a *shuriken* from her hand. The deadly throwing star flashed through the air and struck the soldier in the neck. He choked and stumbled. Miyuki leapt into the air, executing a flying side-kick that sent the samurai sprawling to the ground. As she landed, the next samurai swung his sword to cut off her head. Pulling a straight-bladed *ninjatō* from the scabbard upon her back, Miyuki blocked the attack and engaged in a vicious sword fight with the man.

Weapons clashed as Jack, Saburo and Yori fought the other samurai warriors. Jack was confronted by three at once and had to use all his skill to keep them at bay. His swords whirled above his head as he deflected each of their strikes. Meanwhile, Yori was thrusting the iron tip of his *shakujō* at any samurai who dared to get close. He winded one in the stomach and was driving another back when Jack caught a movement in the bushes. The samurai archer was taking aim.

'Yori, watch out!' cried Jack.

But with no cover nearby, Yori was an easy target.

Using a lightning-fast Autumn Leaf Strike, Jack disarmed his nearest assailant then kicked him hard in Yori's direction. Just as the archer released his arrow, the samurai staggered backwards into the line of fire. The arrow hit him square in the chest and, groaning with pain, he crumpled to the earth. But the precious seconds Jack took to save Yori's life now put his own into harm's way. Seizing on Jack's momentary distraction, one of the samurai lunged with his sword. The steel tip was set to impale him when another blade came out of nowhere and deflected it aside.

'Saved your life yet again!' Saburo panted, jumping between Jack and his assailant. With a furious shout of *kiai*, Saburo charged forward and forced the warrior to retreat.

Grateful as he was, Jack had no chance to thank his friend as yet another samurai advanced on him. At the same time, Jack saw the archer now had him in his sights. While the samurai proved no match for his sword skill, Jack couldn't hope to stop the archer. Almost at full draw, the man was ready to release his deadly arrow.

Then Jack recalled a ninja technique from the Ring of Fire.

Fending off his samurai attacker with his *katana*, Jack held his *wakizashi* aloft and angled its polished blade to catch the sun. The man was dazzled by the burst of light. He lost his aim and the arrow shot wide.

But Jack knew this was just a short reprieve. The archer would kill them one by one if they remained in the open any longer.

Jack turned to his friends. 'Time to get out of here!'

Miyuki was still battling her samurai. The man was strong and threatened to overpower her. Just as defeat seemed inevitable, she reached inside her jacket and threw *metsubishi* powder into her attacker's face. Blinded by the mix of sand and ash, the samurai was powerless to stop Miyuki side-stamping his knee and crippling him.

'This way!' cried Miyuki, as the samurai collapsed in agony before her.

Without a moment to lose, the four friends sprinted from the clearing into the dense undergrowth. Behind them, they heard roars of rage as the surviving samurai soldiers crashed through the bushes in hot pursuit.

JACK FLETCHER IS BATTLING
THE HIGH SEAS . . .
YOUNG
SAMURAI
THE RING OF
WIND
CHRIS BRADFORD
THE ADVENTURE CONTINUES
MARCH 2012

JACK'S BEST MARTIAL ARTS MOVES

KICKS (GERI)

MAE-GERI – This front kick is extremely powerful and can even push an opponent to the ground.

YOKO-GERI – This side-kick is devastating on contact but be careful, it's easier to see it coming than a front kick.

MAWASHI-GERI – Often used to start combat, this roundhouse kick is when you swing your leg up in a circular motion.

USHIRO-GERI – This spinning back kick is one of the most powerful kicks in martial arts.

CHO-GERI – This is called the butterfly kick because all the limbs are spread out during the kick so you look like a butterfly's wings in flight.

PUNCHES (ZUKI)

OI-ZUKI – This lunge punch or jab is the most basic of punches but can definitely come in handy

GYAKI-ZUKI – Even more powerful is the reverse punch or cross punch, which employs most of the body in its motion.

KAGE-ZUKI – You have to be very fast for this hook punch but it's one of Jack's favourites as it's hard to block.

URAKEN-ZUKI – This back fist strike is even quicker and is achieved by forming a fist and striking with the tops of the two largest knuckles.

WHAT'S YOUR FAVOURITE?
Let us know at youngsamurai.com

ENROL FOR
SAMURAI
SCHOOL AT
www.youngsamurai.com
• Practise martial arts with Chris Bradford
• Learn about samurai weaponry
• Discover the secret techniques of the ninja
• Take a class in holding chopsticks
Explosive extracts, extreme competitions, podcasts and author videos
Sign up for all the latest news to keep your adrenalin racing

WANT MORE ACTION? MORE ADVENTURE? MORE ADRENALIN?

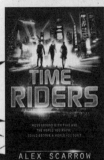

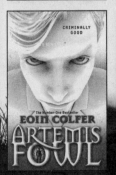

GET INTO PUFFIN'S ADVENTURE BOOKS FOR BOYS

Bright and shiny and sizzling with fun stuff . . .

puffin.co.uk

WEB CHAT

Discover something new
EVERY month – books, competitions
and treats galore

WEB NEWS

The **Puffin Blog** is packed with posts and photos from
Puffin HQ and special guest bloggers. You can also sign up
to our monthly newsletter **Puffin Beak Speak**

WEB FUN

Take a sneaky peek around your favourite **author's studio**,
tune in to the **podcast, download activities** and much more

WEBBED FEET

(Puffins have funny little feet and
brightly coloured beaks)

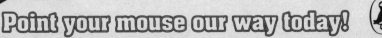
Point your mouse our way today!

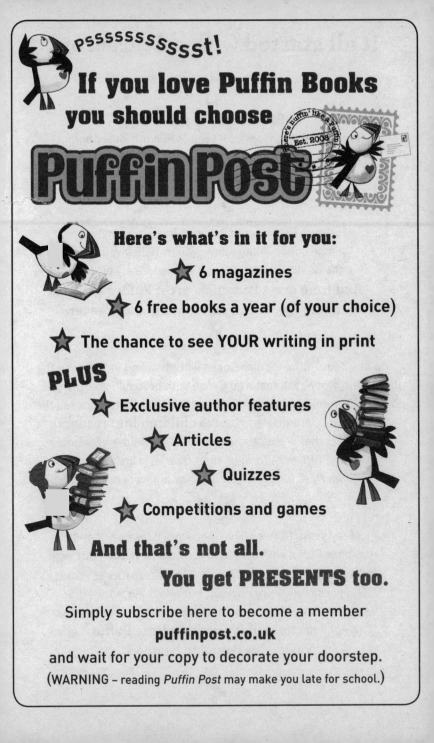

It all started with a Scarecrow.

Puffin is seventy years old.

Sounds ancient, doesn't it? But Puffin has never been
so lively. We're always on the lookout for the next big
idea, which is how it began all those years ago.

Penguin Books was a big idea from the mind of
a man called Allen Lane, who in 1935 invented
the quality paperback and changed the world.
**And from great Penguins, great Puffins grew,
changing the face of children's books forever.**

The first four Puffin Picture Books were hatched in 1940 and the
first Puffin story book featured a man with broomstick arms called
Worzel Gummidge. In 1967 Kaye Webb, Puffin Editor, started the
Puffin Club, promising to **'make children into readers'**.
She kept that promise and over 200,000 children became
devoted Puffineers through their quarterly instalments of
Puffin Post, which is now back for a new generation.

Many years from now, we hope you'll look back and
remember Puffin with a smile. **No matter what your age
or what you're into, there's a Puffin for everyone.**
The possibilities are endless, but one thing is for sure:
whether it's a picture book or a paperback, a sticker book
or a hardback, **if it's got that little Puffin
on it – it's bound to be good.**